When this novel first appeared, its author was not well known. There had been one previous book by "John Sedges," a novel called *The Townsman,* which was a best seller and had been greeted with high praise by the critics. But the identity of "John Sedges" remained a mystery.

Now the secret has been disclosed. "John Sedges" is Pearl Buck, famous author of such books as *The Good Earth* and *Letter from Peking,* the only American woman to win both the Pulitzer and Nobel prizes. The great talent which has made her internationally famous shows clearly in this story of American life after the Civil War.

THE ANGRY WIFE
was originally published by
The John Day Company.

# Pearl S. BUCK

## The Angry Wife

A POCKET **CARDINAL**® EDITION published by
**POCKET BOOKS, INC. • NEW YORK**

THE ANGRY WIFE

John Day edition published September, 1947

A Pocket *Cardinal* edition

1st printing..........March, 1959
6th printing............May, 1966

**This Pocket *Cardinal*®️ edition includes every word contained in the**
original, higher-priced edition. It is printed from brand-new
plates made from completely reset, clear, easy-to-read type.
Pocket *Cardinal* editions are published by Pocket Books, Inc.,
and are printed and distributed in the U.S.A. by Affiliated Publishers,
a division of Pocket Books, Inc., 630 Fifth Avenue, New York, N.Y. 10020.
Trademarks registered in the United States and other countries.

L

# THE ANGRY WIFE

of peace and to work speedily toward nothing less than a total ban after these very words which accompany but to facilitate their increase

# One

"WE ARE FORTUNATE," Pierce Delaney said to his wife.

She did not answer. Outside the window open by her couch, the deep stillness of late October afternoon lay across the landscape of Malvern. The air was warm and fragrant. The servants had been picking the purple grapes. She could not learn to call them servants instead of slaves. Pierce was going to pay them wages. Georgia, her own maid, would get wages!

"Aren't we fortunate, Luce?" Pierce's big voice demanded.

"I wish you wouldn't call me Luce," she answered. "I like my own name."

"Lucinda," he said, smiling. "It's such a prim name."

"Nevertheless, it's my name," she replied.

But he could not quarrel even in fun. He wanted peace, now; as long as he lived he wanted only peace. He stood before the high window and gazed at the landscape for which he had been as homesick, all during the war, as he had been even for his family. There were not many in the world to match it for beauty. Beyond the rich level lands of his farms the foothills rose, softly wooded, into the blue heights of the Alleghenies. It was country fit for all his dreams of peace and he would spend his life in fulfilling them. Only to live, after these years, would be enough, but to live here was heaven.

Without turning he spoke. "The war is over, Tom and I are both alive, the house isn't in ruins. Not many families have as much!"

"Pierce, *darling—*"

At the sound of Lucinda's voice he wheeled. She was lying on her rose satin sofa, her white arms flung above her head, her white hands clasped. Her slender body was hidden in a froth of creamy lace and silk, except for her little bare feet.

He took off the stiff leather belt of his uniform, threw it on the floor and went across the bedroom. He knelt beside her and lifted her into his arms. The moment stood still for him, clear and deep. For the first time he felt sure of being alive. He was at home again, in his own house, with Lucinda, his wife. His two children, his sons, were sound and full of health. Even the work on the land had not stopped. Everything he possessed had miraculously escaped destruction. His mind raced back over the years through which he had just passed. They were already compressed into a single experience of torture, in which he saw the faces of his own men whom he had not often been able to save. They were not all dead—a few had escaped, many more lay in hospitals. But most of them were dead. Kneeling there with his face in the laces upon his wife's bosom, he read upon his brain the figures of the dead. They were so young! This was their tragedy—so young to die for so vague a cause. Thousands of young boys in uniforms had died to compel the nation to remain a union, thousands in grey had died for the right of a state to be free if it liked. Somewhere between them the fate of black men and women had been entangled.

Feeling the beat of Lucinda's heart under his lips, aware of the softness of her flesh, breathing in her scent, he asked himself if even the death of many could hold united those who wanted to be free of one another. It might have been easier if he and his family had lived in the high North or the deep South. But Malvern, his inheritance, lay in the borderland. Men from the south and the north had swept across the mountains to rest here in Malvern Valley, under the great oaks, even upon the verandas of the house. He had been home for a few days of furlough when Grant's men had come marching by, and looking down on them from an attic window, hiding himself, he had been horrified to see how much his enemies looked like his own men. There was only the slight outward difference of the uniform. The boys' faces were the same.

More than Malvern lay in the border country. In the months when the war drew nearer, grim and inevitable, he had had to decide whether, when war was declared, he would go North or South. He hated slavery, while he loved his own slaves. Some deep conservatism in his being, love of form and order, necessity to preserve and persist, made him know that union was essential for their country, still so new. A handful of states, flying apart in quarrels, would mean early death to the nation. But he had stayed by the South. The last moment had come, and in its clarity Lucinda and Malvern had outweighed all else. Heart and not head had decided. He knew that he would fight and perhaps die for her, here in his house. But Tom, his brother, had gone North.

"When do you think Tom will get home?" Lucinda asked.

She curled herself into his arms. When she made herself small in his arms his heart quivered with tenderness. It seemed impossible that she had borne him two sons. He thought of them playing somewhere about the place, sturdy, blond, gay and quarrelsome, affectionate and rebellious, as he and Tom had been in this house of their fathers. By her own strength Lucinda had kept them untouched by the miseries of the war. She was a strong little thing!

"Joe will be here at any moment with him," he said. He laid her gently back on her silken pillows and got up and walked to the window. Almost unconsciously he had picked up his belt and now he stood by the window, strapping it about his waist again.

A slender, hard waist, Lucinda thought with pleasure. The war had done him good. She felt idly complacent. She was safe. The house needed new hangings and new carpets. She wanted to cover the mohair furniture in the parlors with satin as soon as she decently could. Enough of the slaves had stayed on, for wages, to make her life still possible. Nothing would be changed.

She felt joy running in her veins. Her heart softened. She

got up and went over to the tall figure at the window. He was staring out into the sunshine, his face grave and his steel blue eyes tragic. She hated the look. He was remembering something she did not know.

"Pierce," she said, "Pierce, darling—"

He turned to her quickly, seized her in his arms again and held her with pain and love. How much he could never tell her!

"Everything is going to be the same," she whispered.

"I'll make it the same," he said passionately, and felt his throat grow tight over tears. Strange how a man could go through death again and again, could lose what he loved most! For in the hour of battle he had loved his men better than anything. There had been moments when if sacrifice of himself and his wife and his sons, his house and lands, all that he was fighting for, could have saved the losing day, he would have let them all go into the loss, for victory's sake. Yet he had never wept, or wanted to weep, as he did now, when he had come home to his unchanged house. It was so exactly the same that he could not keep back his tears. But this Lucinda could not understand, and for no fault of her own. They would have had to live through the same things to have had the same understanding and he could only be thankful that she had stayed safely at home.

The door opened. Someone stood on the threshold an instant, saw them and closed the door.

Lucinda pulled herself out of his arms and smoothed her straight fair hair. "Come in, Georgia," she called.

Georgia opened the door gently and stood, hesitating and shy, aware that she had interrupted a scene of love. Pierce saw the awareness in her dark eyes, in the half smile of her lips, in the timidity of her bearing. She looked at Lucinda and he saw what he had not known before, that she was afraid of her mistress.

"It's all right, Georgia," he said kindly.

"I declare I didn't know you were in here, Miss Lucie," the dark girl said.

"Don't come in without knocking, Georgia," Lucinda said sharply.

"I did knock, Miss Lucie," Georgia said in her even, gentle voice. "When I heard no answer I came in. I was looking for you and Master Pierce to say that Joe has come ahead to tell that they'll be here in just a few minutes. He says Master Tom isn't hurt by wounds but he's starved near to death."

The tears brimmed her great eyes and hung on her lashes. These lashes, black and long, held the drops and she put up her hand and wiped them away.

"Starved?" Lucinda repeated.

"It's that damned prison," Pierce muttered. He turned to Georgia. "Tell Annie to have some warm milk ready. A half cup of milk with brandy will do him more good than anything. You can't feed a starving man real food. God, I knew they were starving the Yankee prisoners—but my own brother!"

"It comes of his joining the North," Lucinda said bitterly. "If he'd—"

"Never mind now, sweet," Pierce interrupted her. "The war's over."

"I'll hate the Yankees as long as I live," she retorted.

Georgia went away. The moment which she had interrupted was gone and Pierce bent to kiss his wife quickly. "I'll go along down myself, Luce, and see that everything's ready. I wish I'd gone to meet him. But he sent word he was all right . . . Luce, who's going to nurse him?"

"Bettina," Lucinda replied. She sat down in her rose colored chair. The satin was frayed and Georgia had darned it carefully. "I couldn't spare Georgia," she went on, "but the boys are so big now I thought we could turn them over to Joe."

"Good," he said.

He hurried out of the room into the wide hall. At the door of the nursery he saw the two sisters, Georgia and Bettina, in whispering talk. They looked alike, both tall, both golden-skinned, dark-eyed, slender. But Bettina, the younger, showed the Indian blood in her black ancestry. Georgia did not.

Georgia's face was soft and oval, the cheeks smooth, the lips full. Bettina's cheeks were flat, her nose sharper, her eyes keener, her hair less curly. Where the two girls had come from Pierce did not know, except that they had been part of Lucinda's father's estate, and when he died they were for sale. He had bought them because Lucinda wanted them. "Wonderful workers," Lucinda had called them. He scarcely knew them, because a month after they had come into the house he had gone to war.

"Bettina!" he said abruptly. There was something so delicate, so sensitively aware of him in the faces the two women turned to him that he was disconcerted. He had seen this delicacy often enough in the faces of slaves, even wholly ignorant ones, a refinement of the human being so extreme that he was always made uncomfortable by it. It was the result of utter dependence, the wisdom of creatures who could only exist by pleasing their masters. But in these two women it was pathetic and shameful, because they were not ignorant. He must ask Lucinda why they were not ignorant.

"Did you want something, Master Pierce?" Bettina asked. Their voices were alike, deep and soft.

"You're to take care of my brother."

"Yes, Master Pierce," Bettina said.

Pierce paused. "You two," he said abruptly, "don't call my brother and me masters. I lost the war—Tom won. I can't be called master any more—Tom won't want to be, if I know him."

"What shall we call you, sir?" Bettina asked.

It was disconcerting that both of them spoke with a clear English accent, without a trace of the shambling dialect of slaves. It was suddenly monstrous that he had bought these women. But he had not heard them speak when he bought them. They had simply stood hand in hand, their heads downcast.

"You—you can just call me mister," he said abruptly.

"Yes, sir," they breathed. They looked at one another. He saw they would simply call him nothing, ending every sentence with "sir."

He looked out of the window. A slow procession was winding along the road between the oaks—Tom! He ran down the stairs, threw open the front door, leaped the stone steps and lifted from the litter his brother. But could this be a human creature, this tall stick, this gangling monkey, this handful of bones, loose in a bag of skin?

"Tom!" he muttered strangling, "Tom, boy, you're home!" Then he said sternly. "Look here, we'll soon have you—you fed—well again—"

The dark skeleton face could not smile. The fleshless lips were drawn back from his teeth, fixed in a grin of agony. Tom's voice came in a faint gasp:

"Home—"

Pierce carried his brother up the steps, and was horrified to feel the looseness with which Tom's head upon the stem-like neck hung over his arm. His own people had done this—in a secessionist prison they had starved his brother! He had tried to reach through the walls of war to save Tom, but hatred had been stronger than love. Then he pushed aside anger and pain, in the way he had learned to do, to save his own being. Fifty thousand men had been starved to death in those prisons, but Tom was still one of the living. And the war was over.

"Everything is going to be all right, Tom," he said gently.

He carried his brother through the great dim hall, up the stairs into the west bedroom. The room was full of late sunshine, and on the hearth a fire burned. Bettina stood at the bedside, holding the sheets ready, and Georgia moved the copper warming pan to and fro. Georgia was crying silently, but Bettina's face was grave. She put out her arms and slipped them under Tom's bony frame, and lowered his head gently to the pillows. Then she drew the covers over him.

"Where's the brandy milk?" Pierce demanded.

"Here, sir," she said.

A spirit lamp stood on the table, and she poured the milk from a small skillet into a blue flowered cup set in a saucer.

The ghastly lips drew back still further over Tom's strong white teeth. "My cup—" he whispered.

"Annie told me it was, sir," Bettina said softly. She took

up a thin old silver spoon and began to feed the milk to him.

"Don't—know you," Tom whispered.

"Bettina," Pierce said. "I got her—and Georgia—after you left home, Tom, I reckon. It was just before the war. Of course they're free now, working for wages."

"Sir," Bettina begged him, "it doesn't matter."

Across the hall Lucinda's voice floated clearly. "Georgia, Georgia!"

"Don't let her come in yet," Pierce said.

"No, sir," Georgia agreed. She wiped her eyes and hurried out of the room.

Bettina slipped to her knees. Tom was swallowing drop by drop, as she fed him. He looked up at his brother from bottomless eyes.

"I can't—eat," he whispered, and two small thick tears forced themselves from under his papery eyelids.

"You'll be eating everything a month from now," Pierce said.

"I thought I'd die," Tom whispered. He longed to speak, but Pierce would not let him.

"Don't think about it," he urged. "Just rest, Tom—it's all over."

Drop by drop from the silver spoon Bettina fed him. Pierce gazing down at Tom's face saw her slender hand holding the spoon steadily, putting the drops between the waiting lips until the cup was empty.

In the warm silence Tom's eyes closed. Bettina looked up. "He's falling asleep, sir," she whispered. " 'Tis the best thing."

She rose and noiselessly drew the old red velvet curtains across the western windows. "I've tried to get a doctor from Charlottesville," Pierce whispered back. "But there's not one even there."

"We'll heal him ourselves, sir," Bettina said.

"It'll be mainly on you, Bettina," Pierce said, "Neither I nor Miss Lucie know much about such things."

"I'll do it, sir," she said softly. "I'll make it my task."

Where did she get such words? He wasted a moment in wonder.

"I shan't leave the house tonight," he told her abruptly. "Call me when he wakes."

"I will, sir," she promised. She moved silently and swiftly across the room and held open the door, to his vague annoyance. She was so little like a slave. "You feel quite safe alone with him?" he demanded. "You think you can manage?"

"He's safe," she said calmly. Then she smiled a sweet and bitter smile. "I don't forget it was to free me that he's like this—"

He paused on the threshold, and comprehending these words, saw for an instant into her soul. He was made intensely uncomfortable. "Maybe," he said drily and went on.

He went across the hall to his own bedroom. The door was open into Lucinda's room beyond and he walked to the threshold.

"Ready for dinner?" he asked. It was an idle question. She had put on a pale blue satin, wideskirted. There was lace at her bosom and she was fastening about her neck the gold chain and locket he had given her when he went away to war. Inside it was his picture. He tried to fasten it for her, and the locket flew open. He saw his own young face, smiling out of the small oval.

"The catch doesn't hold," she said.

"I don't look like that now," he said. "I'll have to get another picture taken for you."

"I like this one," she said, looking up at him.

He looked down at her. "Meaning you don't like the way I look now?"

"Of course I do," she said. She closed the locket with a snap.

He turned away. He knew of old that she would not allow probing beneath the level of her serenity.

"Where are the boys?" he asked abruptly. The house was too quiet.

"They're having their supper," she said.

He was staring out the window again at the mountains and Lucinda saw the bitterness of his mouth.

"How is he, Pierce? Georgia says he looks awful. She said you said I wasn't to come in."

"I don't think there's any use in your seeing him just yet, Luce." He turned, sat down, felt for his pipe and remembered that he was in his wife's room and did not draw it from his pocket. "He'll look a different fellow in a few days. Now he looks what he has been through—like hell."

"Does he know people?"

"Yes—even knew he'd never seen Bettina before."

"I don't suppose he asked for anybody—the children—"

"He's not up to that yet."

Her eyes were fixed on him strongly. "What is it?" he asked, trying to smile.

"I have a queer feeling you haven't really come home."

"It takes time," he agreed. "You know, Luce, I have to bring myself home—bit by bit. I've lived so many days and nights away. Sometimes the nights were the worse—wondering about you, when the letters didn't come."

"Pierce, you won't be restless now? I mean—war's awfully exciting, isn't it?"

"No—unless you like horror," he said gravely.

He looked around the room. "There's nothing more exciting to me than this—being here at home—in your room. Luce, we'll have lots more children, won't we? That's what's exciting —you and me and our children growing up."

She drooped her beautiful blonde head. Somehow she had managed to keep her skin like a child's in spite of these years of war. She was young, and so was he—she twenty-six, and he not yet thirty. They could have a half dozen children, easily. Her shining yellow hair, real yellow, rare as gold, was twisted about her head in a crown, not braided or curled, and her eyes were blue like his, but more blue.

"How do you keep your dresses so pretty?" he muttered foolishly. He wanted to take her to bed now, this instant, and suddenly his physical need stupefied him with its intensity. He had been home for a week but it seemed to him he had only just seen her.

"Georgia irons them every day," she said.

She was perfectly aware of what his look meant, the flame in the eyes, the concentration in his gaze, the slight tightening of his lips. But she saw no need to yield to it at this moment. After all, he was home to stay now. Old routines must be set up again. She rose, linked her hands together and yawned behind them prettily, smiling at him.

"Here come the boys," she said and threw open the door.

The two boys were leaping up the stairs ahead of Georgia. They ran into the room, Martin, the elder, was eight and Carey five. "Where's Tom?" Martin demanded. He was not afraid of his father because he had forgotten how it was to have a father in the house before. He had been loudly disappointed because Pierce declared himself too big and too old to play all the time.

"Hush—Uncle Tom's asleep," Lucinda said, smiling. She was very proud of the two handsome blond boys she had borne.

"How big is he?" Martin demanded.

"As big as I am," Pierce said, "but very thin."

"Big as you!" Martin wailed.

"Maybe taller," Pierce said firmly. "Looks like Tom's grown during the war."

The interest went out of Martin's face but he hid his disappointment by pushing his younger brother. Carey fell and cried.

"Oh, you naughty boy," Lucinda said. "Pierce, why must they always fight?"

Pierce laughed. "Tom and I always fought," he said. The small scene made him feel at home as nothing had. All of them were under one roof again, his children, Tom, he, his wife. They were a family. How passionately he had longed for the ties of a family about him! That was the worst of soldiering, after the sheer terror, horrible wounds—or death. A soldier was cut off from everything. He had not so much as a room of his own. He became only an atom, scarcely identified, adding his mite of energy to the great blind force of war.

"Shall I take the children to bed now, ma'am?" Georgia's voice, sweet and deep, came from the door. She had been standing there in silence, waiting, and when Carey fell, she came in and picked him up. Now he clung to her.

"Go with Georgia, boys," Lucinda commanded.

Georgia carried Carey away in her arms and Martin leaped froglike from flower to flower in the rose-patterned carpet on the floor. The door closed on them.

"They seem to like Georgia," Pierce remarked.

"Oh, they like both the girls," Lucinda said. "Maybe they like Georgia a little better. She's gentler than Bettina." She went to the mirror and examined her hair in a hand glass and tucked in a smooth end.

"Where did your father get them?" he asked.

"They were payment for a betting debt," Lucinda said in a careless voice. "He went to the races in Kentucky—you know he always did. Mother scolded and he went just the same." She laughed. "He always won, you know, so her scolding never did any good. But she was cross when he came home with two more colored wenches! We had so many already."

"Good pair, though," Pierce said.

"Yes, but Mother said they didn't fit anywhere."

"You mean—they were rebellious?"

"Oh no, Mother wouldn't have stood for that. But they'd been taught to read and you never know—" her voice trailed. "For instance," she said, looking over the top of the ivory glass at her husband. "Why should Georgia suddenly begin to say 'ma'am' to me, instead of 'mistress,' the way she always has?"

Pierce laughed, aware as he did so of something like an old timidity before Lucinda. Well, he wouldn't be afraid of his wife, not after four years at war and two of being a major! "Why, I told her to do that, Luce," he said. "I told her I didn't want to be called master. We've lost the war. Our only hope for the future is to remember we've lost it and begin to live in the new way."

"I haven't lost any war," she said.

He laughed at her. "You little Southern rebel," he said. "Of course you have!"

He seized the mirror and put it down, swept her into his

arms and kissed her hard. Then he held her at arm's length. "You're going to lose all your battles with me, hereafter," he said. "I haven't been a soldier for nothing all these years."

Yes, he told himself—he was going to keep the upper hand in his own home.

"Pierce, you're ruining my hair," she wailed.

"Damn your hair," he said.

"Look here, my beauty," he told her in the night. "Don't bear me a boy this time, if you please. I want some daughters —pretty ones! I shan't keep the ugly ones."

Lucinda laughed into her down pillow. "What will you give me for a girl, Pierce?" she asked. The room was flickering with firelight. He had heaped logs on the hearth and blown out the candles. They had no coal oil for the crystal lamps but plenty of candles. Georgia knew how to make them and scent them with bayberries and juniper.

"Girls actually aren't worth as much in the market as boys," he said. "Let's see—I always give you diamonds for the boys, don't I?"

"My diamond bracelet for Martin and the diamond brooch for Carey," she said promptly.

"Pearls for the girls?" he suggested.

"Sapphires," she bargained.

"Sapphires," he promised. "But you're greedy, you little wretch! Sapphires—I shall have to get them from Paris."

"At that it'll be less trouble for you than for me," she said, laughing.

"All right, wretch," he promised. He pulled her into his arms—"anything—anything—little wretch!"

But in the middle of this soft night, in the quiet of the house where he had been born and lived out all his childhood and youth, in the full sight of the thinnest crescent moon he had ever seen, a rim of silver at the edge of the shadowy full moon hanging above the mountains, in the depth of the great bed where he lay with his wife, he knew that he was changed. War had made him hard. He valued as he never had the few good things of life, love and passion, sleep, morning, food, work, the wind and the sun. But he would never play again as he had played. He would never again be idle, never gay in the old unthinking fashion—

"You hurt me," Lucinda said suddenly.

He paid no heed to her complaint until he heard her sob.

"What the devil is the matter with you?" he demanded.

"I don't like you," she sobbed childishly. "You weren't like this—before."

He released her instantly, "You can scarcely expect me to be exactly what I was before." Lying naked in the bed his formality suddenly seemed ridiculous to him and he burst into loud laughter.

"Pierce, you stop laughing!" Lucinda cried. She beat his breast with her fists when he went on laughing. "Pierce, stop it—you're crazy!"

He stopped laughing as suddenly as he had begun. "Oh well," he said. "Maybe it's worth a sapphire."

He fell asleep as quickly as though neither passion nor anger had been. The war had taught him that.

In the bedroom across the hall Tom woke. Something warm and sweet was in his mouth. Food again! He began to eat with a new hunger and saw a woman's face bent over him. It was a brown face, but the lamp shining from the table behind, lit the dark hair curling about it. She was feeding him in teaspoonfuls and he was swallowing. His mind was clear, as it had been most of the time even in prison, but to know did not mean he would have strength to speak. Fellows had been taken out of the prison in the dead cart when they were alive and knowing, but too weak to protest against their own burial.

"More," he said distinctly.

"There's plenty more," Bettina answered. "I made a full bowl."

He wondered drowsily what it was. Something sweet and something smooth, slipping down his throat. A custard, maybe, with eggs and milk and white sugar. Only where did she get eggs and milk and white sugar in a war? He felt impelled to answer his own question. He opened his eyes with effort.

"We won—war," he announced.

"Surely we did," she agreed. She lifted another spoonful and put it to his mouth.

When he could swallow no more because sleep made it impossible, she put the dish down. The light fell on his face. The terror was already fading from it. In a few days, when his lips were not fleshless, he would not look so like a skeleton. Then the door opened and Georgia came into the room. She wore a long white dressing gown and she had loosened her hair. It flowed down over her shoulders, fine and curly and black.

"How is he?" she whispered.

"You don't have to whisper," Bettina whispered. "When he sleeps he hears nothing."

They stood looking down at him, side by side.

"He's so young," Bettina said.

"I heard them say twenty-three," Georgia answered.

"Then he went when he was nineteen. How long was he in prison—did you hear them say?"

"That I did not," Georgia answered.

They lingered, looking at his face, at his hands, lying helpless on the white coverlet. "He has nice hands," Georgia said, "I like a man to have nice hands. Remember Father's hands, Bettina?"

Bettina nodded.

"Shan't I take a turn with him, so you can sleep?" Georgia asked.

Bettina shook her head. "I want to be here when he wakes," she said.

She gave her sister a gentle push. "You go to your bed," she commanded her. "It's me that she set to nurse him back to health and strength."

She watched her sister's figure glide across the floor and she watched while the door latched. Then she sat down again in her seat by the bed, her eyes fixed on his face.

Down the hall Georgia walked, barefoot, without sound.

She passed "their" bedrooms—her mistress's and master's—She remembered what he had told her.

"Surely, I'm free," she thought. "I could go away. I don't have to take even their wages." She heard voices murmuring, and under the door a crack of light showed. The high transom was bright. They were still awake! But she had waked, too, out of dreamless sleep. The house seemed strange now that the master had come home.

"That's what he is," she thought, "even though he tells me I'm not to call him that. A house must have a master."

She had always come and gone into that room, and her mistress had never seemed to care. It was as though she were nobody at all, until now. But now the whole house was different. Her mistress was different, too. Women were always different when men came into the house.

She went noiselessly past the door. Then she reached the attic stairs. "God help me they don't creak," she thought.

It was the one thing she and Bettina had asked, that they might sleep in the house instead of out in the quarters. Her mistress had looked at them coldly. They had stood, hand in hand, waiting for her question. But she had not put the question.

"Very well," she had said in her cool voice. "You may sleep in the attic. But you'll have to be quiet. I don't want to hear even your walking around."

Up in the attic she and Bettina had made a home for themselves. They had found an old rope bottom bed and a discarded bureau. Rags they had made into rugs and they had crocheted covers for the bed and the bureau top. But they had learned to walk as softly as shadows in the top of the great house and to talk in whispers.

She took off her dressing gown and crept into the bed. Still she could not sleep. She lay quivering, aware, feeling, not thinking. There was no use thinking in a life like hers. She was a creature in the sea, tossed here and there by tides she did not understand.

"But wherever you are," her mother had said, "begin to live

right there and look after yourselves. Only thing, I hope you will always be together."

Her mother had died so long ago she could remember her now only by summoning her consciously to memory. All she saw was a dim dark face, darker than her own or Bettina's, dark but beautiful, more like Bettina than like her, more Indian than Negro. But her father she remembered well. He was an old white man, always old. They had lived with him in a great house with pillars to hold up the heavy roof of the porch. Once there had been a white mistress in the house but never had there been children. She and Bettina were his only children. He had treated them as his children, too, and had made the slaves treat them so after his white wife died. It had been easy, for there were no visitors. Long before Georgia's memory visitors had stopped coming. She and Bettina both knew that it had happened when he took their mother into the house. She had not been one of the slaves. She was a stranger whom he had bought in New Orleans and she had kept herself a stranger always. But she had been wise. She had lived in the house but she allowed none of the slaves to wait on her or on the children. She had made herself a housekeeper, and she thanked the slaves carefully when they helped her, and she never gave an order. It was always "please, will you"—and "I'm sorry to ask you"— Behind the extreme courtesy they had lived together, the three of them, separate from everyone, even the father.

"He's your father, but you can't act like his children," she had told them, "even if he does treat you right," she had added.

So she and Bettina had grown up as solitary as orphans, even when the tall thin old Englishman had held them on his knees and kissed their smooth golden cheeks.

After their mother died, when she was eleven and Bettina nine, they had gone on alone together, growing up, slender, silent, obedient always to the old man. "Sir," they had always called him, neither master nor father. He used to look at them. She remembered and never could she forget how he used to look at them, pitying and frightened, as though something he had done in a moment had surprised even himself.

"I don't know what's to become of you two girls," he used to mutter. He was very old, then, too old to do anything but let them wait on him.

"Don't worry about us, sir—" she had always said. That, too, was her mother's teaching . . . "Don't ever let men get to thinking you trouble, father or husband. Men don't like trouble with women."

She had kept these teachings in her heart and had taught them to Bettina who could not remember the least image of their mother.

After a while the old man had given up even his worry. He grew older and slept more often, and had taken much waiting upon, until the day when he died in a moment and they had found him dead.

"What's goin' to become of us, Georgia?" Bettina had asked.

"We'll have to wait and see," she had answered.

"Maybe he's left his will for us," Bettina whispered.

"Hush," Georgia said. One of the teachings of her mother had been, "Don't expect anything. Then what you get seems good and enough."

But there was no will and no mention of them and when a cousin came as the next heir, he sold the house and the land and the slaves, and they were sold, too. If they had not been slaves before they now became slaves.

Thus had they gone into the next great house. It was no question there—they were slaves. And then, because they had worked well and always in that deep silence which they kept about them like a dark velvet curtain, Miss Lucie had brought them here when again the great house fell. Great houses always fell. She lay gazing up into the thick beams above her head. Would this great house fall, too?

Pierce, waking just after dawn, got out of the bed. He moved as stealthily as he knew how, but Lucinda waked.

"Go to sleep, Luce," he commanded. "It's the middle of the night for you."

"Where are you going?" she asked. Her blue eyes opened wide at him.

"I'm going for a ride," he said. "I'll be back in time to breakfast with you."

He stooped and kissed her mouth. Her breath was not quite sweet in the morning. He knew it and yet it always shocked him a little that it could be, so fastidious was she in every detail of her person. Inside the lovely shell of her body surely there should be no corruption. She was asleep again, lying placidly on her pillow, her hands on her breast. Lovely she was, and he had no complaint against her. By the time he got back she would have washed her mouth with one of her fragrant waters. He had no need to notice an offense not greater than the scent of a faded rose—he who was fresh home from the stench of dying men on a battlefield! Yet that stench had so pervaded him for four years that now his nostrils were always to the wind, like a dog's. He smelled what he would never have noticed in the days before he had smelled death.

He splashed in his wash basin in his dressing room, blowing out gusts of bubbles through the water, he sponged his body, brushed his teeth and put on clean garments under his riding suit. Clean he would be so long as he lived. He had had enough of filth.

Clean to his marrowbones he went out of the door and into the great upper hall, down the winding stairs which were one of the beauties of Malvern, and into the lower hall. The hall ran through the house, and front and back doors were wide open to the morning.

At the table by the door Georgia was putting white and purple asters into a yellow bowl.

"Hello, Georgia," he said.

She turned her head, and he saw with discomfort that she was really very beautiful. He did not want a beautiful slave in his house. Though she wasn't a slave any more—

"Good morning, sir," she said.

"A fine morning," he said abruptly.

"Yes, sir."

"I suppose nothing's been heard of Tom yet? I didn't go in
—didn't want to wake him."

"No, sir," she replied. "Bettina hasn't come out. Likely
he's sleeping."

She pronounced her words so purely that he was curious to
know where she had learned them so. But he refused himself
the luxury of curiosity and went on down the steps, into the
cool bright morning. At the stables his groom was already
brushing his horse.

He looked up with a grin. "Sure is good to have somepin
like a horse again, marster."

"The stables are pretty sorry, Jake," Pierce agreed. "But
give me time—I'll be looking around for some real horseflesh
in a month or so."

"Sure will be good to git the stables full," Jake said.

He slipped the saddle on the mare, steadied her with his
hand on her neck, murmuring and hissing through his teeth to
soothe her.

"She's raring to go," Pierce said fondly. "But it won't be to
war any more, Beauty—"

"Sure is good they ain't any mo' wa'," Jake said.

"You're going to get wages from now on, Jake, like all the
rest of the sl—servants," Pierce said.

"I'd rawther you kep' the money, please, marster," Jake
laughed, and his open mouth was like the inside of a water-
melon.

"You'll be having to buy your food, though, and clothes for
you and Manda and the children," Pierce said. He tested the
stirrups as carefully as though he were going into battle. A
horseman was no better than his stirrups. He heard a gasp
from Jake.

"You ain't goin' to feed us no mo'?" Jake's face was lined
with terror.

"Now, Jake, what do I give you wages for?" Pierce demanded. He leaned against his horse. This sort of thing was
going to take a mighty lot of patience!

"I don't want no wages," Jake wailed. "I wants our food and
cloes like we allays had had!"

"Great day in the morning!" Pierce shouted, "why, the war was fought so you could be free, man!"

"But my food and cloes!" Jake moaned.

Pierce broke into sudden laughter and leaped on his horse. "Oh well, I reckon you won't starve at Malvern," he said. "And if you want, I'll give you food and clothes instead of wages."

"Thank you—thank you, marster!" Jake bellowed after him.

That was the trouble, Pierce thought. You fought a war for people, you all but died, or you rotted in a prison, the way Tom had rotted nearly to death, and you come home and the people don't know what it's all about, or why you fought and rotted. They want everything just the way it was before.

In the brilliant morning sunshine, cantering across his own lands, his face grew grim. "I'm going to live for myself from now on," he muttered.

He looked across the lands of Malvern, his land. Two hundred years ago his great-grandfather had come from England, a landless younger son, and had bought this valley set high in the mountains of the Alleghenies. He had cut the forests and ploughed the earth, he had built the foundations and the heart of the big house. The soil was rich, and the encircling fields were still fringed with virgin forest, great oaks and beeches and maples.

"I will restore my soul," Pierce said to himself.

He turned his mare's head away from the line of cabins to the north of the road. He did not want to see his own black folk, not even to hear their greetings. He was tired of them because he had fought to keep them. Well, he had lost and they were free. He still believed that it was the wrong way to free them. That was what he would have liked to have told that tall gaunt man in the White House, had he not been killed. All during the war he wanted to go and tell Abe Lincoln, "Man, I don't want slaves! I'll be as glad as you could be to have everyone of them free and wage earning. But it's got to be done slowly, the way our family has been doing it, freeing the men when they get to be thirty-five, freeing the women when they marry. Then they're fit for freedom. The Delaneys have been freeing their slaves for fifty years."

Well, almost freeing them! They had their papers, even if they didn't get real wages. They were like Jake, still wanting their food and clothes and cabins. It scared them if they had only cold money in their palms. They couldn't imagine money turning into food and clothes and cabins.

His horse picked her way delicately about something in the road and he looked down and saw a yellow backed turtle slowly making its way across the dusty stretch. It went on, regardless of the peril it had so narrowly escaped. He laughed at its earnest persistence. It was the comforting and delightful thing about land and forest, and beast and bird—they went on, oblivious of wars.

"I'm going to be like that," he thought. He lifted his head, gave his mare rein and she broke into a gallop. He brought her home an hour later in a froth, and leaped up the steps to have breakfast with Lucinda and the little boys. They were already at the table, when he had washed and dropped into his seat. He had not changed his riding things. After breakfast he wanted to go out again, this time on business. But he must see Tom first.

"Hello, you two," he said to his boys. He reached out his hands and rumpled both blond heads. "See how pretty your mama is?" They turned at the question and stared at her.

"Are you pretty, Mama?" Martin asked, surprised.

"How pretty, Papa?" Carey asked.

Lucinda bore the scrutiny of three pairs of male eyes with lovely calm. She smiled at Pierce as the one most important.

"Awfully, awfully pretty, you little savage," Pierce said and tweaked his son's ear. "Heard anything of Tom, Luce?"

Georgia came in with a plate of hot beaten biscuits, and Lucinda turned to her.

"Has Bettina said anything about your master Tom?" she asked.

"She came out to wash herself," Georgia replied in her soft voice. "I asked her then, Miss Lucie, and she said he was hungry and wanting real food. I was to ask you, please, sir, if you thought a beaten biscuit and soft-boiled egg would harm him."

"Give him anything he wants," Pierce said. "God knows he deserves it."

"But, Pierce, a beaten biscuit?" Lucinda asked.

"Tell him to dunk it in milk," Pierce said.

"Yes, sir," Georgia replied. She poured two cups of coffee, pure amber, from the silver pot on the buffet, set them on the table and went away.

He glanced at her back as she went out. She wore a white dress, much washed and soft, and she had her hair on top of her head, and her neck rose straight and golden.

"How much wage are we going to pay those two girls, Luce?" he inquired.

Lucinda fluttered her white hands. "Oh, Pierce, it's so silly! Besides, how are we going to know? I always give Georgia my old dresses, and she eats the leftovers in the pantry—she and Bettina—they don't eat in the kitchen. How are we going to count all that? I'd rather just give her pin money."

"Have you asked her what she'd rather have?" he asked.

Lucinda frowned and shrugged her shoulders under her lace sack. "I don't think Georgia would know."

Georgia came in again, this time with a plate of ham, sliced thin, to go with the scrambled eggs and kidneys.

"Well, ask her," Pierce said with sudden firmness. But Lucinda pressed her small red lips together firmly and ignored him and he was angry. The army had spoiled him for being ignored. Men had obeyed him to the tune of hundreds and he was not to be disobeyed at home.

"Georgia!" he said abruptly. She looked at him, half alarmed, and he saw into her black eyes, eyes so great and deep that he felt uncomfortable again. "Do you want to be paid wages?"

She answered, faltering. "Yes, sir, I do if you say so—"

"Georgia, you may leave the room," Lucinda said sharply.

The girl disappeared from where she stood as though she had not been.

"You shouldn't frighten her, Luce," Pierce said.

"You shouldn't interfere between me and my maid, Pierce," Lucinda replied.

Then they thought of the children and fell into silence. Pierce ate heavily and in great bites, champing his jaws, his eyes on his plate. Lucinda was full of graceful movement. She poured herself a fresh cup of coffee, buttered a bit of the beaten biscuit split on her plate and she tucked in the end of Carey's napkin into his neck. Between these feather soft motions of hands and arms, between the turns of her head and the lifting and lowering of her lids, she watched Pierce.

He threw down his napkin. "I'm going to see for myself how Tom is this morning," he said abruptly.

"Do," Lucinda said pleasantly. "And tell him I'll be in as soon as I have the children settled."

He opened the door into his brother's room and the weight moved from his bosom. He had been away from women too long. It was going to take time to get used to them again, even to Lucinda. There was something secret about women living in a house when a man had been living in the open with men. He looked at Tom warmly.

"Why, you're looking wonderful, Tom," he said. "Great goodness, man, I didn't know what you were yesterday—a scarecrow!"

Tom was lying against fresh pillows, his hair brushed, his nightshirt immaculately white. Bettina was folding a tartan shawl over his shoulders.

"I feel—good," Tom said. His voice was faint enough but stronger than it had been yesterday.

"And you slept?"

"Without waking—"

Pierce sat down in the armchair by the bed. "Tom, you talk differently—more like the Yankees."

"I've heard nothing but Yankees—except the prison guards."

Pierce looked grave. His handsome face, always quick to show his feelings, fell into lines of concern. "Tom, did you know the names of any of those sons of bitches? I'll challenge any man of them we know."

Tom shook his head. "They had it in for me—because I'm from the south. They treated me worse than a Yankee."

"Probably did," Pierce said. "I feared for you. First I heard you were dead, Tom. Then I got word you were a prisoner. I moved heaven and earth, of course, but I couldn't break through."

"They had it in for me," Tom said again slowly. "From the top down—not the slightest favor."

"Tom, did they—hurt you?"

"Yes," Tom said. He paused as though he would not go on and then the words burst out of him in a retch. "They whipped us, starved us—more of us died than were lost at the front. Pierce, you know how many men Grant lost? I mean from the Wilderness to the James River—I tell you it wasn't anything to what we lost last July and August—in Andersonville—the awful heat—the miserable holes we lived in—and all around us woods to make cabins if they'd let us—but they wouldn't let us."

Tom was crying, the tears running down his cheeks at last. He had tears today to weep out his heart and Pierce felt his throat grow tight.

He threw his arms around his brother. "Tom, don't you remember it! It's all past. You're home, boy. Why, you and me, we're going to make Malvern like a heaven—"

"What's the use of a spot of heaven—in the middle of a hell world—" Tom was shaking in a chill.

"Here, Bettina," Pierce cried in terror.

Bettina came quietly to the bedside. "Leave him to me, sir. You'd best go away for a space, if you please."

"I reckon you're right. Give him something to calm him, Bettina—"

He hastened out of the room and paused at the door, remorseful at his own inability to endure the sight of his brother. It was a shameful sight. A man had to mend himself. Tom would thank him for going away when he was all in pieces. He closed the door softly, pulled out his handkerchief and wiped his forehead.

"Got to get myself to work," he muttered.

He tiptoed through the halls and out of a side door to the stables again. He did not want to see Lucinda or the children. He'd get along down the lanes and across the country, be by himself awhile, maybe stop in at the town and get him some tobacco. Full of misery, he strode into the stable. It was a great empty place, inhabited once by a string of race horses and farm beasts, nearly all of which had been destroyed in the war. Cattle had been eaten except for two old cows, and horses had gone to the army. There was no sign of Jake and he must saddle his mare himself.

Then once more the good work of his hands comforted him. He brushed his horse's coat and put on the saddle blanket and tightened the girth. Beauty looked at him gaily and tossed her tail. He was comforted by her simple presence, by her rolling dark eyes and her willingness to bear the burden of his body.

"You're my sweetheart," he told her and leading her into the yards he swung himself astride her back and touched her into a gallop. He had to get to work on Malvern, root himself here again, make it his being as once it had been before the war tore him out and threw him into the alien world. He had longed for Malvern every moment he was away. Even when he was at Charlottesville, at the University, he was always homesick. Now Lucinda, the children, all of them, and even himself, were only part of the place.

"I've got to get Tom on his feet," he thought solemnly. "Get him on his feet and then on a horse! That'll cure him. Then we'll get Malvern going again—"

He was inspired by the thought of a horse for Tom. He would ride over to Jackson's stable and see what they had in the way of horses. Twenty miles, a little over—he could do it easily by dinnertime. Then he would go in and tell Tom and cheer him up. Nothing was so cheering to a man as to know he had a good horse waiting for him. Given a few weeks and he and Tom would be riding over the land together. Then women and house would be left behind and in their right place.

"You have to tell somebody, sir, that I see, and you can

tell me," Bettina said to Tom when Pierce was gone. He looked into her grave dark eyes.

"I'm simply—dissolved," he gasped. Yesterday it had been impossible to talk. Today with his first shred of strength he wanted to talk.

"That is right," she said. Her voice was kind and warm but without pity. "That is natural."

"I've—been through so much—" he whispered.

He looked up, searching for her contempt—"A man pitying himself," he went on.

There was no contempt in her beautiful face. "Sometimes a man must pity himself. He alone knows what he's been through."

"You see that?"

His tears dried and he felt stronger. He cleared his throat. "It was unnecessary—what we went through—"

She drew the armchair to the side of the bed and sat down, her elbows leaning on the bed, her chin on her clenched hands. "Tell me," she said.

"You can't imagine—" he began.

"I know I can't, so tell me—" she repeated.

"A poor dreary village—in the forests—in the morning—the sun would never come up. I used to wait for it—and then when it came it poured down so hot that you longed for night again, and when it went down it went down as though it had dropped into a well and all the mosquitoes and flies sprang at you like tigers out of the dark—"

"I know," she whispered, "I was born in Georgia."

"You know, all those forests—we could have built ourselves houses. The Confederate government owned all the sawmills —you know that? They could have put up houses for us—but we lived in holes and tents and there was a big pen—"

He pushed up his sleeve and showed her his bone-thin arms. They were covered with scars. "Burned," he said, "they burned us with pine sticks lit into coals at the end. What did they do that for?"

"Men do such things," she said. "I've seen men hang another man and burn him before he died."

"But we were all white men," Tom said.

"It doesn't matter, white or black, when the feel for it gets in them. Happens to black more often because the black men are in white men's power. But I reckon when white men get under the power, the same things are done to them."

"I couldn't save myself," Tom went on as though he had not heard her. "I used to curse and swear and rave and hit at them. After a while you learn better. You just look down at the ground and don't even mumble. You just take it, whatever it is—think about something else if you can—but you take it."

"I know," Bettina said, "how I know!"

The room was full of peace and stillness. Years ago some ancestor had paneled it white wood, and had set into the space above the mantel piece the portrait of a young girl, young as spring in her white and green gown. Her hair was the color of daffodils, but she held a gold cross in her hand. Why did a white girl hold a cross? What did she know about the meaning of a cross?

"You've never been a prisoner," Tom said restlessly. "You can't know."

"I know how it feels to have to take things," she answered. "I know how it feels to be helpless."

He came out of his absorption in his own misery enough to look at her with faint curiosity. "Nobody is mean to you here —in our house."

"I lived a long time enough before I came here," she said, sighing.

But his curiosity could not reach beyond himself today. His own body was still his chief concern. "How my back hurts me!" he muttered.

"Turn yourself over, sir. Turn over and I'll rub you well."

He turned himself painfully, groaning, and she helped him, half lifting him. Her slender arms were unexpectedly strong and he felt them so.

"You've got strength," he murmured into his pillow.

"I've got to have strength," she replied. She began to rub his back as she spoke, and the strokes of her hands were long and strong. He yielded himself to their comfort.

The lands of Malvern lay across a wide shallow valley and over two ranges of hills. Riding until noon Pierce had cut diagonally across from the northeast corner to southwest. Not too many of the fields were fallow, but the war had forced idleness on the land. With Tom and himself both away he could not expect to see the land looking as it should. But it was there and it still belonged to him. He was stripped and penniless, as every man on the Southern side was, but he could borrow for seed, and he knew his land. Give him a year, and it would be pouring out its gold again. Labor he would get somehow, for whatever pay. He wanted only to look ahead.

At the southwest corner Malvern joined its fields to that of his nearest neighbor, John MacBain. Pierce held his horse just short of the border and looked across a meadow. Part of the MacBain house had been burned down. He had heard of it, but he had not seen it. Now it was plain. The east wing was grey and gaunt, a skeleton attached to the main house. Strange how crippled the house looked—like a man with his right arm withered! No, he was not going to let himself think about crippled men.

He loosened the reins and went cantering over the meadow. He'd stop and see John MacBain. They had been good neighbors always, and their boyhood friendship had held.

He tied his horse to the hitching post by the stile near the front door and then mounted the wide stone steps. The front door was open and he was about to shout when he heard his own name called.

"Pierce Delaney—by Gawd!"

It was John himself— By-Gawd MacBain, people called him.

Pierce swung on his heel and saw him lying on a cot in the shadow of an ancient climbing rose that hung in festoons from the second story of the portico.

"Why, John," he exclaimed. "What's damaged you?"

"Sit down," John said. His voice was still deep but the substance had gone out of it. It sounded hollow, as though it came from a cavern.

"I hadn't heard you were sick," Pierce said. He sat down and laid his whip on the floor.

"I'm not sick, I'm wounded," John said. "Got a Yankee bullet in me."

"Can't a doctor get it out?" Pierce asked.

"Not to guarantee my life while he's doin' it," John said.

"But you can't just lie there!" Pierce protested.

"At least I'm alive," John said. He gazed at Pierce from under the bushy red brows that gave ferocity to his deep-set grey eyes. "I aim to live," he said doggedly.

"Of course," Pierce replied. His determination never again to think of the wounded failed him. Here was John, wounded for life! He knew the look of the desperately wounded, the secret hopelessness behind the eyes, the hidden knowledge of death. He looked away and over the meadow to Malvern.

"Well, I just thought I'd stop by and see how you were, John," he said at last.

"Thank you kindly, Pierce. I hear Tom's home."

"Starved nearly to death, John, but we'll mend that as fast as we can."

"You can't hardly blame our side for starving Yankees in jail when our own folks lived on dried beans and cornmeal," John said. He stared up at the cobwebby ceiling of the portico. "You 'member my twin boys?"

Pierce nodded. "Lucinda told me—"

"They're both dead," John said. His hollow voice tolled the words. "No milk, no eggs—nothing they could eat, poor little fellers! Well, that leaves me alone with Molly."

"You'll have more boys," Pierce said.

"Nope—I reckon not."

Pierce turned his head at the agony in John MacBain's voice.

"No more boys," John said. "The Yankees got me there, Pierce."

"You mean—"

"Yes."

Pierce felt the old insufferable weight in his breast. His chest grew tight when he was forced to face suffering. So often, when at the end of a day and the battle was over, he had scarcely been able to breathe when he had seen the rows of his men, the dead and the wounded, lying on the ground, waiting to be carried away. It had been his duty to see them, and he had done his duty.

"John, if I knew what to say—"

"There's nothing to say, I reckon, Pierce. It's my wife Molly I worry about. She's still young."

They heard Molly's clear voice at this moment. She was talking to someone, directing and scolding at the same time. Her skirts rustled and she was at the door.

"John—" she began and saw the visitor.

"Why, Pierce Delaney!" she cried. Her round pretty face lit and she put out both hands to him. "John and I were just wondering—how is that poor Tom?"

"Nothing wrong except what some feeding will put right," Pierce said. He felt her warm strong little hands in his and felt sorry for John MacBain and let them go.

"Well, it's good to see you," she said. Her eyes traveled frankly over his tall figure. "And you're out riding? My Gawd, it's good to see a man riding as though there hadn't been a war."

"My Gawd," the ribald called Molly MacBain. By Gawd and My Gawd.

John MacBain, watching them, shouted suddenly. "Molly, go and fetch some of the blackberry wine! Pierce has rid half a day—"

She bustled away, and John closed his eyes. "What I told you, Pierce," he muttered. "You dassent to tell. She don't want a soul to know it. I don't know why I told you. But I felt I had to have a man know it."

"Surely I won't tell," Pierce promised.

"Not even your wife," John said.

"Nobody," Pierce promised.

But he could not forget it. Molly came back with wine and small cakes. "They're only cornmeal and sweetened with molasses and riz with yeast," she said in her busy gay voice. "My Gawd, what it will be to have baking powder and sugar! How long will it be, Pierce?"

"Who knows?" he said. He tasted the wine and bit into a cake. "These are good," he said politely.

"Oh, I make do with what I have," Molly said. She went to John's cot and pulled a cover straight and Pierce watched them. Should he speak of the twins or should he not? What would be right for Molly—no, for John, for whom he cared far more? He looked across the sunny meadows where the two little boys used to play. They were just toddling around when last he saw them.

"I am mighty grieved to hear about the boys, Miss Molly," he said abruptly. The cornmeal cake clogged his throat.

She turned and stood rigid for an instant. "Thank you—" she said at last. "Thank you kindly, Pierce. But I just—I just can't think of them."

Her small full mouth quivered, and her eyelids glistened. She gave him a look and ran into the house. John closed his eyes and lay rigidly still.

"If there is anything I could do," Pierce began.

"There isn't, thank you, Pierce," John did not open his eyes. "We've just got to live along—"

"Yes, I reckon," Pierce murmured sadly. "Well, John, maybe I could help you with the place, anyway. We'll be ploughing again this spring, and I could make shift to do some of your fields if you're short of help."

John opened his eyes. "Short—I'm without help!" he cried. "Two old niggers—that's what's stayed with us. They can scratch a kitchen garden—that's all."

"Then I'll rent your land from you, if you like, until you can get up and around once more."

"How come you got help?" he demanded.

"I'm payin' wages," Pierce said simply.

"I ain't goin' to take your paid help," John declared.

"There's no other kind to be had, John," Pierce told him.

John lifted his head from his pillow. "By Gawd, Pierce— what did we fight the war for, if you're goin' to pay niggers?"

"We lost the war, John—"

"Not me—I didn't—so far as I'm concerned, the war is goin' on forever."

The voice was brave, but its hollowness made the words a boast. Pierce did not say what he thought. He had his two sons alive and Malvern must go on in the new times as it had in the old. He picked up his whip and got to his feet.

"Of course I know how you feel, John," he said amiably. "And I'm not going to argue with you. I've had enough of fighting. I'm going to live in peace—with all men. And if I never set foot on any land except Malvern, I'll be content. But I'll farm yours if you want me to—"

There was a second's silence. John's head fell back.

"Your family all right?" he asked.

"Yes, they are—I don't know why I'm lucky," Pierce said. He tapped his riding boot softly with the crop of his whip. "I thank God," he added simply.

"Not many of us got anything left to thank anybody for," John said bitterly. "But I won't put my burden on you, Pierce. I reckon I can carry it."

"You are a strong man, John," Pierce said kindly.

They were both silent again and then they had a common impulse to part.

"Well, goodbye," Pierce said. "I'm going over to Jackson's to look for a horse for Tom. If you change your mind about your land you have only to let me know."

"Thanks—I can't answer for myself—I might stay," John replied. "Or I might go away."

Pierce mounted his horse behind the rose bush to spare John the misery of seeing him ride off well and whole. He cantered south to Jackson's, very grave and sorrowful. Of all men John was the least suited to such a wound, John who never willingly read a book, who lived to hunt and ride and eat and drink. And Molly was not like Lucinda. Luce could make shift without a man, he thought cruelly. Sapphires he had promised if it was a girl. Diamonds he had given her for the boys. She would never give herself entirely for her own passion. That was because she had none. Well, he was glad he had never liked Molly MacBain, since they were neighbors and likely to be neighbors all their lives. She was not quite pretty enough—a little on the common side, he thought, and cursed himself.

"I'm a damned difficult combination," he thought ruefully. "I like them to look like queens and act like gypsies. The two don't come together."

The brief frankness with himself made him ashamed. He thought of Lucinda with tenderness, and suddenly feeling the sun beat down on him he touched the mare with his whip and she broke into a gallop. He had the decent man's dislike of allowing himself to think secretly about women. It was a thing to struggle against after adolescence, a childishness to be outgrown.

He forgot women thoroughly when he reached Jackson's horse farm. By some miracle, Jackson had a two-year-old bay.

"She ain't quite gentled yet," Jackson said. He stroked the bay's shining bronze flanks and she tossed her head.

"Tom will want to do his own gentling," Pierce said.

He examined her, from eye to tooth to fetlock, and settled on a price.

"Too high," he thought as he rode homeward. He would be afraid to tell Lucinda.

"I don't have to tell her," he thought and rode on. He was astonished at his new freedom. Once he would have felt he had to tell her everything. But the war had separated him from her. He had learned to live to himself—or almost!

"Georgia, hurry—here comes your master!" Lucinda cried. She sat by the long window of her room on the rose satin hassock and Georgia knelt beside her, mending a torn ruffle. It was part of Lucinda's pattern for herself that she always met her husband when he came home. She liked to think of herself throwing open the big door and standing there, a picture against the great hall.

"Hurry—hurry—" she said impatiently.

Georgia bent her dark head and her fingers flew at her task. The needle broke suddenly and she held it up, terror in her eyes.

"My thimble's got holes in it, ma'am," she said— "The needle caught."

"Oh, Georgia," Lucinda cried. "The very idea—"

"Yes, ma'am," Georgia agreed. "Let me just pin it, ma'am."

"You know we haven't any pins—" Lucinda retorted.

"Yes, ma'am, but I'll just use this broken needle, 'tis good for naught, now."

"But do we have another needle? Really, Georgia, to break a *needle*—"

"I have two more, ma'am, I saved—"

"Well, then—"

Lucinda stood, shook her ruffles, and ran downstairs lightly. Behind her Georgia picked up bits of thread from the rose flowered carpet. She stood up and saw herself in the long oval mirror above the dressing table. It was an accident, and she hesitated. Then she tiptoed nearer and gazed at herself. She was pretty! She and Bettina were both pretty, but maybe she was a little prettier even than Bettina. But what use was it? Whom could they hope to marry?

"Unless we should go up north—" she thought.

Plenty of brown people were going north. Brown was what she called herself and Bettina. Their father had taught them. "Don't you call yourselves niggers," he had told them. "You're my daughters, damn you! Brown—brown—that's what you are. Brown's a good color, isn't it?" But when he got old and drowsy he had not cared what color they were.

"Wonder how would I look with my hair up high?" she thought.

She glanced at the door. They'd be downstairs now together —no danger of their coming up. The mirror in the attic was a cracked old thing and she could never see herself in it. Besides, she was ashamed to fuss with herself before Bettina. Bettina was younger, but she acted older.

She loosened her curly black hair and let it fall on her shoulders. "I daren't use her combs and brushes, though," she murmured. She was sorely tempted. She washed them out every day anyway, and she would wash them out right away. Upstairs she and Bettina shared a bit of broken comb. She didn't

know what a brush felt like in her hair though she brushed
ma'am's hair an hour every single night before bedtime until
it shone like the copper kettle. She lifted the silver-backed
brush on the toilet table and then jumped. There in the mirror
she saw her master standing. She put the brush down softly
and without turning around she bundled her hair back into
her net.

"Are you beautifying yourself, Georgia?" Pierce asked, and
laughed.

She did not answer nor did she turn. She was too honest to
excuse herself.

"You better not let your—you better not let her see you,"
he said.

"No, sir—I know I am doing wrong," Georgia said in a faint
voice.

He was watching her face in the mirror. It was downcast,
and the heavy fringes of her black eyelashes lay on her pale
gold cheeks. "Why, the girl is a beauty, poor thing," he
thought.

"Where's your—" he stopped, and Georgia lifted her eyelashes.

"Hang it," he swore, "I keep trying not to say 'your mistress.' "

She turned and smiled at him with pity. "I wish you
wouldn't bother. I don't mind," she said.

"It was only yesterday I decided I wouldn't let you say
master and mistress any more," he reminded her.

"Yes, sir, but I know how you want to do, and so I don't
mind," she said.

The girl's lips were red and her teeth very white. He did
not remember ever having seen a brown girl's lips so red.

"Then where's your mistress?" he asked. He heard the
harshness in his voice and could do nothing to quell it. For the
first time the future loomed as something monstrous. The end
of this war meant that Georgia and all like her were free and
they were his and Lucinda's equals. The distance that had
once been between had been taken away. Anything could
happen, and there were no laws to check it. If there were to

be new barriers, they must be made by people like himself, or there were no barriers—he refused to think further. There must be barriers, of course, between white and black.

"Pierce!" Lucinda's voice floated up the stairs.

"She's downstairs to meet you, Master Pierce," Georgia said. As though she felt new distance shaping between them she returned to her old shape of his name.

He turned and left her standing there. From the head of the stairs he looked down at his wife at the foot. She had left the big front door open and she stood against a silver screen of light. Her golden hair caught it and the whiteness of her skin caught it and her eyes were like the sapphires she loved. She saw him and ran up and he met her halfway and took her in his arms.

"Pierce—in broad daylight—" she protested.

"Day and night," he muttered, "night and day—"

He held her and for once she stood pliant in his embrace. But it could not last. The boys were running in from outdoors and behind them Joe was making efforts to catch them.

"Mama, Mama!" Martin screamed, and then saw them on the stairs. Lucinda turned in Pierce's arms and smiled down at her two sons proudly. They stood gaping up at her and Joe turned and pretended to look out the door. Let her sons remember their mother, young and beautiful, standing in their father's arms!

"What you doin', Mama?" Martin asked.

Carey put his thumb in his mouth and continued his stare.

Lucinda forgot her role. "Take your thumb out of your mouth, Carey Delaney!" she cried.

She freed herself, ran down the stairs and pulled his thumb out of his mouth. It came out with a soft plop and she wiped it dry on her lace handkerchief. "You want to have buckteeth when you grow up?" she inquired. "Girls don't love men with buckteeth."

Carey gazed at her placidly. She flicked his cheek with her thumb and finger, and walked away into the drawing room. As soon as her back was turned he put his thumb into his mouth again.

Pierce, watching from the stairs, laughed. "Don't you obey your mother, sir?" he inquired of his younger son.

"Not when she ain't here," Carey replied. He took his thumb out for these words and put it back. Regarding his son's round red cheeks and bright blue eyes, and seeing the small gold curls which perspiration plastered to his forehead, Pierce burst into laughter, loud and fond.

"You're a man," he declared.

His laughter penetrated to the drawing room and Lucinda stopped, listened and frowned. Pierce's laughter! He laughed easily, at jokes to which she always listened without understanding them. Since he had come home he laughed more than ever, but about nothing.

She shrugged her shoulders and dismissed the laughter for something far more important. A deep discontent ate its way into the pleasure of her days. Malvern had been conceived and born in Virginia, even as she had been. It had never come into her imagination that at any time of her life she would be living outside Virginia. But the war had dealt cruelly with her. Malvern lay on the eastern edge of the western counties that had seceded to make a Union. Now, irrevocably, she lived in a state that was hateful to her. Virginia was old and stable and proud, the home of aristocrats. But West Virginia was an upstart.

She gazed moodily at the gray mohair of the drawing-room furniture. It had come, a generation ago, from France and even its fine close texture had yielded to the war years. It looked well, but she knew that Georgia's fine stitches were woven in and out of it. She would not allow the children to sit on it, and even now, alone in the room, she sat in a wooden Windsor armchair.

She turned her head and saw Pierce at the open door in the hall. He was standing, his feet wide apart, his hands in his pockets, staring out over the land.

"Pierce!" she called. "Come here!"

Once he would have come instantly but now the imperiousness in her voice stirred distaste in him.

"What do you want?" he called back.

She rose in a flutter of ruffles and lace and ran out into the hall and pausing behind him she reached up and slapped one of his cheeks lightly and then the other.

"You hear me call?" she demanded.

"I answered, didn't I?" he replied.

"But I want you to come when I call!" she complained.

She clasped her hands through his arm and dragged him half-unwillingly, half-laughing, into the drawing room.

"I want to know when I can have new satin for the furniture," she demanded.

Pierce shook himself free from her. "Jiminy, Luce, do I have to tell you again that we have no money? If you can raise your own stuff you can have it. But you can't buy anything. Well, we're going to raise sheep. Malvern hills can grow good wool."

Lucinda pouted. "I don't want wool. Moths will chew it. I want satin."

"Then you'll have to wait until we can trade wool for satin, my girl," he said firmly.

"Pierce, I can't believe you haven't got anything!" she protested.

"I have money to burn, and that's all it's fit for," he said. "We lost the war, honey! How come you can't understand what I tell you over and over? Our money is worthless. But we're lucky we have the house and the land and a fair number of slaves ready to work for wages. And thank God, we're not in a Southern state. We can begin to build new railroads and factories and open up the mines."

"And I hate it that we're not in Virginia any more," she cried.

"It's the saving of us that we're not," he said gravely. "We'll escape a lot of woes."

It occurred to him that he had not seen Tom since he came home to tell him that he had bought a horse, and in his impetuous fashion he forgot his wife and turned and strode upstairs.

Lucinda watched him, her hands folded one over the other

as years ago her English governess had taught her to hold them.

"Put the hands into graceful rest when not in use," she had proclaimed. She had taken the small Lucinda's hands and laid them one upon the other just beneath the place where later her breasts would bud. There Lucinda now held them unconsciously when she did not embroider or pour tea. Their quiet was deceiving. Both her sons knew that those slender white hands, lying as quiet as the two wings of a resting bird, could fly out and leave a smart upon a small boy's cheek, and then in the next second lie at rest again. When she spoke, they watched not her face but her hands.

She listened and heard Pierce's step enter the bedroom above the drawing room. Then she went and stood in the tall French window that opened upon the terrace. Malvern lands were spread before her eyes. Sheep! Yankees raised sheep. She stood, seeing nothing while within her something grew hard and firm. She would not allow Pierce to change her life. She belonged to the South and in her the South would live forever. She would keep it alive.

"I had nothing to do with the war," she told herself. "It's just the same as if it had never been—for me, anyway." She sat down again and began to plan the colors of her satin.

# Two

"Tom!" Pierce's voice was softened to suit the pale face on the pillow. It was morning, a summer morning, and he was on his way to the farms.

Tom opened his eyes.

Pierce tiptoed in, and the boards creaked.

"You don't need to do that," Tom said. "I'm better."

"You ought to be," Pierce said, "after all these weeks."

Bettina was sitting by a window darning a nightshirt. Now she rose and stood waiting.

"I'll look after him awhile, Bettina," Pierce said. "You can go and get some fresh air." He sat down in the armchair near the bed.

"Yes, Master Pierce," Bettina replied. She picked up a few threads, straightened the bed covers, and went out. Pierce, watching Tom's face, saw his eyes follow the girl's figure until the door closed. He coughed.

"Does she take good care of you?" he asked.

"Yes," Tom said.

"Lucinda says both those sisters are good at nursing," Pierce went on.

"Bettina says she took care of their father for a long time," Tom said.

Now that he was alone with Pierce, Tom did not know what to say.

"Their father was old Colonel Halford, who used to live down in Mississippi," Pierce said. "Luce doesn't know much about him, though." He sighed. "It's queer even for me to remember we don't live in Virginia any more. Luce is taking it hard. But I can't move Malvern."

"When I look at Bettina," Tom said strangely, "I know what the war was for. To think she could be bought and sold!"

Pierce said, "Now look here, Tom, you're mighty weak. It'll likely be months before you feel just right."

"I'm weak," Tom agreed. He lay listless for a moment. He felt now that he could not begin talking to Pierce. He felt crushed under his brother's health and strength. The war had made Pierce coarse and tough. While he had been shut up in a Confederate prison, Pierce had commanded a regiment of men. Authority had hardened him. All the days and weeks and months that he had been idle and starving and struggling to live for his own sake and wondering every hour of the day and night why life was what it was, Pierce had been too busy to think. They had both been changed and in opposite directions. He closed his eyes.

"Tired?" Pierce asked.

"I reckon I'll be tired forever," Tom said.

"Now don't you get to feeling sorry for yourself," Pierce advised him. "Especially when you have as nice a horse as still lives outside a soldier's stomach," he added and laughed.

Anger burned under Tom's eyelids and gave him strength. "I'm not in the habit of feeling sorry for myself," he said sharply. Then he relented. "Thanks for the horse—I reckon I'll be riding again one of these days."

"Of course you will," Pierce declared. He went on, because he could not think of anything to say to that closed face. "Tom —your mare came today—ready to train to do anything you like. Canters naturally, like a girl waltzing."

Tom opened his eyes, and Pierce went on with enthusiasm. "You'd better look, Tom. I'm going to pace her under your windows and you'll be up and on her back in no time."

The room was full of Pierce's big voice. The noise of it echoed in Tom's ears and made him faint. He had the feeling that Pierce was using up all the air in the room and he gasped. Pierce stood up in alarm. "Are you feeling worse, Tom?"

"Yes," Tom whispered. He longed suddenly for Bettina.

Bettina knew how to make him feel strong. She could lift up his head and put the pillows right.

"Bettina!" Pierce shouted out of the window. "Bettina, you come here right away!"

Out in the kitchen summerhouse Bettina was drinking a cup of sassafras tea. She had poured the boiling water from the kettle always hot on the range, and had taken her cup to be out of Annie's way. She heard Pierce's voice, and threw what was left of the tea on the roots of the climbing rose and went quickly upstairs.

Pierce was poised in anxiety and met her at the door. "Looks to me like Tom's fainted," he whispered. "Better see what you can do—quick."

"Yes, sir," Bettina said. She moved to the bed. Pierce paused in the doorway. He was no good in a sick room. Tom was sick, he supposed, weak, anyway. He had helped many a man to die, but he did not know what to do with a starving man.

"Better give him more real food," he told Bettina. "Get him full of something strong."

"Yes, sir," Bettina said.

Pierce stood a moment longer and then could not bear to stay. "I'll be downstairs in the library if you call," he said. "Or I'll be out at the stables."

"Yes, sir," Bettina said.

But she knew the moment that she looked at him that Tom had not fainted. She closed the door softly and then stood beside the bed, smiling. His eyelashes were quivering. He opened his eyes and saw her standing there.

"Kneel down," he commanded.

She knelt, wondering. He turned himself and put out his arms and she drew back.

"Oh no," she whispered. "Oh no, Master Tom—"

"Yes, Bettina, yes!"

A moment ago he would have said he was really fainting. But now he felt a strange tingling energy. He seized her arms and held her fast. "You belong to me," he said. "I fought for you—I made you free."

She pulled back and was amazed that she could not wrench herself from his hands. "Then leave me free!" she cried, and glanced fearfully at the door.

To her surprise he loosened her as suddenly as he had seized her. "You're right," he muttered. "Of course—I fought to make you free of everybody—me, too, God knows!"

He lay back on the pillows and flung out his hands. "Go on away," he said. "I don't own you—"

One of his hands fell near her breast. She put out her two hands and took it and held it pressed against her. On the pillow his thin face turned to her.

"You don't own me—" she whispered. "Nobody owns me any more. I do belong to myself. But seeing I belong to myself —why, I reckon I can do what I like—with myself—"

She put her lips into the palm of his hand and he felt them soft and hot.

"I can *give* myself—" she faltered, "seeing how I am free—"

He turned to her and she leaned to him. He put his arms about her and kissed her full. She turned her face away at last.

"Oh, my Lord," she breathed.

"Why didn't you tell me you loved me?" he complained

" 'Tisn't for me to tell— Oh, Master Tom, it isn't even what I want—"

"Hush," he said, "don't call me master—never, so long as we live!"

The first harvests of Malvern were being reaped. Pierce rose at dawn for the joy of seeing his harvests, and rode about his fields. In his barns could be heard again the sound of cows lowing and the whinny of horses. Not all were paid for, but with the harvests he had money in his hand and he was not afraid.

The year had been an unusually good one. Winter had been mild toward the end, and spring had come with a rush of rhododendrons in the woods. He had forgotten all beauty in the years of war, and now it seemed to him he was seeing everything for the first time, the ruddy blossoms of the red maples, the early green of lilac, the redbud and the dogwood. During the spring he had searched avidly for each sign of life and growth. Sugar was still scarce and there was excuse for the making of maple sugar, as his father and grandfather had done before him, and as he had not done since he was master. He had ordered staple crops sown into the freshly ploughed fields, wheat for bread and corn and oats for man and beast, barley and rye. There was still no coffee to be had, but the rye made a fair drink when it was roasted slowly with black molasses. There were no dye stuffs to be had either, and he had superintended the making of dark brown dye from the black walnuts and saffron yellow from sulphur and red and purple from wild berries. Lucinda put up her nose at his household interests, but he could not sufficiently satiate himself with life after the years of death. He had even busied himself in the dairy, ordering great flagstones to be laid and new shelves to be built. It gave him solid comfort today when he rode over the land to know that in the dairy at Malvern crocks were full of butter and jugs full of buttermilk and that cheeses already stood in the presses.

He drew up his horse this July morning under an early-bearing apple tree and plucked a green-skinned sweet apple and ate it as though he sipped a glass of the finest wine. Come October he'd be having apple butter again, and this winter there would be hams and bacons. Give him five years and Malvern would be on its own feet once more and marching on! And with all this, scarcely a hundred dollars of real cash had lain in his palm during the year. He had worked without money, paying his help in kind, and feeding the family what Malvern had. It had been bare eating in the winter. He and Lucinda had sat down to a dinner table more than once where linen and silver were fine, but the Spode dinner set, which his grandfather had brought from England, had held nothing except cornmeal mush and black peas, and the soup had been brewed from cabbage.

Well, that was over. Malvern was in fruit again. They were eating roasting ears and greens and their first new potatoes, grown from a half bushel he had traded with Molly MacBain for a hen and a rooster. He smiled at the thought of Molly,

and flushed under the summer sun. Lucinda was to have her
child in early autumn. She had announced it to him last night,
although it had been obvious to him for months that she was
pregnant. But he knew better than to mention it to her before
she chose to tell him.

"Mr. Delaney," she had said last night in her room.

"Well?" he had asked. He was lounging in her low chair
preparatory to dressing for dinner. She made him dress every
night now as she had before the war.

She herself was already wearing her yellow taffeta, which
she complained was in rags and tatters, except that Georgia
held it together by delicate darning. She had looked neither
ragged nor tattered, however, as she sat in her highbacked
chair, her hands folded together like magnolia petals.

"You may expect an addition to your family, Mr. Delaney,"
she said.

"Indeed!" he cried. He sat up and took his hands out of his
pockets. "When, may I ask?"

"In the first two weeks of September, likely," she said.

She sat very straight and full of dignity, and he smiled and
went over to her and took her head between his hands and
kissed her forehead.

"Careful of my pompadour, please," she cautioned him.

He sat down again. "And what shall her name be, Luce?"
he inquired.

"I had thought of Sapphira," she replied. "It's a Bible
name," she added.

He reflected. "Wasn't she a liar, Luce?" he asked.

"She obeyed her husband, I believe," Lucinda replied. "It
is in my memory that her husband bade her tell a lie."

He had burst out laughing. "Why, Luce, all women are
liars! They don't need to have men teach them."

"Indeed they are not," she had cried.

"Indeed they are," he had cried back at her, "and if you
plague me I shall utterly destroy your pompadour."

He knew by now that a threat to disarrange her hair was
the surest way to subjugate her, and she knew that since he
came back from the war he was capable of doing it. Twice

when she had plagued him he had tumbled and tossed her and left her half crying with rage.

Riding over the fields solitary in the morning he smiled, thinking of the evening. He was tender toward her always, even when he was rough, accepting her little tempers and tantrums with loud laughter, and holding her hands when she fell into a rage. For she could beat him when she was angry and this amused him mightily. It seemed to him that she was the essence of all that was feminine and he loved her profoundly, more he knew, although he would never acknowledge it, than she could possibly love him. He did not blame her for this. She loved him as well as she could, and she could love no one better, or so he believed. With that he could comfort himself. Yet he wondered if there were somewhere, in some women, something more than she could give him. He blushed now when he thought of this. Luce had given him sons and she would give him daughters. He had no reproach against her. But it was strange how war loosened the withers of a man's soul. Many imaginings came into his own mind now which before the war he could not have had. He was beset by the continual knowledge of the shortness of time and the richness of life. War had shown him both.

He lifted his hand and drank in the morning sunshine. Once when he and Tom were children they had kept a pet crow, and on a fine morning like this one, the crow would bathe its body in the sun. It would ruffle its feathers and hold them apart for the sun to penetrate into the skin, and then, still unsatisfied, it would turn its beak to the sun and open it wide and let the sun pour down its throat, as though the light were food. He opened his own mouth now and felt the sun warm on his tongue. He could almost taste it, sparkling and pure.

At the boundaries of Malvern he found John MacBain, leaning on a fence, his straw hat pulled down over his eyes. He was on his feet again, thin as a withe and leathery, alive, but with a curiously dead look in his eyes.

"You there, John!" Pierce called and cantered his mare. Then he jumped down and threw the reins over the beast's neck and sauntered toward his neighbor.

"Feeling well again?" he asked.

"Well as I'll ever be," John MacBain replied. He was chewing a twig of spice bush.

"You look pretty good," Pierce said gaily. He was warmly aware of the blood coursing through his own potent body, and of his child in Lucinda's womb. He was too kind to dwell upon his own good fortune. "Going to farm again, John?" he asked.

"No," John MacBain said. "I'm thinking of moving away—take Molly to Wheeling, likely, and get me a job in the railroads. Railroads are the coming thing in the state, I hear. The city'll give Molly life, I figure. It's hard on her just fussing around an empty house."

"I hear about the railroads, too—" Pierce said. He did not want to talk about Molly.

"Or mining," John MacBain said moodily. "There's coal mines opening toward the north of the state. I want to do something I never did before—start out fresh."

"We'll miss you for neighbors," Pierce said.

"I'll rent you the land but I shan't sell the house," John said. "I was born in it and so was my father. We'll be back and forth, likely—summers, anyway."

"That's good," Pierce said.

The bleakness in John's eyes was a grey wall between them. He felt the constant knowledge of impatience that haunted them, and unable to think of further talk, he mounted his horse again.

"Well, see you again, John. Let me know before you go. Lucinda will want you both over for dinner."

"It'll be a while yet," John said.

Pierce rode away, feeling the envy in John MacBain's eyes burn into his back. War was cruel and unjust—as cruel and unjust as God, who gave down rain on the good and evil. He resolved that as little as possible would he consider anything except the joy of life itself, of food and sleep and riding and hunting, of wine and children and sunshine and earth and the seasons. He would live for himself and his own, "so help me God," he thought, "from now until I die." He hardened his heart toward John MacBain and toward every maimed and wounded creature, and was arrogantly proud that he was whole.

It was nearly one o'clock when he rounded the turn of the road and cantered up the avenue of oaks that led to the house. He dismounted and tossed the reins to Jake who came running out to meet him.

"She's lathered, you see," he reminded him.

"I'll rub her down good," Jake said.

Pierce mounted the steps of his house and took satisfaction in the mended terrace and the newly painted porches. He owed money everywhere, even for the fresh white paint on the house, but men trusted him and Malvern. Their confidence was in tomorrow, and tomorrow would come. He leaped up the last steps and met his brother coming down the stairs into the hall, and was struck again, as he continually was, with Tom's good looks. The youthful sallowness and slimness were gone. He had actually grown taller this last year.

"Tom, you should have ridden out with me this morning!" he shouted. "God, how the land is producing!"

Tom smiled. "You should have called me, Pierce," he replied. "I found you gone when I came down for breakfast. Bettina said you'd been gone an hour."

"Oh well, I'll let you be an invalid another month or two," Pierce said indulgently. "Where's Luce and the younguns? I'm starved clean to the bottom of me."

"Lucinda has been sitting in the summerhouse," Tom replied. He stood leaning against the door jamb. "Here comes Bettina with the children."

Pierce turned and saw Bettina walking across the green lawns. She held a book in her hands, and the two boys were tugging at it. She stopped, and dropping on her knees she opened it, and they pored over it together.

"Queer how those two girls know their books," he said. "I wonder who taught them."

Tom did not answer and Pierce looked at him and saw what made him aghast. He had been trying not to think of it—but now Tom was well and it had better be said. Tom—Bettina! He felt suddenly sick.

"Reckon I'll go and wash," he said. "If you see Luce, tell her I'll go straight to the dining room."

"All right—" Tom's voice was dreaming, and Pierce mounted the stairs on tiptoe. Did Lucinda know? Or was there anything to know? And what would he say to Tom? Nothing, probably! What a man did with a colored wench was his own business. Still—Tom! Here at Malvern!

He went into his dressing room and poured the water out of the jug into the ewer, and felt the blood suddenly begin to pound through his body. Tom was not at all the sort of fellow to take up with a wench. Damn Lucinda for bringing two such pretty girls into the house! Now there would be mulatto children running around, cousins to his own children, and nobody saying a word because nobody would dare.

"I shall ship that Bettina away," he thought angrily. He scrubbed his hands and went down to the dining room and held his head very haughtily while his family gathered. Lucinda sat at the foot of the table and Tom at her right and the two boys opposite him. Pierce busied himself with his soup and then with carving the fowl. Lucinda asked him questions and he answered them. Yes, the wheat was very fine, as fine as the oats had been, and if the hot weather held the corn would be good, too. They were lucky.

"Then why are you so cross, Papa?" Martin asked.

Pierce cursed himself for not being able to hide his thoughts even from a child. "I have worries," he said shortly.

They were all silent after that, and in silence they ate the green apple tart which was their dessert. He called for the new cheese and Georgia brought it to him, and he took it coldly from her. He would settle his house once for all.

Lucinda looked at him inquiringly when he rose.

"I wish you'd come into the office, Lucinda," he said still coldly. "I have something to talk about with you."

She followed him and Bettina came in for the children. He cast a swift look at her and imagined that under her gathered skirt her body swelled, and he grew deeply angry. How dared Tom do such a thing in this house!

He shut the office door firmly behind Lucinda and sat

down at the desk and shuffled some papers. She sat down in the leather armchair which his father had brought over from London years ago for this very room.

"Well, Pierce?" she inquired.

Then he found himself unable to speak. The blood came up under his collar.

"Put down those papers," she said. "Tell me what it is you have done."

He put down the papers at once. "I haven't done anything," he said savagely. "It's your own colored girl I want to talk about."

"Georgia?"

"No, Bettina."

Now he wished he had never begun. For it was not only Bettina of whom he must speak, but also his own brother. Instinctive loyalty beset him. Must he betray his own kind? Women never understood these things.

Lucinda's face had grown sharp. "Pierce, what do you mean? Tell me this minute. What's Bettina done?"

"Nothing that I know of. Probably just my imagination."

But she knew him. The faint look of guilt that haunts a man's face when he speaks to his wife of sex now haunted his and he was betrayed.

"Pierce Delaney, do you mean—"

He banged both fists on the table. "I don't mean anything. I don't know whatever got into me to think I had to tell you."

But she pursued what she smelled as relentlessly as a cat pursues the scent of a mouse. "If I thought that Bettina could be carrying on right under my own eyes in my own house, I'd—I'd have her strapped. I don't care how light-colored she is—she's nothing but a nigger. What has she done? Why—why, Pierce, she hasn't said anything to you?"

He sighed in a great gust. "Good God, no! Now I've got you started, I wish I hadn't spoken."

She forced him on. "Well, you have spoken, and you might just as well go on and tell me everything, because I'll find out anyway."

He now saw how slender was the proof of what he suspected. What had he seen? Nothing except such things as the look on Tom's face when Bettina happened to be crossing the grass with the children.

"I haven't seen a thing," he protested, "not a living thing."

"Pierce Delaney!" Lucinda screamed. "You stop!"

He began to sweat and he pulled out his silk handkerchief and mopped his forehead and his cheeks. "Well, nothing I could really say I saw," he amended.

But she squeezed it out of him word by word and he told her.

"Maybe Tom was only smiling at the sunshine or something," he groaned at last when he had faltered out his suspicion. "Maybe he was pleased because I said the crops were going to be good."

"Oh, fiddle!" she cried, in such profound contempt that he felt allied to Tom as never before.

"Anyway, I certainly am not going to accuse my own brother," he protested. "Not without some proof."

"Pierce Delaney!" she said sternly. Her hands were clenched under her breasts. "You know as well as I do that you saw something or you wouldn't have tried to tell me and then take it back. Whether you speak to Tom or not is just nothing. It's I who will speak to Bettina."

She rose, spread her skirts and floated out of the room like an outraged swan, and he groaned again and laid his head down on his arms and knew that he must go and warn his brother. For a moment even Malvern was filled with misery. Then suddenly he lifted his head. He had thought of escape. He would go and find Georgia and warn her and she could warn Bettina, who would warn Tom. He jumped up, suddenly nimble at the thought of mercy for Tom, and went out into the hall.

At this hour of the day, where would Georgia be? In her room, maybe, in the attic, or maybe in the pantry, where Lucinda had said they took their fragmentary meals, standing at the tables. He walked softly through the halls toward the pantry. The front door was open as he passed and out on the lawn the children lay stretched on a blanket on the grass for their naps, while Joe sat near them, back against a tree, droning out a story. The air was still and hot and filled with noonday sleep. He opened the door to the pantry and saw no one. Beyond the door into the kitchen he heard the mumble of Annie's voice complaining to her little slaveys, and he walked away again into the great front hall, and stood listening. Would Lucinda have found Bettina already? Where was Georgia?

He remembered that there was a winding little stair that went up out of the back porch and he walked there and began to mount it softly. It led, as he well remembered, straight past the second floor into the attic. When he had been a boy he had escaped his father's wrath more than once by that stair, dragging little Tom after him by the wrist. Under the attic eaves they had hid until wrath was spent and they dared come down again. He had not climbed the stairs since he had first gone away to the university, the year before he was married. Now the steps creaked under his weight but he went on.

The door at the top was closed and he knocked softly.

Georgia's voice called, "It's not locked!"

He had a second's wonder, "locked against whom?" and then he lifted the old-fashioned latch and looked in. She lay on the bed, dressed, but with her hair down and hanging over the pillow. At the sight of him she leaped up and gathered her hair together in one hand.

"Oh—I thought it was Bettina!" she gasped. Her cream-colored face went pale.

"Don't be frightened, Georgia," he said quickly. "I had to find you—I had to tell you. Look here, I say—please listen, Georgia, because I've got to tell you—"

She had her hair knotted now, looping the ends through without hairpins. "Yes, sir, please—"

"Your mistress thinks—she has an idea that there's something going on between Bettina and my brother."

Georgia's very lips went pale. "How did she know?"

"Then there is something?"

"I can't tell you, Master Pierce."

Against his will he saw her black brows clear against her

skin and the separate blackness of her long lashes set into her pale eyelids.

"I only wanted to warn you," he said sternly. "I think Bettina ought to be prepared. It's natural that her mistress can't be pleased. I'm not pleased myself."

Georgia's dark eyes fell. Her narrow hands fluttered at her apron. "No, sir. I'm not pleased, either. I told Bettina so. And Bettina isn't happy. She knows she can't—" Georgia stopped.

He wanted to ask "Can't what?" But his dignity would not allow him. He was in a dangerous place, and he wanted to be out of it.

"You had better find her and tell her," he said severely.

"Yes, sir. Thank you, Master Pierce."

He turned to the door abruptly and crept down the stair again. Once he wondered if the girl were staring after him and he turned and took a quick glance. But the door was shut.

He reached the back porch and then his office in safety and he opened a door in the panel and took out a decanter and a glass and drank deeply of wine. The smell of October grapes reminded him of the day when he had come home, he thought to peace at last. "God," he muttered with bitterness, "what peace!" and drank again.

Upstairs in her own room Lucinda sat alone. She had come in, her skirts swirling, and had at once locked the door and sat down to think. Why she locked the door she did not know, but it was her first instinct. Now and then she locked it against Pierce in the night when she wanted to sleep, and in bed she lay wakened when she heard him turn the knob and find it locked and then curse and swear softly under his breath. He had learned that it was useless to call her. Nothing would persuade her to unlock the door after she had locked it. She would lie laughing into her pillow because she felt arrogant and powerful. She had a whip in her hand over Pierce, her husband, whom she loved.

She wanted the door locked now against him because she wanted to be alone. Her room was silent and safe, closing her in from everybody. She had made the room exactly what she liked, and somehow even during the war she had kept it so.

The flowers on the carpet were clear against the deep white pile of the background. It had come from Paris, and it would last forever. Georgia cleaned it with cornmeal twice a year even when cornmeal was their only food. The dirty meal was given to the pigs so it was not all waste. But she would not have dared to let Pierce know.

So it was with the organdy curtains at the window. Somehow they were starched, even when there was no white bread. Georgia made the starch out of potatoes, long soaked.

She sat thinking and staring out of the window, and little darts of fear and premonition ran needling through her veins. She tried to ignore them. It was Tom, not Pierce. But Pierce had not been really angry with Tom. Pierce sided with Tom in his heart. Men stood together against women, and Pierce stood by Tom. She longed for a woman friend to talk with, a woman who would feel as she did against men, and made up her mind that she would ride over and visit with Molly Mac-Bain. Maybe she would tell her and maybe she wouldn't, but anyway it would be strengthening just to talk with a woman. When she came back she would decide about Bettina. She put aside an uneasy thought that maybe she ought not ride now that she was going to have a baby. Pierce would be cross with her about it. She had not ridden for a month—let him be cross, though! She wanted to disobey him. But she delayed decision, nevertheless, and went on thinking.

If she talked to Bettina it would set the girl up. Her own mother had never noticed her father's mulatto children. They grew up in the servants' quarters and everybody knew and nobody said anything. It was her father who had bought Georgia and Bettina and now that she thought of it she remembered how her mother had looked when he had come in and thrown down papers.

"I've brought you two likely house girls, Laura," he had shouted.

Her anger against Bettina grew. Why, maybe even in her own mother's house, her own father—

She began to cry softly. It was sadly hard to be a woman, so hard to hold her own when she had no real power at all and had to ask for everything she wanted, even new satin to cover the parlor furniture! She had to get what she wanted any way she could. She thought of all the things she wanted. Every room in the house needed something new. Pierce didn't understand that the house was her world, her place where she had to live. Men went out but women stayed at home and in the home they had to have new things sometimes or go crazy fretting and mending. She wiped her eyes and sighed and then got up suddenly and put on her grey riding habit and went downstairs, feeling sad and a little weak.

Out on the lawn Joe was waving a branch over the sleeping children and no one else was to be seen. She did not want to meet Pierce and she had a conviction that Bettina and Tom were together this very minute, probably up in his room. Bettina still came and went there. It made her physically sick to think of it, here where she lived, in her own home! She clenched her hands against her breast and thought of marching upstairs. But she did not. A woman had to think how to do a thing like that. Just to make a fuss wasn't enough.

She went outside the open door and down the steps and Joe got to his feet. She motioned to him and he came softly across the grass.

"Tell Jake to bring a horse around quickly, and don't wake the children."

"Yassum," Joe whispered. He went noiselessly away and she sat down on the bottom step and pulled her hat over her eyes to shade her skin from the sun. If she walked around the boys would wake out of sheer contrariness and she wanted to ride off by herself. Maybe she would go to see Molly. Maybe she wouldn't. She just wanted the feeling of running away. If Pierce worried about her, let him be worried.

She saw Jake leading the horse and got up and went to meet him, so that the horse's hooves would not clatter on the gravel. Joe stooped and she stepped into his hand and sprang into the side saddle and lifted her whip.

"If your master wants to know where I am, tell him I've gone for a ride and that's all."

"Yassum," Joe said. He stood looking after her thoughtfully

and scratching himself, his head, his armpits, the palms of his hands. "Reckon there's some kinda ructions," he mumbled to himself. He tiptoed back to the tree and looked down on the little sleeping boys. A small breeze had sprung up and he sniffed it. "Reckon it'll keep off the flies," he mumbled. He settled himself under the tree, his head on a root, folded his arms and dropped into instant sleep.

Upstairs in her room Georgia sat crying softly and waiting for Bettina. She was afraid of her younger sister, and yet the time had come when Bettina must tell her everything. If the two of them didn't stand together, then what would happen? They had always told each other everything and had made their little world secure here in this room. But she knew Bettina had something hidden. Bettina didn't talk any more. At night when they lay in bed where they used to talk, whispering so that nobody could hear, now only she talked, and Bettina lay listening and answering a word or two, and then lying awake. She knew Bettina lay awake, because in the night she heard her sigh.

"Honey, can't you sleep?" Every night nearly she waked to ask the question.

"I can sleep after awhile, maybe," Bettina answered.

In the morning she made excuses that the night air was hot or the moonlight too bright. But the real reason was that there was something always awake in Bettina nowadays. She couldn't get to sleep any more, not the old deep sleep when they never even dreamed, because they were so tired when night came and morning came so quickly. And now she knew what it was in Bettina.

Still she did not come, and at last Georgia dared wait no longer, lest her mistress call and hear no answer. She washed her face and put on a fresh white cotton dress and went downstairs into the pantry and began to clean the silver.

In Tom's room Bettina sat with her hands in her face, listening and shaking her head again and again while he talked. He still had to rest in the afternoon and she read to him to help him rest. But today he had begun talking and talking.

"Bettina, you've got to do what I say," he insisted. "We can't go on in the house like this. It's horrible. It makes our —our relationship just like any—any—"

He tried to pull her hands away from her face and she struggled against him and then yielded suddenly and sat looking at him, her face all bare and quivering. They knew each other so well now. She knew him to the bottom of his soul. In the long hours when she had been caring for him he had told her everything, every suffering, every loneliness, from the pain of a younger brother growing up in this house, Pierce always the stronger and the handsomer and the more brilliant and the more loved, and he always second, to the agonies of the prison camp and the slow starvation of body and soul in the war.

And she had told him everything, too, and he knew what it was to be a woman like any other but inside a dark skin, and what it was to be a servant in this house and forever a servant somewhere. She told him of her mother and how her mother had taught Georgia and her to keep themselves apart and to cling always a little higher and nearer to the white people. But she did not tell him what her mother would have said now. Her mother had not known what it was to love a man so much that it no longer mattered that he was white. She had separated herself even from her mother because she loved Tom more than she loved herself.

"So I want you to marry me, Bettina," Tom was saying, "and you'll be my true wife."

She was shaking her head again and he reached out his hands and took it between his palms and held it so that she could not shake it. "Yes, you will marry me," he insisted. "The war was fought so you could be free to marry me. It makes everything worth while to me—all I've been through. It makes me understand the good of suffering. We're free to marry."

"No, we're not," she said stubbornly.

They had been through all this before and would go through it again and she would always say no, over and over. For of course he couldn't marry her. It would ruin him. He'd have to leave Malvern, and Pierce wouldn't give him any money.

"Why not?" Tom demanded. He knelt in front of her and held her hands so that she could not cover her face again.

"The war didn't change how people feel," she said. "It's how people feel that counts. They feel toward colored people just like they did before the war. Miss Lucie, she hasn't changed. It doesn't make any difference to her that Georgia and me get wages. She still thinks she owns us, I know."

"But she doesn't own you," Tom said impatiently. "It's your fault if you keep feeling she does."

"I don't feel she does," Bettina said with patience. "What I'm saying is about her. You and she belong to the white people and I belong to the colored folks. She feels the colored folks still belong to the white people, and it don't matter about the war or the law or anything so long as she feels that way and so long as you are white and I'm not. That feeling is going right on and the way she feels is the way she's going to act, and she isn't ever going to act like I was your wife, no matter if we marry, and if she don't act that way, it won't be that way, because she won't let it."

"Good God, Bettina, Lucinda isn't everybody!" Tom cried.

"She's like everybody," Bettina said simply. She gazed at him sadly and smiled.

But he would not accept the smile. "You don't love me enough," he complained.

"I love you enough to have the baby and if you want more, I love you enough for any more," she replied.

He groaned. "But what are we going to do? We can't stay here—"

"You can stay here," she said steadily. "And you can find me a little house somewhere near enough and there I'll live, and you can come whenever you can. It'll be my life."

He was not strong enough for her. He bent his head on her knees and she laid her cheek against the back of his head.

"It'll be a happy life for me," she whispered. "Happy enough—"

Lucinda's horse was tied to the fence and she and Molly were talking upstairs in the bedroom. She had decided suddenly that she would go and see Molly MacBain because she was disturbed by a thought which had come to her as she was cantering through the woods along the Malvern stream. Pierce had made a path for horses along the stream before the war and had ordered it cleared as soon as he came home, but she had not ridden along it until today.

"Maybe the war has really changed things," this was the dreadful thought. "Maybe colored women aren't any more just—property. Maybe Tom can really marry Bettina—legally!"

She had touched the horse with her whip and had decided to go and talk everything over with Molly.

"Honey, how glad I am to see you!" Molly had cried. "John's gone to Wheeling and I'm all alone and lonesome."

They had begun by blackberry wine and cookies on the porch and then Molly had taken her through the house and here in the bedroom, where no one was near, Lucinda had told her.

"Molly, I surely do need your help, honey," she had said abruptly, sinking down on the window seat.

Molly had listened avidly.

"Tom has taken up with my girl Bettina," Lucinda said.

"You don't tell!" Molly breathed. "Why, when did it happen?"

"I shouldn't have let her have the nursing of him, I reckon," Lucinda said.

"You mean—there's a baby?" Molly asked.

"I don't know how far it's gone," Lucinda replied. "Of course if it's begun, a baby will be the end of it and maybe half a dozen. It's so sickening—not that I care about either of them, Molly. But what bothers me is whether Tom could make it legal."

Molly looked puzzled. "Make what legal, honey?"

"I mean really—marry Bettina," Lucinda said. She flushed with embarrassment. It sounded silly even to imagine such things.

Molly began to laugh. "Honey, whoever heard of a white man marryin' a nigger?"

"Things are so queer now," Lucinda said defensively. "It would be just—dangerous—for ladies like us—if colored wenches could be married—why, we wouldn't have anything left—none of us would be safe in our own houses—"

"Now, honey, stop your foolishness," Molly cried. "Men don't marry women they can get without marryin'."

The two women looked at one another. Each remembered the teaching of their mothers. "If Bettina's given herself," Molly went on, "what is there she can make him marry her for now?"

Lucinda smiled. The worry rolled from her mind.

"Maybe it's a mercy that things have gone so far," she said cheerfully. "Thank God, it's not Pierce! But it's still sickening. Molly, what do you suppose is the matter with men?"

She was a little shocked by the greedy interest in Molly's blue eyes. Molly's red lips were parted and she wet them.

"So long as it isn't your Pierce, it isn't so bad," Molly agreed. She felt hotness creeping up her neck, and her eyelids fluttered before Lucinda's surprised look. "Men are—well, just that way," she said. She patted both sides of her fluffy red hair. "We have to put up with them, Lucinda." Then she laughed. "Maybe God felt sorry for women and gave us a little whip of our own to do the drivin' with!"

She felt relieved to laugh because Lucinda was staring at her so hard. She considered telling Lucinda in return about John and how he was wounded and then decided she would not. She had a whip over John, too. John was afraid all the time. Poor old John! "What does Pierce say?" she inquired.

Lucinda shrugged. "Oh Pierce—"

"He can't approve?" Molly cried.

"Oh, he doesn't approve," Lucinda said impatiently, "but after all, Tom is his brother—and when you come right down to it, men are all the same about that one thing, Molly."

Molly laughed again, her eyes shining. She put out her soft plump white hand on Lucinda's slender one. "Honey, if I were you, I just wouldn't pay any mind to it. I'd just live as though the whole thing was beneath my notice. That's the way ladies have always done, you know, and it's the best way. My own mother used to say that we had to realize men have a lower nature and the less it was noticed, the better."

Lucinda drew her hand away gently. "I do believe you're right, Molly," she said with gratitude. "So long as you don't think harm could come of it . . . It isn't like it was before the war, you know. I get to worrying for fear Bettina would be uppity."

"I wouldn't notice anything," Molly said smoothly. "If she gets uppity I would just send her away like a servant. There's that good thing out of the war—you can send 'em away."

"You could sell them before," Lucinda reminded her. "I wouldn't like to lose Georgia, and if Bettina went, Georgia would probably want to go, too. We'd lose two good house girls without getting a penny for them, though Papa could have sold them for a thousand dollars apiece. I know, because Mama scolded him so, when we didn't need them. It isn't fair, do you think, Molly? I mean, for that poor white in Washington just to write a few lines and say that your property isn't your property!"

"I'm glad he was killed," Molly said simply.

They rose, feeling that everything had been said and decided, and went downstairs, their arms about one another like girls.

Lucinda kissed Molly when she went away. "You have certainly made me feel better," she said. "I'm going home and I'm not going to speak of it again, not to Pierce or anybody."

"I'm sure that's best, honey," Molly replied.

She looked at Lucinda a moment and then laughed. "Why do you stay 'way out here in the country, honey? We're goin' to Wheeling, John and me."

Lucinda looked at her, speechless. "Why, Molly, leave your own house?"

Molly's eyes flitted restlessly about the room. "I feel to change. I'd like to travel. I tell John he's just got to get rich. Honey, he's goin' into the railroad."

"Railroad!" Lucinda cried. She thought of the smoking,

puffing, bell-topped little engine that ran choking and sputtering westward from Baltimore. "I don't see how that'll make him rich," she declared.

"Railroads are goin' to grow," Molly said firmly. "We've borrowed money and bought stock—"

Lucinda felt a jealous envy of possible riches. She hid it behind her pretty smile.

"I certainly do hope you will get what you want, Molly dear," she said. She rose as she spoke and brushed Molly's red cheek with the palm of her hand. "Of course, I have the boys. Pierce would kill me if I didn't let them be brought up at Malvern—and I've a girl here under my belt."

She pressed her waist. A flicker in Molly's eyes made her suddenly smile. "Goodbye, honey!" she said and tripped away.

So meditating, Lucinda rode home through the mild evening air. An instinctive resolution was growing within her. She would say nothing at all about Bettina, not to Pierce, not to Tom, and not even to Bettina herself. She would ignore the whole matter, as generations of women before her had ignored the doings of their men. After all, Tom was only a brother-in-law. Sooner or later he might even be leaving Malvern. There was no use upsetting her house over Tom. Besides, she wanted to think about railroads. Why should Molly MacBain be rich?

When her horse ambled into the yard again, she smiled at the two boys who ran to greet her.

"Is your papa home yet?" she asked.

"He ain't come," Martin said.

"Don't say ain't," she commanded him. She handed the reins to Joe, who came forward scratching himself. "You surely are going to have to start some schooling, Martin . . . Joe, have you got fleas?"

"No'm, I hope I don't," Joe answered grinning. "But maybe I has," he added, and led the horse away. "I'm liable," he muttered. "I shore am liable. Until there's soap again, fleas take advantage."

But Lucinda was walking toward the house, her long riding habit sweeping the grass, a hand on the shoulder of each son.

She felt strong and clear for the future. The ride had not hurt her, and she would not even tell Pierce she had taken it.

When Pierce came home that night he found his house quiet, his children cleaned and fed their supper and ready for bed. Tom was outstretched on the long chair on the terrace, and opposite him, in the calmest of moods, Lucinda sat on a garden seat. The sun had set and a pure light flowed over the landscape.

Pierce approached, aware suddenly of the beauty of the scene, and warmth welled up in his heart. If things were quiet, it meant that Lucinda had decided to keep them so. He drew near, his intuition alert. Lucinda turned up her face for his kiss. He smelled a faint perfume upon her skin, and beneath his eyes hers were calm. Yes, she was all right. She was in a good mood. God knew why, after the fuss she had made after luncheon, but he was grateful. Maybe she had talked with Tom and they had decided something. He glanced at Tom.

"Hello, Tom," he said. "You're looking well enough to be your old self."

"I feel well, at last," Tom replied.

"The children are waiting for you to kiss them good night, Pierce," Lucinda reminded him.

"I'll go upstairs," he said. He was bewildered by the utter peace, but he was too grateful for it to speak of it. He went upstairs slowly and turned into the nursery. Georgia was there with the boys, reading to them while they lay on their stomachs, listening. She ceased when he came in, and the boys shouted to her to go on.

But she rose and stood waiting, her eyes fixed on Pierce's face. He saw her eyes, doubtful and defensive, and looked away.

"Tell your father good night," she said in her soft voice. The boys rose and jumped up and clung to his legs and he leaned to them and kissed them, and then, his arm on their shoulders, he looked at her again, and made up his mind to be completely casual. "Had you a chance to talk to Bettina?" he inquired.

"No, sir," Georgia said simply. "We've both been busy. Tonight, I'll ask her, sir."

"Good," he said heartily. He looked down at his two sons. "How'd you like me to find you a pony?" he inquired.

They screamed their joy at him and he promised. Then as he went to the door, Martin called after him, "What's school, Papa?"

"Who said school?" he asked.

"Mama said I need to go to school."

"So you do," Pierce replied.

"Then I could ride the pony to go," Martin said.

"So you could," Pierce agreed.

He went to his own room and changed his clothes into the semiformal garments that Lucinda required of menfolk in her house at dinner. The coat was tight. Outdoor life had thickened him. Must he struggle into the coat? To think he had a son old enough to go to school! Only, there were no schools! A tutor, he supposed, must be found, unless Tom wanted to teach the boys. The idea struck him as a happy one. Tom would make a good schoolmaster. Yes, it would give him something to do, take him out of the house.

He had one of his waves of simple happiness. The mellowness of the light in his room, the comfort of his bed and chair, the cleanliness of floors and walls and white curtains at the window, the reality of his home all conspired to make his mood. No, hang it, he would not disturb all this for a fancy that Tom had for Bettina. He tied his stock and ran lightly down the stairs, and at the sound of his step Lucinda and Tom rose and met him in the hall and they went into the oval dining room, she between the two of them.

That night after Lucinda had gone upstairs he turned to Tom. They had come into the drawing room after a pleasantly satisfactory dinner. The windows stood open to the terrace, and Lucinda had played her harp for them. He had watched her white hands on the strings and had admired her head in profile as she leaned it against the gilded frame. All his love for her had surged into his heart and melted his mind. In spite of her pregnancy her figure in its full skirt still looked graceful. She was a beautiful woman and he was proud of her. She plucked the strings and broke into occasional song. Her voice was light and musical, and he loved to hear her sing. He had a vision of himself, a happy man in a happy home, this pretty woman his wife, bearing his children. Such homes as his were the foundation of the re-established union in the nation.

When at last she had risen to leave them he went with her to the door and kissed her hand and watched her go upstairs. She paused on the landing and looked back at him and smiled, and so easily was his sense of romance stirred that even though he knew well enough that she saw herself in every act she did, yet he admired the picture she made.

He went back into the room and sat down and lit his pipe. "This autumn, thank God, we'll have real tobacco of our own again," he said to Tom. "But I never plant much, you know—it's greedy stuff on the land."

"It's a wonder what you've done to Malvern already," Tom said. He lay back in his chair lazily, not looking at Pierce. Outside the window the mountains were black against a dark and starlit sky. The light of the new oil lamps in the room was dim, for Lucinda had turned them down when she began to play.

He was thinking about Bettina. Should he tell Pierce what they had decided to do? He made up his mind that he would. He hated the thought of deception and hiding.

"Pierce," he said.

"Well?" Pierce's eyes, gleaming over his pipe, were suddenly aware.

Tom sat up. "I want to tell you something—"

"All right, Tom."

"I suppose you know I've fallen in love with Bettina."

Pierce drew hard on his pipe and blew out the smoke. "You don't fall in love with a colored wench, Tom!"

"I've fallen in love with Bettina," Tom said firmly. "I want to marry her."

Pierce put his pipe down and faced his brother. "You can't marry her, Tom."

"I can, but she won't have me," Tom said.

"You mean you've proposed to her—as if she were—"

"I proposed to her, and she refused me," Tom said stubbornly.

Pierce laughed loudly. "Good God, Tom! Then she's got better sense than you!"

Tom gazed gravely at his brother's laughing face. "To me, it's the same as marriage," he said in his even quiet voice. "I've told her so. I'm going to get a house for us to live in, Pierce."

Pierce stopped laughing suddenly. "Tom, you can get a house for her, but you can't live in it."

"Yes, I can."

"Not if you're my brother," Pierce said sternly. "Tom, for God's sake, think of our family and the children!"

"I'm thinking of Bettina and myself," Tom said in the same unchanging voice. "This is what I fought the war for, Pierce—so that I could marry Bettina."

"You fool, you didn't even know Bettina till you came home!"

"Nevertheless, it was for her I fought." Pierce looked at his brother's face. It was still the face of the little boy who had been his stubborn follower. Nothing would make Tom different, not even growing into manhood. He was stubborn to the bone.

"Well, Tom, there's not a thing I can do about it," he said, "except turn you out of the house and disown you as my brother."

They looked at one another. "All right, Pierce," Tom said.

They parted and Pierce went upstairs, and Tom went out on the terrace and paced up and down. Far up in the top of the house a dim light burned. It was in Bettina's room, but he could not go up to it. In this house she was beyond his reach. He could only take her away.

In the attic room Georgia was crying softly.

"I don't see how I can stay here all alone, sister." But she was sobbing quietly lest she be heard downstairs.

Bettina sat on a box by the window, her cheeks on her hands, staring out into the tangled branches of the ancient trees that leaned against the house. "I never thought I'd love any man so much that I wouldn't marry him," she said. "Mother didn't know what love was, Georgy. She told us to go quick with the whitest man we could get to ask us. Well, I've found the whitest man in the world, and he wants to marry me and I won't let him—"

Georgia stopped crying and looked at Bettina sadly. "I wouldn't know what to do with such love as that," she said.

"I have to give in to it, because I know I can't live without him," Bettina went on, "but I don't have to let it hurt him, and I never will."

She had paid no heed to Georgia's weeping. Georgia's face took on a look of awe. Bettina was far away from her, in some world she did not understand. She was left alone behind. Her lips trembled again but she wiped her eyes and stopped crying. She sighed and rose and let down her long hair and began to comb it.

"Mother always said we were as good as anybody," she said.

"We are, but it doesn't make any difference, if other people don't think so," Bettina replied. "Anyway, I'm not thinking of us."

"Will you tell *her* you're going?" Georgia asked.

"No, I shall just go," Bettina said.

"What'll I say if she asks me?"

"She won't ask you."

"You mean she'll pretend she doesn't notice?"

"She'll know, but she won't say a word."

"How do you know that, Bettina?"

"I know *her*."

Georgia put down the comb and braided the thick waving mass down her back.

"When are you going, sister?"

"Tomorrow, honey, I'm going to move into Millpoint.

There's a little brick house there. I've seen it when we go to church. It's been empty this long while. I've saved all my wages."

"Does—*he* know?"

"No, he doesn't. I'm going myself. I don't want him to know when I go nor where. I want him to say he doesn't know a thing about me. Maybe she'll ask him, and that's what I want him to say. But if he asks you, you can tell him."

They undressed in silence and climbed into bed together and suddenly Bettina clung to Georgia. "I know I'm right," she whispered. "I'm right—but tell me I am!"

Searching for words to comfort her Georgia laid hold on truth. "You're free anyway, Bettina. If you don't like it you can always move on."

Bettina's hold relaxed. "I hadn't thought of that, Georgy— it's true. If I don't like it, nobody can hold me."

They fell asleep, their arms wrapped about one another as they had slept always since childhood.

Lucinda knew before the day had begun that Bettina had left the house. She knew by the look on Georgia's face. Georgia came into the big bedroom in the morning, tiptoeing, drawing a blind against the sun, glancing at the bed, opening the drawers softly to fetch clean garments.

"Why do you keep looking at me?" Lucinda asked sharply from behind closed eyelids.

"I'm not sure if you're awake, ma'am," Georgia answered, in the softest of voices.

Lucinda did not speak again. But she heard Georgia go into the boys' room and call them and help them wash and dress. That was Bettina's work. Bettina was gone!

She sat up in bed, smiling, listening. It was much the best way, of course. If Bettina had run away, it would save trouble. But she would not ask a word. It gave her tremendous power to know and to say nothing. If she said nothing, no one would know how much she knew. Let them wonder why she did not speak.

She called across the hall through the half-open door, "Don't bother with those great boys, Georgia—they're big enough to take care of themselves. They don't need anybody."

There was a pause and then Georgia's voice answered, "Yes, ma'am."

A moment later she was back again. "Shall I bring up your breakfast, ma'am?" Her cream colored face was flushed and her eyes were miserable, but she held herself very straight.

"No, I'm coming down," Lucinda said briskly. She tossed back the covers, and slipped from the high bed to the floor. "Go on away," she commanded, "I don't want anybody, either —it's too nice a day. I'm going to dress in a hurry."

"Yes, ma'am."

Georgia seemed to drift from the room and Lucinda shut the door, smiling.

The day was shining bright, the air so clear that the Alleghenies rose like alps against the brilliant sky. Tom was restless with new life. He felt completely and finally well at last. He had waked and felt himself strong enough for anything, strong enough to beat down Bettina's fears and leave Malvern forever. He wanted to be free of Malvern and free of his family. They'd go away somewhere, he and Bettina, and start for themselves—change their names, maybe! Let Pierce keep the name of Delaney, if he wanted it. He'd take Bettina's name. No, they'd take a name for themselves that no one had ever borne.

By mid-morning he knew that Bettina was not in the house. Never before had so many hours passed without their meeting somewhere, in a passageway or a corner of the garden, or in his own room which she came to make neat. He waited there until long past the hour for the making of his bed. Then he went out and lingered about the halls until he saw Georgia steal in swiftly and he came back and caught her spreading his sheets. He closed the door and leaned against it.

"Where is Bettina?" he demanded.

Georgia looked at him with sadness in her dark eyes. "She's gone to Millpoint," she said simply. "You'll find her in that little brick house we pass on the way to church—that is, if so be she was able to rent it."

"We can't live in Millpoint," he said sharply.

"No, sir, but she can," Georgia replied. She went on spreading the sheets, tucking in the corners hard and square, making his bed. He wached her an instant then turned and went out to the stables, saddled his mare and cantered down the road to Millpoint.

He knew the road as he knew the palm of his own hand. Every Sunday of his childhood he and Pierce and their parents had driven over it in the carriage, on the way to church and home again. He knew the brick house. It had belonged to a widow, a seamstress who had come to Malvern every spring to mend and sew the dresses the house women wore. His mother had never trusted her own gowns to Minnie Walley. Old Walley was a poor white farmer up in the hills from Malvern, but his daughter had bettered herself and they had all called her Miss Minnie instead of just Minnie. When she died the house had belonged to nobody, he supposed. He did not know when she had died—during the war, maybe. It seemed to him she had been there always.

He found Bettina behind shut doors, scrubbing the floors of a small sitting room. There was still furniture in the house, Miss Minnie's furniture, plain deal stuff except for a fine rosewood sewing table by the fireplace.

Bettina was on her hands and knees, and she sat back on her heels when he came in. He closed the door and stared down at her.

"We can't live here," he said abruptly.

"I can live here," she said sweetly.

"Where you live, I'll live," he said.

"No, Tom," she replied. Her red lips were firm and stubborn.

"Do we have to go over all this again?" he demanded.

"No, Tom."

"But you've run away from me!" he cried.

"Only run away from the big house," she corrected him.

"Who says you can live here?" he asked.

"I can rent it for five dollars a month. I went up to Walley's place and her son is there—home from the war without his leg. He's glad to have the cash."

"You haven't five dollars a month," he said cruelly.

She clasped him about the waist as he stood before her.

"You're going to give me the money, dear love," she said. "You're going to house me and feed me and clothe me, because I'm your own. But I won't marry you, for it would be wrong. I'll live with you forever but I'll not marry you and bring you down in the world to where I was born. I'll kill myself before I do that, Tom."

He groaned because she was so beautiful and so wise and because she was stronger than he.

"You're going to stay at the big house and claim your birthright, my darling," she said.

He stared down at her, his heart cold in his breast. "You deny me a home of my own. I shall have to live in my brother's house all my life."

She let her hands slide down his thighs and his legs and she bent until she was crumpled at his feet. "It was such bad luck for you to love me," she mourned. "Bad, bad luck, my darling —I ought never to have let you love me." She lifted her face, "Tom, promise me something?"

"Why should I, when you will promise me nothing?"

"Promise me, my dear—"

"Well, maybe—"

"If ever you see the white lady you could marry, dear heart —promise me you'll marry her."

"I'll never marry, Bettina—"

Then for the first time she broke into weeping. "Oh me, oh me—" she wept.

But she did not weep for long. She wiped her eyes on the skirt of her blue homespun dress and tried to smile. "It's noon, and I haven't any food for you fit to eat—"

"What have you for yourself?" he asked.

"Some bread and milk. But some day soon I'll have chickens, Tom, and fresh eggs for you—maybe a cow—and a little garden. You'll see—but not today, my dear."

"I'm not hungry—"

He stared about the disordered house, and wondered bleakly if he really were in love. And she caught the bewilderment in his eyes and begged him to go away.

"Go home, Tom darling. Come back when I'm all settled. Give me a couple of days, darling, and then see if there isn't a fire blazing in the stove and something cooking, and a clean soft bed and a chair for your own. Tom, lucky the house is back from the road and the lilacs are so high. You don't even need to come down the main road, my love—look, there's a winding path along the little stream at the back—Deep Run, they call it."

She coaxed and pushed him to the back door on the pretext of showing him the stream and suddenly he found himself outside and he heard the bar drawn, and then she opened the door quickly again lest he feel shut out.

"Come back to me day after tomorrow, in the evening, after the sun has set," she said softly. She smiled her sad and brilliant smile and closed the door again. And he went soberly back to Malvern.


Pierce was on the terrace sipping brandy and water. He had had a long talk with Lucinda. That is, he had sat listening to her for well over an hour, emitting cries of astonishment from time to time at what she told him and declaring that it was asking too much of him when she forbade him to say one word to Tom about Bettina's running away.

"Damn you, Luce, the fellow's my brother, after all! I talk about everything with Tom."

"You'll talk us all into a peck of trouble if you talk with him about this," she counseled him. She looked so dainty as she sat in the shade of a pear tree that overhung the terrace, that he could have picked her up in his arms and squeezed her, except that nothing, he knew, would make her more furious. She became violently angry if, when she was dressed for the day, he disturbed the fastidious perfection of her gown and hair.

"There's a time for all things, as the Bible says, Pierce!" she would cry at him.

Once he had exclaimed with violence, "Hang the Bible, Luce—you're always bringing it up against me!" She was then genuinely and deeply shocked.

"Pierce! You aren't a fit father for our children if you speak so about the Holy Bible!"

"The Bible's all right in church, Luce—or on Sundays, but to lug it into our daily affairs—"

"Pierce, hush—and I mean it!" she had cried, stamping her foot.

He was continually bewildered by her genuine reverence for all the conventions of religion and her extraordinary ability to act swiftly with complete disregard for common morals when she felt inclined. She lied easily, laughing at herself and at him when he was shocked.

"But, Luce," he had complained, after hearing her tell a neighbor's wife that he was going to run for governor. "You know I haven't any idea of going into politics. I wouldn't demean myself."

"Well, she was boasting so," Lucinda said calmly.

"But it's a lie, Luce," he went on, "and I shall have to deny it—it'll be talked about everywhere."

Lucinda had laughed loudly. "Nobody'll know whether you will or you won't," she said triumphantly. "They'll watch you and wonder and be afraid maybe you will and they'll be polite because they won't know."

"But to lie—" he had repeated feebly.

"Oh, hush up, Pierce," she had said rudely. "Men do much worse things than lie, I'm sure."

"I don't know what," but he had sputtered and turned red and subsided when she became hysterical with scornful laughter.

This morning after protesting he had subsided again, half-convinced that maybe she was right about Tom and that to talk about the affair with Bettina was to make it too important. He sat ruminating and idle on the terrace, putting off his riding about the farm, listening to her. Like most women she

kept on talking after she had really finished everything she
had to say. He let his mind wander. Then suddenly he was
drawn back to attention by her changing the subject completely.

"And, Pierce, anyway, you aren't going to just sit here at
Malvern all our lives and play at farming."

He came out of his vague reflections made up of pleasure in
the warm sunshine, the safety of home and the beauty of the
hills rolling away from the house, and a vague secret envy of
Tom in his new romance with a beautiful female creature. In
the heart of his own life he wanted romance—with Lucinda, of
course. "Playing!" he shouted.

"Well, you're not a farmer, Pierce Delaney," Lucinda said.

"Well, I just am, Luce," he said. "I don't see myself living
anywhere but at Malvern. Besides, what would I do?"

"Of course we'll live at Malvern, dummy," Lucinda said
with impatience. "But we can't get rich on Malvern."

"Who wants to get rich?" he inquired.

"I do," Lucinda declared.

"On what, pray?"

She looked so pretty that he was charmed and amused by
her audacity. Had she been tall and vigorous he would have
been angered by it. But she was tiny, a toy of a woman, and
he could never take her with full seriousness.

She leaned forward, held her breath an instant and then
blew it out.

"Railroads!" The word came from her lips like a rainbow
bubble.

He had been walking about lazily but now he sat down.

"Tell me, pray, just what you know about railroads," he said.

"You can get rich on them," she said confidently.

"How do you know?" he asked.

"Because John MacBain is going to get rich that way—
Molly told me so."

"Molly been here?" he asked abruptly.

She looked at him, and decided to tell. "I rode over there,
and we talked and she told me."

"You rode! When?"

"When you made me so mad—"

"Mad! I'm mad at you now—" he was suddenly swept with fury at her. "Lucinda, what right have you to risk the life of our child—my child?"

She smiled at him radiantly and stood up and put her hand on his lips. "Hush—you know how I am when I'm mad."

The touch of her small fragrant palm against his lips made his knees weak. "But, Luce, darling—when I've got home and everything is perfect again—"

"I won't any more—I won't—I promise, Pierce."

She knew the time had come for capitulation and she leaned against him and sighed and clung to him, and he lifted her and carried her into the house and put her on a couch.

"You're tired," he scolded her. "Now you lie there and rest, and don't you get up until I say so." He lifted his head and bellowed "Georgia!"

Georgia came into the room as softly as a shadow.

"Fetch your mistress a half glass of sherry."

"Yes, sir—"

She had been sewing. A thimble was on her finger but she slipped it into her pocket and went away.

"You behave yourself—" Pierce said sternly to his wife upon the couch.

Lucinda looked at him with meekness, well aware of her outstretched beauty. "I will," she whispered. But he saw mischief playing about her lips and he dropped to his knees and kissed her hard.

"Oh you damned little Luce!" he muttered.

They heard the clop-clop of horses' hoofs and she gave him a push.

"Tom's coming," she murmured. "Go on out and meet him. And Pierce, mind you don't say a thing—"

He went out, committed to her demand, and sat down on the terrace and took up his half-finished glass. A wasp had fallen into it and he cursed it, and flung the drink away.

Ten minutes later he heard himself use Lucinda's very words. They came out of his mouth as though they were his own. "Tom, I've been thinking—I believe the best way to get rich is railroads in this new state."

He said the words not because he cared about being rich or about railroads but because he saw misery in Tom's face and weariness in his eyes and he knew that whether Lucinda was right or wrong, he would not speak of Bettina because he did not want to speak of her. Tom's heart had turned down a dead end.

Tom did not look at him. He felt in his pockets for his short English pipe and answered out of sheer necessity to say something, anything, that was meaningless. "Railroads?"

He found the pipe and lit it, and sank down on the marble step at the top of the shallow long steps leading from terraces to the garden. "I was wondering if you wanted to be a schoolmaster," Pierce said, with forced cheerfulness. "Maybe you'd like railroad business." He saw Joe rounding a corner of the house and yelled at him.

"Here you, Joe, bring me another whiskey and water, boy!"

Joe shambled over to him and took his glass and Pierce cleared his throat and went on talking, because there had to be talk. "We have to get a school started somehow—the boys are getting to the place where they must be taught. But I'm no schoolteacher, God knows, and maybe you're not. Lucinda put this railroad business into my head this morning, and though she doesn't know anything, still, like most women, she hits on things at times."

"I thought you were going to be a gentleman farmer," Tom said absently. He was still seeing Bettina at his feet. Even there she had looked lovely and proud and not abased. Her body was straight and slender and soft.

"Well, Malvern isn't going to make us a lot of money," Pierce said frankly. "And Lucinda's set her heart on a lot of things—so have I, for that matter. We want the best—why not?"

"Why not?" Tom echoed. His blond reddish hair stirred in the wind, and he narrowed his blue eyes against the sun and lifted them to the mountains.

"You want to go into it with me, Tom?" Pierce inquired. All his life he had moved swiftly on an idea, either to accept

or reject it. Now that he had made Lucinda's thought his
own, he felt it was a good one.

"I don't think so," Tom said slowly. "No, I believe I'd
rather be a schoolmaster than a railroad man, Pierce. You
wouldn't bring a railroad near Malvern, I hope?"

They were both talking and talking, burying deep inside
themselves the thing they were thinking about.

"I hope not," Pierce said heartily. Joe was back again with
his whiskey and water. "You tell Jake to have my horse saddled after lunch," he ordered.

"Yassuh," Joe said, and dragged himself away again.

Pierce watched him go. "Malvern will never make money if
the help doesn't move faster than Joe," he said. Yes, railroads
were a good idea. So were schools.

"We could start an academy right here in Malvern," he said
abruptly. "Why not? Take the garçonnerie there—we can
throw a couple of rooms together, and make a real school-
room. Martin and Carey will be your first two pupils. Levassie
will send his boys and the Richards their three—"

Tom shook himself. "It'll have to be for everybody's boys
if I teach it," he said abruptly.

Pierce was disposed to be pleasant about everything except
the one thing about which they must not speak. "Surely," he
said, "why not? A small tuition fee, and anybody can pay. I
won't charge you rent, schoolmaster."

They stole looks at one another and a bell rang softly from
inside the house and both men rose quickly, relieved that the
talk was over. Then Tom was moved to truth.

"I suppose you know Bettina has moved to Millpoint," he
said. His mouth was as dry as ashes as soon as he had spoken.

"The less I know about that the better," Pierce said.

"But I want you to know," Tom insisted, out of his dry
mouth.

"Well, you've told me," Pierce said abruptly. They moved together and side by side they entered the house. Pierce clapped
Tom's shoulder heartily. "There's a whole life to be lived without women, Tom," he said. "The sooner you know it the better."

Tom smiled and did not answer.

# Three

RAILROADS! PIERCE LOOKED out of the window of the train sweeping over the rough landscape. He was aware of a region of irony somewhere in his being. Without intending it, certainly without planning it long ahead, he now found himself on this train, north bound for Wheeling. He reviewed the incidents, none of them important, which had led from his own comfortable house to the hard red plush seat upon which he now sat.

It had begun out of a letter he had written after Lucinda had first blown the word "railroads" at him like a rainbow bubble. He had written to John MacBain, in Wheeling, asking again for the rental of his idle lands. John had been willing enough now to rent and Pierce was busy for three months finding hired men enough to farm the five hundred acres. He had collected a conglomerate score of laborers, some black, some white, and had put them in the old slave quarters of the MacBain house. He had ridden over there often enough in the last months to oversee them, and always before his eyes MacBain House had stood gaunt and empty, its burned wing still shattered. Molly had gone to Wheeling and he had not seen her again. She had spent a day with Lucinda before she went, but it was a day when he had been riding over the country, hunting for seed corn. Seed was his treasure, hard to find, almost impossible to buy. He had gathered it by the handfuls, wherever he could find it, paying almost its weight in silver. The mountaineers had hoarded seed but they would take nothing for it except hard coin. He had ridden the mountains until he was stiff-legged, stooping through the doorways of the miserable cabins and tempting ragged men to divide the hidden stores of seed. But he had succeeded. Malvern today was planted to corn, and he had seed for the wheat of next year.

The sight of MacBain House, gaunt against the southern sky, had always made him think of John. Then John had inquired in a letter, "Why don't you get into railroads? They're the backbone of our trade. In the next fifty years all the great fortunes will be built upon railroads. You have your sons to think of, man."

With John's words clear upon his brain he thought of his sons very often. The two boys had grown that summer in one of the sudden spurts of childhood growth. Martin shed baby fat and showed the frame of his manhood, tall and strong, and Carey, because he could not keep up with his older brother, developed a canny hardness that was often shrewd beyond his years. There would be other children and it was true that Malvern would not be big enough to provide for them all, especially in the luxury which was a necessity to Lucinda. The old plantation days were gone. Perhaps John was right, that the fortunes of the next half century were in trade, not farming. Railroads from the East, building up the new West! There was profit in it, and why should he not have his share?

One clear cool September day, he set out for the nearest railway depot. Lucinda was nearing her time, and as always she disliked him as her pregnancy progressed. When this had happened before Martin's birth, it had broken his heart and driven him half mad with grief. He had been desperately in love with her and ignorant of women. When she repulsed him he had been first hurt and then filled with fury. She was ignorant, too, and she could not explain herself. His anger and her disgust had risen to such crisis that one day she had demanded, screaming with tears, to go home to her mother. He had turned cold with fear, but he had taken her there himself, and she had stayed until Martin was nearly due. He insisted that his children be born at Malvern, as he and Tom had been. Lucinda's mother and father had both come back with them. He would never forget Lucinda's father. He had died during the war, but Pierce remembered the cynical, lordly old man when he had tried to tell his son-in-law that he must not think that Lucinda really hated him.

"Give her time, my boy," the tall, angular Virginian had cried. "Dash it, Pierce, no man can understand a pregnant woman!"

"I suppose not," Pierce had said drily. They had looked at one another and laughed.

He had given her time, and Lucinda had returned to him sweetly and when Carey was born he had been ready for her hatred. That was during the war, and he was taking saltpeter like the rest of the men and they were all too busy to think about women.

But this time it had been hard. Lucinda was different. There could be no doubt that the war had made her self-sufficient and independent. She had got used to managing without him. She knew she could live without him—dangerous knowledge for any woman to know that she could live without a man! She had been more than usually absorbed in her pregnancy.

He frowned, remembering how often she was cruel to Georgia. Not that he cared what she did to her own servant, except that Georgia was a human being, after all, and unfortunately delicate and fine. Lucinda had lain abed on the long hot days, fretful and complaining and commanding Georgia to fetch and carry, until the girl had looked faint with weariness. But Georgia never complained. Pierce wondered sometimes at her unvarying sweetness. She was too patient. He would not have blamed her had she flung out at them all. He had been silent. He had not reproached Lucinda for a long time. He had not indeed meant to reproach her at all, but one day, before his eyes, her white hand had darted upward so quickly that it made him think of a snake's tongue, and she had slapped Georgia's cheeks.

Georgia stepped back, her palm on her cheek, her eyes wide. Pierce had been reading aloud to Lucinda. It was evening—night, in fact, and he had paused to light the lamp. His eyes had been turned from the bed, then the sound of the slap had made him start.

"For God's sake, Luce!" he had shouted.

"I've told you not to shake my bed!" Lucinda said fiercely to Georgia.

The girl had looked from her mistress to him, and for one full second he had found himself gazing into her great brown eyes. Then she had turned and fled from the room, her soft white skirts flying behind her.

"She's so clumsy," Lucinda complained. She closed her eyes.

He had not answered for an instant. Why were women so cruel? Then, pondering, he suddenly understood Lucinda's cruelty. She was revenging herself upon Georgia for Bettina. She never mentioned Bettina, she never reproached Tom, but she was taking her sharp revenge on Georgia. He went and stood beside the bed, and he looked down at her. He loved her, but into his love welled a deep sadness. She was so pretty, his Lucinda, his wife, often so good, a good mother, and to him, when she was herself, a good and dutiful wife. She had a dear and lovely body. But what was it that twisted her soul? He did not know. He only knew that something made her smaller than his love deserved. The war, perhaps, had shown him too much nobility among men, and he measured her by it.

She had opened her eyes and now looked up at him with her clear blue gaze. "Well?" she asked.

"I wish you wouldn't be so hard on Georgia, Luce," he said gently. He had not wanted to reproach her. He only wanted her to be big enough for him to love utterly. He longed for wholeness of her soul and for largeness in her spirit, because he wanted her perfect for his love. He was loath to judge her or see her smaller than the image his love made of her.

He had been horrified by the flash of rage that lit her eyes and changed her face. "Don't you dare stand up for a nigger, Pierce Delaney!" she had screamed at him. She sat up in bed, her hands clenched. It had seemed to him that even her golden hair stiffened and sprang alive with her fury.

And then in her rage she had flung at him the unspeakable insult, which even yet he could not forget or forgive. She had cried at him, "Don't tell me you're going to take up with Georgia—like Tom has with Bettina! Men are all the same— you are all beasts—every one of you!"

She had covered her face with her hands and sobbed. But he had turned and walked out of the room.

Outside he had met Tom. He was choosing a walking stick from the stand in the hall, debonair in a new grey suit and a white felt hat. Pierce saw every detail of Tom's well-being.

"Where are you going, Tom?" he had asked. He was prickling with rage and hurt and yet he could not tell Tom what Lucinda had said.

Tom had answered in his usual calm way. "Bettina expects me, and I won't be back until Monday morning."

He had not answered. Instead he had walked to the front door that stood wide open to the evening air. Mosquitoes were beginning to whine about the terraces. Damn Tom for his calmness! Damn him, too, for his happiness.

"By the way," Tom said behind him. "I must tell you, Pierce, that Carey is making the most extraordinary progress with his reading. I think he will be ready for his second year's work soon—a clever boy. Martin could do as well if he weren't all for play and horseback riding."

"Martin's smart enough," Pierce replied.

"Of course he's your favorite," Tom retorted. He ran lightly down the marble steps, smiled at Pierce and waved his stick. Pierce stared after the graceful figure walking briskly down the road between the oaks. Down by the stile Jake was waiting with a horse. What did Jake think of Tom and Bettina? He wondered morosely, and his mind ran ahead of Tom into the little brick house at Millpoint, where Bettina waited. Angrily he saw her soft dark beauty, her readiness, her warmth. For weeks Lucinda had not let him come near her. Yet she had flung at him the insult. It was then, at that very moment, that he had decided to go to Wheeling and see John Mac-Bain.

The train pounded around a curve in the mountain road.

Pierce loved mountains. As a boy he had spent days of hunting in the mountains that circled Malvern. But always after a few days he grew oppressed with loneliness, and was compelled to go home again and feel the walls about him safely, and see his parents and Tom.

He became aware now of something very like that loneliness. He was thinking about Lucinda. He had never spoken to her of the taunt she had flung at him nor had she. When they met they had both said nothing. Perhaps he had forgiven her, after all. At any rate, he wanted to forgive her. He sighed loudly as he thought of her.

"I'm weak," he thought mournfully. "At least, where she is concerned."

In the army he had been hard enough—no, even there he had been secretly tender to those who depended on him. He stared at the flying landscape and was troubled afresh at his own confusion.

When he got to Wheeling he would use that newfangled telegraph and send word to Lucinda. She was safe not to have the child until he got back, but he wanted her to know where he was in Wheeling, in case something went wrong. He had told Georgia to be watchful.

"Georgia, you keep a sharp eye on your mistress," he had told her. It had been hard for him to be natural with her. Lucinda's foolish words stuck in his mind like a flung dagger he could not pull out. They'd be in him always, maybe. He had looked away from Georgia's beautiful, waiting face. "If you think anything doesn't look right, you're to tell my brother, and then he'll get a telegram to me."

"Yes, sir," Georgia had said.

And then the girl's gentleness had moved him in pity to go on, "You don't blame her, I hope, Georgia, for all her fancies and tempers these days? She doesn't mean anything."

"Oh, no, sir," Georgia had replied, flushing under her pale golden skin.

"She's always like that before the children come," Pierce had gone on. He wanted to stop talking and yet he wanted to go on. He wanted to say that she must understand that Lu-

cinda might go on being cruel because of Bettina. But Georgia
had said it for him.

"It isn't just that, sir," she had said simply and plainly. "I
know she feels upset about Bettina, and she can't say so, and
she doesn't know it, but she takes it out on me. But I don't
mind, sir. People can't help themselves, I reckon. Anyway,
if it's for Bettina, I can bear it."

"It's very clever of you to understand," he had said quickly
and had turned away. He must not discuss Lucinda, his own
wife.

Over the hills the trees were beginning to change, ready for
autumn. Malvern was green, but as he had come north he
could feel the stopping of summer growth. A touch of frost
and the mountains would flame. He gloried in the beauty.
Everything here was fortunate. They had been spared the
misery of carpetbaggers. Lucinda's brother, Randolph, had
written how at night he had gone out under the white sheets
of the Kluxers. "It's life and death, these days," he had written, "and I don't choose death, not at the hands of slaves I
have fed and clothed all their lives."

Well, thank God, West Virginia was on the side of victory.
It was his state now. He lifted his head and breathed in the
dusty air of the swaying car, bumping over the faulty road-
bed. It was a state carved out of the old, born for the new.
He and Lucinda were happy—they must be. He put her out of
his mind impatiently. Too much of his life was spent in thinking of her. Lucinda had a way of making herself felt. Without being aggressive or even talkative, she impinged. His
smile grew grim as he thought of her. The years which the
war had wasted must be repaired. His ambition, leashed to
Malvern, broke its bounds. If John MacBain could grow rich,
why not he?

Late at night a week later he sat talking in John's library
before the fire. He had looked about the big dark room with
some amusement.

"I never knew you to read a book, John," he had remarked.
John laughed his silent grey laughter. "They're only wall-

paper as far as I am concerned." He yawned as he glanced about the shelves. "They came with the house—Molly's notion, this house."

"Expensive notion," Pierce said drily. He had eaten an excellent dinner with grateful surprise. Molly's somewhat slipshod housekeeping had changed with the city. Two light colored men in white linen jackets had served them deftly and Molly had sat at the foot of the table in a yellow taffeta gown, her green eyes brilliant and her red hair piled on her head. After dinner she had gone to a concert on the arm of a young man who had called for her with a horse and carriage and he and John had come to the library and had talked about getting rich while they smoked and drank whiskey and water.

"Molly has to amuse herself these days," John said. He glanced at the big marble clock on the mantelpiece. It was after midnight. "She'll be home soon. I don't care for music myself. But I want to be fair to her—"

He sat hunched forward in his leather armchair, his long hands hanging slackly between his knees. Intimate words hesitated in the air and Pierce avoided them hastily.

"I'm mighty appreciative of this evening, John," he said in his rich amiable voice. "When I came here last week, I thought no more than that we'd talk things over. Tonight—well, I feel as if I'd found the end of the rainbow."

"You came at the right minute," John replied. "The new stock was put on sale that night at midnight."

"Still, if you hadn't helped me by taking a mortgage on my land—though I never thought I'd mortgage a foot of Malvern —I shan't dare to tell Lucinda," Pierce said.

"You needn't tell her," John assured him. "A year and it will be paid off. Don't forget I didn't want the mortgage. I wanted to make it a loan—so far as I'm concerned, it's no more."

He spoke absently, listening for the hall door to open. "Molly isn't satisfied with this house," he said irrelevantly. "She's seen a big place on a hill—Morgan property. It's too big for us—why, it's even got a ballroom!" He looked at Pierce sorrowfully.

"Women are insatiable, I reckon," Pierce said lightly. He filled his pipe, and then, seeing John's listening look, he put it down again. Molly would be home at any moment.

"Go on and smoke," John ordered him.

"No—I'll wait—she might come in. I don't like to smoke before a lady," Pierce replied.

The moment hung between them again, hovering on the edge of the intimacy he dreaded. Then it closed down upon him and he could not avoid it.

"Insatiable—you've hit the word," John said slowly. "But it's not her fault. . . . Pierce, I've done you a friendly turn."

"You have, John," Pierce met his eyes fully and with deep dread. Was his friend about to ask a price of him?

"I like you better than any man I know—or am likely to know in this damned city, by Gawd," John went on.

"We've grown up as neighbors," Pierce murmured.

John looked up sharply. "Understand—what I'm asking isn't a price, though, Pierce. I want you to have the loan—whatever you say."

"I'm sure of that," Pierce replied. He sat gazing steadily into the fire.

John looked away and wet his lips. "I want to ask you a queer thing—queer enough so I reckon no man asked it ever before of another man."

Pierce tried to look at him and could not. He picked up his pipe and lit it.

"Molly's still—young. Too young to live—without more children, Pierce . . . Pierce, I want you to father me a child."

It was out. Pierce heard it and knew that John had pondered over it long, in the secret darkness of many nights. He could not look at him for pity. His blood drummed in his ears.

John went on. "If Molly had a child—or two, maybe—she'd be more content—with me." He got up and kicked the fire and the lumps of smouldering soft coal fell apart and blazed. He leaned on the mantelpiece and stared into the flames. "I've thought it all out. Why should she suffer—because of what the war did to me? It'll happen—sooner or later—with some man. Pierce, let it be you!"

He turned abruptly and their eyes met. Pierce saw agony in John's eyes and felt tears come into his own. But he shook his head.

"John, I—can't. I've got to love a woman before I can—can—besides, Lucinda's the only one for me."

The door opened in the hall. They heard Molly's voice calling a gay goodnight. Then she was at the library door, her cheeks crimson, her eyes shining. "Oh, it was heavenly!" she cried. Then she stopped and looked from one to the other of them. "Why, you two," she exclaimed. "What's wrong with you? My Gawd, you look like a couple of thieves!"

"God forbid," Pierce said heartily. He turned to John and they broke into common laughter, and in its gust they were restored.

When Pierce reached home his daughter was already born, a week earlier than she was expected. Jake brought the news to him proudly at the station, and Pierce hastened the horses home.

He tiptoed into Lucinda's room before he had changed his clothes. She was asleep, her cheeks pearly pale. He stood looking down at her with unutterable tenderness, grateful for his own good fortune. The strange thing John had asked of him he would never tell her. She would never believe that he could have refused. He smiled half ruefully at her invincible female distrust and she opened her eyes and, seeing him, she held out her hand and gave him a smile ravishing and mischievous.

"Pay me!" she demanded.

He laughed, put his hand into his pocket and brought out a velvet box. "It came last month from Paris," he said.

"You monster," she murmured, "to keep it so long—"

"You had to fulfill your part of the bargain," he said.

She pouted, her hand still waiting, he still withholding, "If it had been a boy you wouldn't have—" she began.

"Certainly not," he said firmly.

"Give it to me, Pierce!" she cried.

He withdrew his hand and the box. "Show me your girl, madame!" he said with mock severity.

"Silly," she said, but she pulled the ribbon bell rope that hung beside her bed and Georgia appeared at the door.

"Bring the baby," Lucinda said to her arrogantly.

"Only if it is a girl," Pierce amended.

Georgia smiled her soft warm smile, "It is a girl, sir—"

She went away to fetch the child and Pierce sat down on the bed and smiled down at his wife and teased her in the extravagance of his love. "Hardhearted as ever, I see, even to your daughter—keeping her out in the cold, in another room!"

Lucinda had always refused to have the babies in her own room. Now she pouted again, prettily. "She cries more than the boys did."

"Ah, maybe you've met your match, Luce," Pierce retorted.

Georgia came in, the pink bundle in her arms, and Pierce rose as she drew back a corner of the silk afghan. He looked down into the face of his daughter. She was asleep. He studied every detail of her round pretty face. Her tiny features had a firmness which disconcerted him. Neither of his sons had looked so complete at birth. He held his gift toward Lucinda. "Here," he said hastily, "take it! I can see she's a female."

Then he waited for the first look in Lucinda's eyes when she saw the bauble. She opened the box. "Oh, Pierce," she breathed, "how beautiful!" She lifted sapphire earrings and brooch from the grey velvet. "Oh, perfect!" she sighed.

"You're a damned expensive woman," he growled proudly, and at his voice the baby opened her eyes and gave a soft cry.

He turned at the sound of this new voice, and gazed down into large, deeply violet eyes.

"Sapphira," he said to his daughter, and smiled in pride that somehow held a heartbreak in it which he could not understand. "I have a notion that you're going to be expensive, too," he said wryly.

# *Four*

---

PIERCE DELANEY LOOKED down the long table loaded with
silver and fruits and flowers. He sat at one end and John
MacBain at the other in the immense dining room of the
mansion in Wheeling which had belonged to the Morgans and
now belonged to the MacBains. At John's right Lucinda lifted
her blonde head. The fairness of her hair had not dulled in
the ten years since Sapphira had been born—Sally, Pierce
called her. There had been two others after her, his third
son, and then last year, the baby. The light shone down from
the great crystal chandeliers and Lucinda's piled curls
gleamed softly. She had rouged her cheeks a very little. He
did not approve of it, and yet he had not the heart to reproach her when the touch of color added so much to her
calm beauty. She was still slender.

At his own right Molly MacBain leaned her elbows on the
table. Her arms were bare and white and her elbows dimpled.
He knew just how those dimples were placed in the outer
curve of the smooth flesh but still the knowledge did not disturb him. His eyes rested with secure pleasure on her rosy
face and bright black eyes.

"You're prettier than you were ten years ago, Molly," he
said genially.

She laughed at him. "I've never been quite pretty enough
for you, Pierce," she said frankly. "But it don't matter to me
as much as it did. Look at John—he's like a hen ready to lay
an egg! That means it's time for the speech-making."

Up and down the long table the faces of men and women
turned reluctantly toward John MacBain. He had grown

heavy and somber in the last ten years and his head was bald. Now he rose under the waiting eyes and stood an instant, gathering them into his power. They submitted, half amused, but a sigh, like the breath of a slow summer breeze, rose and died down. Here and there a pretty woman turned unwillingly from the man with whom she was talking and silence fell.

Pierce looked with affection and amusement at his old friend. Ten years ago he had taken the train to Wheeling in search of John. He had done it for Malvern's sake. The hungry acres had eaten and drunk his money and were draining him. He knew that if he were to complete his dream and leave the inheritance as a great estate to his sons he would have to find money elsewhere. Malvern was repaying him richly now, thanks to his railroad shares. In less than a year he had repaid John's loan, and he had insisted on high interest.

This was John's dinner, John's house, John MacBain, the vice-president of the greatest railroad in the East. When the president died, John might become president. Pierce was only half listening to the earnest heavy voice. He had heard scores of John's after dinner speeches, and he always made the same halts between sentences.

"I am grieved to state that our president is not able to be with us this evening," John was saying. "You may be sure only the most important affairs could have prevented him from taking the chairmanship here at this dinner of the Board of Directors and their ladies, at which I make a report on the new eight-wheel passenger engine of the 2-6-0 type. This engine, number 600, is the largest of the passenger locomotives in this country, and—"

"Oh dear—he's off on engines," Molly whispered to Pierce. Their eyes met, laughing. He was occasionally secretly astonished that in the years he had been John's partner in the railroad business, he had not yielded to Molly. There had been times when he might have yielded to her in a mingled pity for her life and the fullness of his own vitality, and remembering always that John would have said nothing. It had been a temptation again and again. Had Lucinda ever denied herself to him, he might have taken revenge with Molly. But Lucinda, always silent, never denied him anything any more, even when the two younger children were born within three years. His dear little Sally was worth the sapphires hundreds of times over.

"You're mine," Pierce declared often to this his favorite child. "I bought you from your mama the first time I saw you."

"Tell me how it was," Sally always demanded with relish at the thought of her immense cost.

"Your mama sent me word that she had just finished you, down to the last little finger nail, and would I please come and see how I liked you. So I went into Mama's room and Georgia brought you in, and you wore a long white dress. I looked at you and I thought you would do. So I said, 'Well, here's a pair of sapphire earrings for her two blue eyes, and a sapphire brooch for the rest of her.'"

Lucinda, wearing the sapphires at this moment, caught his eyes and smiled at him. He was aware of her cool and watchful smile whenever he and Molly sat together, and he smiled back at her.

It was one of Lucinda's qualities never to utter her suspicions of him. But he could feel them, nevertheless. He retaliated by an amused silence equally unbroken. He did not tell her that he never intended to sleep with Molly MacBain. Let her continue to think that he might! He turned his eyes from Lucinda and looked calmly at John, who stood with his thumbs in his white waistcoat, and gazing at his partner's bearded face, Pierce's thoughts continued about himself.

When his third son was born he had named him John after John MacBain, but the youngest girl was Lucie, after Lucinda herself. He and Lucinda had decided together that they would not plan on more children, but if they came by accident, they would be welcome. Privately to himself he thought he would like to have seven children, another son and daughter. He was proud of Malvern and proud of the half-grown boys and girls of his family, and proud, too, of his wife. Lucinda was a credit to him and she had helped to make Malvern what it was, a gentleman's home, set in the midst of a thousand acres of rolling rich land. He had added two wings to the house, one on either side, and had thrown out a great porch to the west, where he could watch the sun set over the tops of the mountains beyond his fields. At evening the wide valley lay full of mellow light, and when the sun dropped, the twilight was purple. The deep softness of darkness over his land and the stars over the mountains made the night as living for him as the day. In quiet sleep was renewal. He was a fortunate man. Tom, his brother Tom, was the only thorn. He turned away involuntarily from the thought of Tom.

John MacBain's voice took on an added importance. "We are now building our own sleeping cars and parlor cars. We are adding five hotels to the palatial hostels already operating at Deer Park, Relay and Cumberland. We are preparing to establish our own telegraph lines and our own express company. By the end of the decade there will be no railroad in the country so well equipped as our own to handle the transportation of passengers and goods. For this we have to thank not only the genius of our president, but the confidence of the stockholders and of the Board of Directors, during the long years of building, when faith had to be the evidence of things unseen. And now I call upon one of you—Pierce Delaney, old neighbor of mine, friend, partner."

John MacBain sat down and glowed with relief in the midst of handclapping. He looked at Pierce and his thin lips lengthened into a smile. He nodded. The soft rush of women's voices that had begun as soon as the clapping was over ceased as Pierce rose to his feet. Eyes that had turned to John MacBain with affectionate amusement turned now to Pierce with respect and envy.

He rose and stood for a second or two, looking at one face after another. All had become familiar to him in the ten years in which he had been part of the great railroad company from which he had drawn the money he needed for Malvern. He had none of John's devotion to the iron framework which tied the Eastern states to the West. What had been John's

life had been for him only a means to an end. He had chosen
to build for himself his own habitation. To live on his land
as a gentleman, to breed fine children and fine horses and fine
cattle, and when he had no guests, to spend his evenings in
his library—all this had been good. His energies had flowed
into such creation. But John, lacking children, had spent his
energies in making the railroad.

Pierce smiled his famous smile and took his usual pleasure
in seeing the faces around the table warm to him. He liked it
that the men responded to him as instinctively as the women.
He liked men better than women and men knew it and they
admired him and liked him the more. He began in his amiable,
informal fashion, "John is never satisfied unless I make some
sort of speech at these shindigs of his, and yet he knows that
I can't make speeches. I'm a farmer—a West Virginia farmer."

Low laughter murmured around the table. Pierce was quite
aware of his own appearance, gentleman among gentlemen,
and he laughed a little at himself. His white hand, holding his
wineglass, was certainly not the hand of a farmer. "I've never
been a railroad man," he went on. "Ten years ago I came to
find John MacBain in Wheeling, because I needed some
money to fix up my place after the war and I wanted him to
help me get it. Well, he did. Those were the years when our
stock was begging to be bought. I borrowed enough money
from John to get me a little stock and following his advice,
I bought more with what it earned and let my wife and children starve awhile. It did them no harm. Well, the railroad
has treated me—adequately—as it has the rest of you. The
company deserves our loyalty. Furthermore—"

He smiled again, and again they smiled back at the tall
handsome man, still young in his maturity. His voice grew
grave.

"There is a magic in railroads these days. They bind our
nation together with more than bonds of steel. They bring us
together in trade and exchange and friendship. It is doubtful
whether even the war could have achieved our unity as a nation had not the railroads come quickly to take up the task.
Old hatreds still remain, for many of us. Particularly in the

South, the Yankees remain the Yankees. Even the children will scarcely forget. But the railroads are a new force. No hatred is in their history. They heal the wounds of the past, and they reach toward the future. Men of great vision, and John MacBain is one of them, have guided their building westward, and westward our nation has grown. It has been the railroads, too, that have delivered us from the horrid danger of socialism, and it is John MacBain whom we must thank for the fact that labor unions have been kept out of our state. The poison of the northern industrial states must not enter our fair mountain land.

"We have been fortunate," Pierce's firm white hand lifted his wineglass again. "We have been spared the extremes into which our sister states have fallen. We have marched in steady progress upon the wheels of railroad development. Our great railroads have carried all of us to prosperity. Mines have been opened to provide steel and waterways have flourished in carrying the loads of lumber and ore we have needed. The produce of the land has been borne swiftly to all parts of the hungry nation, and we have profited by it all, from the first blow of the miner's pick and the roll of the farmer's wagon wheel, to the flow of gold into our coffers. Schools and churches have been built and cities grow. The force behind all our growth and all our wealth is the railroad. Ladies and gentlemen, let us drink to the new engine, the 600, the great eight-wheeler, designed especially for the bold slopes of our Mountain State!"

They rose, skirts rustling, chairs scraping, and glasses clinked. They sat down again and talk broke out. Greyhaired Jim McCagney leaned his tall Scotch-Irish frame upon his elbows and called out a question.

"Tell us something more about the engine, Pierce!"

Pierce smiled. "You ought to ask John that," he said in his even voice. "But I'll tell you what I know. It's bigger than the Larkins engines. We thought the top had been reached in them. Now I dare to prophesy that we will build something bigger even than this 600, beauty though she is. She weighs eight thousand pounds more than the Larkins and has more than twelve thousand square feet beyond her heating surface."

"Twelve thousand and fifty nine!" John MacBain shouted. "And she weighs one hundred and fifty three thousand pounds!"

"That's enough about engines," Molly cried, springing to her feet. "Let's begin the dancing—"

Laughter broke out and the men rose to pull out the ladies' chairs. They stood watching while the ladies lifted their ruffled skirts and walked out of the doors that were opened for them by footmen. Molly MacBain was proud that everything had gone so well. Her footmen, black as the West Virginia coal, were dressed in maroon uniforms, piped with yellow. She held her head high as she led her guests into her parlors. Beyond them doors opened into the ballroom.

"The men won't be long," she promised them. "I told John I would be real mad with him if he got talkin'."

The ladies smiled and scattered, some to the powder rooms to mend their complexions, and some to sit by tables and look at albums. Lacey Mallows took out a tiny pipe and began to smoke it. Lucinda saw this and pointedly ignored it. The Henry Mallows, living so much in Paris, were rather fast. The others, following Lucinda's lead, said nothing. Lucinda was always in the best of taste and those who followed what she did were sure to be right. She drifted toward a long mirror hung on the wall and saw that she was as fresh and lovely as when the evening began. She sat at its foot and fanned herself gently with a white ostrich feather fan, set in silver filigree and diamonds. It had been Pierce's present when she had given him his third son, John.

In the dining room the men were talking of railroads in frank harsh terms. Cut-throat competition was the threat.

"I don't see how you can keep it up, Mr. MacBain," Henry Mallows said. He had inherited his share of the road from his father who had died last year and the sudden wealth had sent him hurrying home from Paris with his English wife. She was the daughter of the Earl of Marcy, but he tried not to mention it often. In the determinedly democratic atmosphere of his native state he had found it no advantage to him that his wife was titled in her own right in a foreign country.

"It's outdo the other fellow or bust," John MacBain said flatly. "We've got to keep the trade, even if we ship cattle and goods free from California and back again. If another road can afford to ship a cow from Chicago to the coast for five dollars, we've got to do better."

The men looked at one another in consternation.

Pierce laughed. "The other roads are worse off than we are," he said gaily. "They can't afford to make their own rolling stock—we can and do! Of course these cut-throat ways can't last. Some day we'll all be ready to quit. Then we'll act like gentlemen and keep to our agreements. But we won't act like gentlemen until we have to. Human nature! I see it in my own older sons. Those boys of mine will fight about something until they're like beaten cocks. Then when they can't fight any more, they come to terms."

Pierce's children were his weakness, and his friends knew it. "I saw your eldest son the other day at the University," a man said. "I went down to enter my own boy—fine looking fellow, yours! What's he going to make of himself?"

Pierce inclined his head. "Martin will follow me at Malvern," he said modestly. But the modesty deceived no one. Pierce met their smiling eyes and in the silence looked at John. He was sorry the talk had come around to sons. The look of suffering stillness that fell upon John when other men talked of their children was dark upon his face now. Pierce rose, "Let us join the ladies," he said. "Mrs. MacBain extracted some sort of promise from John, I believe—she told me so."

They went out, well-fed men, rich men, determined to hold their riches in a state still poor. They were confident that from their prosperity would flow the prosperity of all.

In the ballroom Pierce went to Molly as a matter of course. The hostess must have the first dance. She slipped easily into his arms, accustomed to the pose. She was growing a little solid, but she was still light and graceful enough when she danced. He was used to her step and he suited his rhythm to hers. They were old friends now, frank enough. He was accustomed to her frontal attacks and he was no longer afraid of her as once he had been in the days when he did not know if he wanted her. He knew now that he did not.

"You men left the table earlier than I dared hope," she said. Her frankest talk was always behind the screen of music when they were dancing. The band she had hired was playing a Strauss waltz, bows sweeping long across violin strings and the piano throbbing.

"The talk got around to sons, and I saw John flinch as he always does," Pierce said.

"I wish John would let me adopt a boy, but he won't," Molly said. "He says if he can't have his flesh and blood he don't want somebody else's."

"I can understand that," Pierce replied. "I wouldn't want Malvern inherited by any except my own."

"If John would take a boy, I'd have one for him," Molly said laughing. "I'd be glad to—especially if you'd father him for me, Pierce. Wouldn't it be kind of nice? He'd inherit our place—next to yours."

He was accustomed to these bold proposals and he smiled. "We've been through all this before, haven't we?" he remarked. But he had never told her that John had once asked him the same thing.

"Only in words," she said wickedly.

He laughed in spite of himself. "Molly, for God's sake," he protested. "You know what a fuss it would make in our families! Lucinda would leave me."

"My Gawd, Lucinda needn't know," she declared.

"Lucinda always knows everything," he said, in pretended rue.

"I can fix it," she persisted.

"Please, lady, leave my life alone," he begged in mock alarm.

Molly dropped into utter seriousness. "Of course I know— you don't want me—"

"I don't want you enough to roil up my life," he countered.

"I'm not young enough—that's the truth!" she declared.

She lifted her lashes and dared him, with eyes too bright, to deny it.

"You'll always be young," he said gaily. "Please, Molly, when your hair is white—and mine too—keep on asking me! Something would go out of my life if you stopped making proposals to me which I can't accept."

The waltz ended at exactly the right moment for him upon this casual gayety, which, affectionate though it was, he kept devoid of passion. She sighed, and he dropped his arms from about her and sighed in mimicry. Then he smiled and went to Lucinda and sat down beside her. She had been dancing with John and he had torn the ruffle of her skirt. She frowned at it. "I shall have to go and get it mended," she said.

"Lend me your fan while you're gone," he begged. "The rooms are too close."

"Sure it wasn't Molly?" she inquired with malice.

"Not after all these years," he returned.

"But you are so handsome, Pierce," she murmured.

"Thank you, my dear," he replied. He took the fan from her hand and sat fanning himself without embarrassment. "I shan't dance until you come back," he said calmly.

She was back in the middle of the next waltz, and took her fan away from him. "You mind looking silly less than any man I know," she remarked. "Dance with me, please, Pierce!"

"Did I look silly?" he asked. They began waltzing slowly. Lucinda did not like flourishes, and neither did he. "But everybody knew it was my wife's fan. Besides, I still love the perfume you use and the fan kept blowing it to me."

She was mollified and smiled. "When shall we go home?" she murmured. Their steps matched perfectly. She saw Lacey Mallows watching them, and yielded herself a little more to Pierce's embrace.

"I always want to go home," he said.

"Molly wants us to stay until tomorrow," she teased.

"Then let's stay," he said promptly. He knew that it was the surest way to get her to go.

She fell at once into his trap. "I sleep better in my own bed," she said.

"So do I," he said; —"with you," he added.

She laughed. "Pierce, you aren't a little drunk?"

"I think not," he said, "but maybe—"

"If we are going home tonight, we'll have to catch the twelve forty—" she reminded him.

"John has the car at the siding. It will be easy," he replied.

At one o'clock they were going to bed in John MacBain's private railroad car. Pierce in his fine linen nightshirt looked out of the window at the swiftly passing moonlit landscape. The whirling mountains were black against the dark blue sky. "God, what grades the men had to climb!" he murmured.

Lucinda came to his side and he put his arm around her to steady her. "The road is astonishingly smooth, considering the solid rock they hewed," he went on. He had blown out the kerosene lamps the better to see into the moonlight. "Tons of dynamite," he murmured. They could see the engine turning a curve and spitting sparks. It turned and curved again and a cliff hid it.

"Oh, stop thinking about railroads!" Lucinda cried.

He looked down at her. The filmy stuff of her nightgown flowed to her feet, and there were ruffles at her bosom and her wrists. Her long fair hair was loose on her shoulders. He lifted her into his arms. "The way you keep hold of me," he murmured into her fragrant neck, "The shameful way you never let me go! How can you go on getting prettier every year? What chance has anybody else, you little selfish thing? Look here—don't you blame me for anything that happens tonight—"

"I won't," she said sweetly. "Really, I won't, Pierce."

But he knew the reason for her willingness. She was afraid, a little afraid, of Molly MacBain. He smiled at his cynicism and accepted his Lucinda for what she was—a pretty woman, and his own.

He reached home in the full pride of possession. Jake met them at the station with the new surrey and the matched bay horses of Malvern breeding, and when they swept up the long drive of oaks which his grandfather had planted, he turned to Lucinda in profound pleasure.

"There isn't a place even in Virginia to match Malvern," he declared.

Lucinda, very composed in her dove-grey traveling dress, smiled. "I shan't be satisfied until we have the new green-house and when that is finished I want a formal garden laid out below the slope."

She lifted her parasol and pointed to the hollow at the foot of the knoll upon which the great house stood.

It was early summer and the green of grass and trees was bright. "It would be pleasant to sit on the terrace and look down on the garden," she went on.

"You always want something more, my pet," Pierce said with amiable sarcasm.

"Why not, when I can have it?" she replied.

He did not answer. The children had heard the surrey and were gathering on the top step to meet them. Martin and Carey were at school in Virginia, but Sally, John and lit-tle Lucie were standing and waiting. Georgia had dressed them in their best and she had curled Sally's hair down her shoulders. The morning sunlight fell on them warmly and Pierce felt his throat catch in absurd sentimentality. "You've given me wonderful children, Luce," he said. He tried to make his voice casual but he knew it was not.

Lucinda smiled and then frowned. "I wish John didn't look so much like Tom. That means he won't be as handsome as the other boys."

As soon as she spoke Tom's name the whole problem of their lives came back upon them. They put it aside again and again, now to go to Wheeling on railroad business, now to White Sulphur on a holiday, but when they came home it was always there waiting. Pierce did not answer her, but he remembered the promise he had given her this time before they went away. He had promised her that he would tell Tom firmly at last that he must marry and settle down. Whether he kept Bettina was no one's business, but he had to keep her elsewhere than in that house by the road, where whenever there was another child, everyone knew it. Tom had now three children by Bettina, children who were own cousins to his children and Lucinda's. This was what Lucinda could not endure. She had faced Pierce with it last week.

"If only our children didn't love Tom so much and hang on his every word!" she complained.

"Tom's their teacher and I reckon it's only natural," Pierce had replied.

"That's what is so disgusting," she had said angrily. "You pay Tom to run the Academy, and we send our children there, and everybody knows."

"I don't consider it my affair," he had retorted to end the talk.

"But it is your affair when your own children are involved," she had retorted in turn. "It isn't as it used to be before the war, when a man could go to a black wench in the quarters or get her to his room and nobody be the wiser and little mulattos were only niggers with the rest. Things can't be hidden the way they used to be—everybody knows about Tom and Bettina. Why, it's as bad as if they were married! As soon as that boy is ready for school—you mark my words, Pierce—Tom will want him to go to the Academy with our own children."

He was outraged by Lucinda's absurdity. "You know Tom wouldn't mix white and black that way," he grumbled.

She had laughed her cruelly light laughter. "Do you think Tom calls his children *black*?" she cried.

"But they are," he had protested.

She had laughed again and suddenly he had hated her laughter. It occurred to him that Lucinda never laughed except at someone else.

"Tom's no fool," he had said loudly.

She had patted the ruffles of her skirt, and made her voice casual again.

"You're too soft, Pierce. You always want to avoid trouble. But somewhere you have to make a stand, even with your own brother."

"Well, well," he had muttered. "Let it be until we get back from John's shindig, then I'll see what's what."

"Is that a promise?"

"Well, yes—it is."

Now the children ran down the steps to meet them and in a moment he had his daughter in his arms. His first embrace was always for Sally and she knew it and all the others knew it. John and Lucie submitted to their mother's kiss and waited until Pierce opened his arms to them. John was a quiet child, undeniably like Tom in his looks, and Lucie was a miniature of Lucinda. Her likeness to her mother disturbed Pierce sometimes, and occasionally it had occurred to him that if he watched Lucie he might understand Lucinda too well. The veneer of manners and behavior which covered Lucinda had not yet accumulated over Lucie, and the child was frankly selfish. Pierce was never willing to face Lucie's faults because he loved his wife truly. He stooped now and kissed Lucie with gentleness. The little blonde girl returned the kiss demurely and without emotion. Pierce never kissed his sons. He put his arm on John's shoulder and walked up the steps with him and Lucinda followed with the girls. John rubbed his head against his father's solid body.

"Father, Uncle Tom is going to put me into Latin."

"Good," Pierce said heartily. "That means he thinks you are a clever fellow and so you are."

He pressed the boy's thin body to his and felt the wave of emotion that always swept him when he held his children. They were so young and touching, so dependent upon him. Their weakness made him strong, and quieted all that was wild and restless in him.

His eyes fell upon Georgia as he mounted the last step. She stood a little to the right, motionless in her peculiar still fashion. She was as quiet as a shadow in his house, but sometimes suddenly he saw her as now, human and alive. The strong summer sunlight falling upon her delicately golden skin and upon the soft waves of her fine black hair revealed her. She wore white, as Lucinda liked her maids to do in the summer, even though it meant that they washed and ironed late into the night, and the secret living quality of her dark eyes shone above the white fichu about her neck. He saw with surprise that her eyes were not black but a warm brown, clear enough to show the pupils. Her face flushed under his hard stare, and she looked away quickly. But her usual expression did not change. Her mouth was composed and its habitual look of sweetness came from the deepest corners.

"We're glad to see you back, sir," she murmured.

Pierce turned his eyes away. "We're always glad to come home," he said.

He passed into the cool shadows of the great hall of his house and John slipped from under his arm. "Uncle Tom said I must come back quickly," he explained.

"Where is Tom?" Pierce asked.

"He's in his study at the Academy," John replied. "Good-bye, Father, I'll see you at noon."

He darted down the wide hall and out the door that stood open into the garden and across the garden to the Academy. Pierce had taken a piece out of his own land for the school building. He regretted it sometimes, for the academies that had been built so painfully after the war by citizens were now being taken over by the state and made into public schools, and he objected to a public school on his property. He was determined to keep the Academy private.

Lucinda was going up the stairs, and the little girls were following the billowing ruffles of her skirts, to see what she had brought them from the city. He hesitated, wanting to follow them himself. He and Lucinda had chosen gifts, a pink parasol for Lucie and a blue one for Sally. Then he remembered his secret gift for Sally, a little gold ring with a tiny sapphire set into the circle. No, he would give that to her later when he was alone with her. She would keep it and say nothing. She was used to having secrets with him and he loved her so much that he had to give her things sometimes just for herself.

Georgia had taken Lucinda's mantle and parasol and was about to go upstairs. He remembered his promise to Lucinda to settle the problem of Tom. One of his impulses swept over him. Why shouldn't he talk to Georgia once more and get her to persuade Bettina to move away? Then whatever Tom did would be his own business. He hated the thought of a quarrel with his brother, but he knew that Lucinda would force him to it unless he could circumvent her. He wanted peace in this house he loved so well, and he loved Tom as he loved all that belonged to him. He had only to remember still how Tom had suffered in the Confederate prison, and how he had looked when he came home to Malvern to feel a wave of new love for the only brother he had so nearly lost. Away from home Pierce was a hard man and he took pride in it. He drove his bargains so close that he had to hire lawyers to keep him inside the law. But his hardness in business was balanced by softness for his family. He did not love humanity but he loved his own, the love he had for Malvern, for his horses and his dogs and even his cattle and steadfast love he had for his family. He fought by any means he could for what he wanted elsewhere but he did not want to fight inside those walls—for anything.

"Georgia!" he said.

She halted at the foot of the stair, soft and obedient, and again he was uncomfortably aware of her as a beautiful woman. Indeed, Lucinda should long ago have married her to some good man.

"Yes, sir!"

Now how the devil would he go on? He plunged in brusquely. "I need some help from you again, Georgia—about Bettina. It upsets your mistress to have things as they are—all the children—"

He paused and felt heat under his collar. Georgia helped him at once.

"I can understand that, sir," she said. "I've often told Bettina it would be better if she moved away somewhere."

"That's it exactly," he said eagerly. "You know how it looks. I'm not talking about Bettina—she's a good girl. I blame my brother entirely."

"You mustn't blame either of them, Master Pierce," Georgia's soft voice was tranquil and sad. "What they're doing

is natural, sir." She paused and then went on, half-hesitatingly.
"I'm afraid it was the way that our father treated us when we
were little—that makes Bettina so—so independent."

Pierce began to hate the moment he had brought on himself. He no longer told the servants to stop saying master and
mistress. Lucinda had not approved his democratic ideas, and
after the troubles in the South with the free slaves he had let
the old ways slip back. It was better, perhaps, not to break
down the barriers. He had come to see that the war had
changed nothing that was fundamental in the relationship
between whites and blacks.

Now in a sudden perception he did not often have he saw
that some deep, insoluble, unreachable wrong had been done
to Georgia by her white father. It was wrong to have given
her this beautiful face, with nothing more than a faint tinge of
the skin and duskiness in the hair and eyes to set her apart
from white women. It was wrong to have given her the delicacy and the keenness of understanding which belonged to the
best blood of the South. The dissipation of valuable blood
suddenly made him angry—his blood, too, through Tom!

"I'm not blaming you or Bettina," he said, "I'm just saying
that we aren't willing to go on like this any more. Now I can
tell Tom to get out or Bettina can get out—one or the other.
It's a shame and disgrace to us as a family to have things as
they are. The girls are getting big—I don't want to have to
answer Sally's questions. Now you know it'll be easier for you
to tell Bettina how I feel than it will be for me to tell my
brother—"

He made his voice harsh with his anger and expected to see
her yield as she had always yielded to command. To his astonishment she spoke with gentle firmness.

"I had rather not speak to my sister about how you feel, if
you please," she said. "Whether you speak to your brother is
according to your own wish." Then while he stared at her she
added the syllable, as though she had forgotten it—"sir."

He was so surprised that he was furious and the palms of
his hands itched to slap her cheeks. But he had never struck
either servant or child and he would not do so now.

"I'll tell Bettina myself, damn the whole business," he muttered.

She bowed her head and went up the stairs with a steady grace which matched Lucinda's own.

He regretted at once that he had spoken to her. There was nothing he hated more than a quarrel with a woman. But having said he would talk to Bettina himself, he would do it now while his anger sustained him. He knew himself well enough to know that if he allowed his anger to cool he would postpone everything as he had so often. But Lucinda would give him no peace!

He picked up his hat and his stick and went out of the house and down the path. He stalked down the tree-covered road, conscious of looking sulky and finding release in it. He frowned hard at a small black boy scuffling along in the dust and the child stopped and stood, his face fixed in terror, but Pierce did not speak. He went on, his cane stirring up small whirlpools of yellow dust, until he reached Bettina's gate.

He had seen the house almost daily in all these years but never once had he opened the gate nor had he seen Bettina except in glimpses of her tall woman's figure, hanging up clothes, raking the leaves, sweeping away snow from her doorstep. A boy was cutting grass now with a shorthandled scythe, and when the latch lifted the child stopped and turned his head. He saw Tom's son, a boy of seven, dark, but with Tom's grey eyes and the Delaney mouth as clean-cut as his own. He would not have believed that he could be so confounded. The child stared, dropped his scythe and ran around the house.

"Luce is right," Pierce told himself. "It's a disgrace."

He went to the closed door and thumped on it and a few seconds later it opened. Bettina stood there in a freshly starched dress of thin green stuff. He knew something was strange about her and then realized that it was the first time he had seen her without an apron.

She did not invite him to come in. "Can I do something for you, Mr. Delaney?" she asked.

He stood staring at her. She had gained a little weight and the thinness of her girlhood was gone. Her body was rounded and matured. She was extremely beautiful—there was no denying it. She was paler than Georgia, and her features were sharper. He took heed of such details because he was as used to scanning the physical details of such people as he was used to marking the looks of cattle and horses.

"Yes, you can do something for me, Bettina, and I'd like to come in," he said abruptly.

She stood aside and he went in and stepped at once into the main room. He saw that the small house was not only clean, but it was kept as a home. There were curtains at the windows, rugs on the floor, a spinet against the inner wall. He saw a big chair which had once belonged to his father and which he had given Tom. It stood beside the south window, and by it were a table and a globe and on the table were books and writing paper. He looked away and saw through the open door opposite him the glimpse of a small cool-looking dining room, and a table set for six. A pot of flowers stood on the table.

He sat down in Tom's chair and laid his hat and stick on the floor. She had not taken them when he came in. She followed him and sat down quietly and it was the first time that anyone like her had sat in his presence. He was disconcerted and sensible enough to be amused at his own disconcertment. A little girl of perhaps three came in, a pretty child, round and plump and fortunately reminding him of no one. She climbed on Bettina's lap and gazed at him with placid eyes. He tried to ignore her but his uncontrollable love of children stirred in his heart. This little thing was a bonbon of a child, something to put on a valentine. He had to acknowledge that for sheer prettiness she outdid his own.

"That's a pretty little trick," he said suddenly.

Bettina ruffled the child's short curls with her fingers. "She's not a good little girl, I'm afraid," she said gravely. "She gets into such mischief I don't know what to do, sometimes."

"What's her name?" Pierce asked.

"Georgy, after my sister," Bettina said.

"I am good," Georgy said in a high little voice.

"Not when you run away down the road," Bettina said.

"I went to find Papa!" Georgy told Pierce confidentially.

In his embarrassment Pierce did not speak. But Bettina said in the same grave voice. "We mustn't go to find Papa. We just wait until he comes."

Pierce could bear no more. "Send her away—I want to talk to you."

Bettina rose silently and slipped the child to the floor and led her away into the dining room. The door closed and behind it he heard her quiet voice and the child's high one, answering. He looked about the room and was deeply troubled. There was no doubt that Tom considered this his home. Above the simple wooden mantelpiece he had hung a small portrait of their mother. Their father had had one painted for each of his children. Pierce's hung in his own room and he had supposed that Tom's was in his. But Tom had brought it here, because this was his true home and not Malvern. Pierce looked at his mother's face, a delicate irregular face, not beautiful—his father had had all the physical beauty—and too sensitive. What would she have thought had she known that she would preside over this house? Perhaps Tom had even taught these children to call her Grandmother. Lucinda was right—it could not go on.

The door opened and Bettina came back and closed it behind her. She crossed the room and closed the outer door, too. They were alone and for a moment after she sat down, he kept silent. Outside in the yard the boy was beginning to cut the grass again, and he could hear the soft swish of the blade.

"You have—three children?" he asked abruptly.

"The baby is asleep upstairs," Bettina replied.

"What's her name?" Pierce asked abruptly.

"Lettice, after my own mother," Bettina replied.

Pierce cleared his throat. He was tired and it occurred to him that he ought to have postponed this affair because of his night on the train. He never slept well except at Malvern in his own bed. But here he was.

"Bettina, you're a sensible woman," he began.

"I hope so," Bettina said quietly. Her black eyes were fixed on his face and the light from the window by which he sat showed them deep and dark. They held none of the golden lights of Georgia's eyes.

"Now, Bettina," he began and his voice took on the tone of argument. "I know you will understand why I felt I had to talk with you. You've been with us at Malvern and you know how things are. Mrs. Delaney is getting very worried about the children and how to explain to them—well, this house and you and—and these children and—and all that. We've always been unhappy about it, of course. As things go, I haven't said anything. Young men usually have a fling, especially when they're just out of the army. I didn't want to say anything at first. I said to myself and I told Lucinda—'it's Tom's own business.' But now—well, it's going on and it is time that things come to an end somehow. Tom ought to get married and settle down, you know."

He stopped, looked at her and looked away. Her face was set in frozen quiet. She did not speak. He felt very unhappy. He resisted his awareness of her as a human being, but it made him uncomfortable.

"I don't know what to suggest," he said. "I still don't feel I can presume to give orders to Tom—exactly. But I think I ought to tell you that when he marries and starts his own family, I'm willing to share Malvern with him or even build him a separate house on any of the land he chooses. When a man is well over thirty he has to get started." He felt that he was right in his point and he gained confidence. "I want to see that you are treated well, Bettina, and I am going to suggest that you move away somewhere with these children of yours, and I'll treat you very handsomely if you do so. You can go north if you like—I'll buy you a house in some town there—and see that you get money every month as long as you live. I'll even put that in my will."

He felt that he could not be more generous and he leaned back in his chair, as he had often seen his father do. She sat in the same pose, her hands on the arms of the Windsor chair. She looked like Georgia, but her mouth was not so sweet. Something about the firmness of that well-cut mouth disturbed him. This was not an obedient woman and doubtless Tom had spoiled her. It always made a colored woman proud to belong to a white man. He pursed his lips and decided to be firm himself.

"That's my proposition," he declared.

She leaned forward a little, clasping her hands on her elbows. "I don't feel it is for me to decide, Mr. Delaney." Her voice was so pure, so cold, that it seemed empty of all feeling. "If—your brother—tells me to go, I will go."

"Now, Bettina, let's be sensible," he complained loudly. "Tom isn't going to tell you to go. We won't pretend. I want you to help me persuade him that it's the best thing."

"Maybe it isn't."

They were beginning now really to talk. He had penetrated that cold shell of hers.

"Bettina, you know it is," he insisted. He tried to keep anger out of his voice. "Surely you want what's best for Tom—as I do."

"You said Mrs. Delaney—" her voice trembled and sudden tears swam into her eyes. Something hurt and quivering looked at him out of those shimmering depths.

"Let's put her aside—damn it all, I love my brother, too. I'm only going to talk about him. Tom deserves legitimate heirs, Bettina. He's going to be a rich man some day, if he stays by the family."

"I don't just think of property," she said in a low voice.

"No, nor I," Pierce said swiftly. "But think of Tom when he's old! He ought to be surrounded by children of his own—"

"These are his,"—she broke in.

"Of his own kind," Pierce went on, "children who can be in his house and who can stand for him. Bettina, don't think I don't feel for you. I feel very sorry indeed, but you know how things are in this world. You can't change them and I can't change them, however much we might wish things were different. And I don't mind saying that if they were different—if you hadn't been—well, what you are—I wouldn't have felt it was my business. But you know how things are—I can't help it any more than you can—it's just how things are—"

Just how things are—just how things are—with this phrase he beat her down. He saw her head droop, and the tears flowed over her lids and down her cheeks and she wrung her slender hands together. He saw her hands—it had often amazed him to notice that her people always had beautiful hands.

"I reckon I can go away," Bettina sobbed.

He rose. "Of course you can," he said cheerfully. "And I'm going to make it easy for you—"

What he had not counted on was Tom's coming. He had thought it was the middle of the morning but the clock had run on to noon. He heard the gate click and saw his brother come into the yard and pick up the little girl and come to the door.

"Wipe your eyes," he ordered Bettina and she obeyed.

But Tom was at the door and in the room. He had to face his brother. "Why are you here, Pierce?" Tom demanded. He put the child down and she ran to her mother and Bettina laid her cheek on her hair, her face turned away.

Pierce looked at his brother. He had seen Tom every day of these years, but he saw him now exactly as he was, a grown man, mature and dignified. He could not endure the steady, cold light of his blue eyes.

"I came to talk with Bettina," he said. "Bettina, I take back what I asked you. You can tell Tom everything I said. Tom, I'd like to see you tonight in my own study. We'll thrash this thing out for fair and have an end to it."

He snatched his hat and his stick and strode out of the house, looking neither to the right nor the left as he went.

In the room he left so silent Tom went to Bettina and knelt and put his arms about her and the child. But Bettina let the child down and leaned her head upon his shoulder and began to weep.

"My dear love," Tom muttered.

"I know what he said was right," she sobbed. "Oh, my mind tells me he is right! God give me the strength—"

"What do you want strength for?" Tom asked.

"Nothing—I don't know—I love you too much, I reckon," she whispered.

"You can't love me too much," Tom said. The child was sobbing and he took her in his arms and held her, rocking her a little while he talked.

"I know Pierce was here to badger you, but you mustn't heed him. It's Lucinda—I'm sure she's behind it. Pierce is so easygoing—he wouldn't care much."

He sat down in the big chair. The love he had for this woman had changed from the wild first passion of his youth. But she was necessary to him, a part of his life. He never allowed himself to wonder whether he had done well in taking her. Having taken her he had kept her and would keep her. He respected her deeply. In her unchanging goodness he had refuge. She was selfless to the last drop of her blood. He had never found the same quality in any one else except in his own mother. His mother would have understood the quality of Bettina's goodness. He knew, of course, that she would never have understood what he had done. He wanted to believe that she would have understood Bettina—that would have been enough. But he was glad she was dead. Living, she would never have entered this house. He did not pretend that what he had done was easy, nor that his life was not beset with complexity. Both he and Bettina were isolated from their communities and he was deeply troubled for the children. Bettina kept them away from other colored children, but he could not lead them to the children of his kind. Leslie, his son, was named for Bettina's father. Both of them had avoided the names of his own family. He had toyed with the idea of naming the baby Laura, after his mother and then had not done so. They had named her Lettice instead.

Leslie came in now, flushed with the sun. "I'm hungry, Mother," he said, hesitating at the door. He knew so well these long conversations between his parents and that in some fashion they concerned him. He had a strange feeling always of waiting for something to happen. He knew that whatever it was must be decided always by his father. Everything in this house waited upon his father.

"We must all eat," Tom said, sighing. "I have to get back to the school."

He did not often come here in the middle of the day, but he had been haunted with some sort of uneasiness when John came back and said his parents were home again. Bettina went out and the little girl slipped from his lap to follow her and he leaned back and closed his eyes. Through the open door he could hear Bettina moving about, setting the table, and pouring milk. Perhaps he had been at fault, too. He had taken his situation for granted—he had let this house become too much his home. Had he come only and occasionally at night, had he returned always for the day to the house at Malvern, had he not behaved as though Bettina were his wife, would it have been better?

She opened the door. "I have everything on the table," she said softly. "I didn't expect you, so there's only what we'd have—cornbread and milk and salad greens."

"I'm not hungry," he said, and went in and sat down. He helped the children to food and helped her, and then himself. But every time he lifted his eyes he found the children watching him timidly. They were too sensitive. They had been born in doubt and they knew their fate was uncertainty. He did not speak and Bettina, too, was silent. He looked at her and saw the shadows under her eyes.

"You look tired," he said. "You'd better rest yourself."

"Will you come back tonight—after you've seen—him?"

"I'll come back and tell you everything," he promised.

He rose early from the meal, refusing the fruit she had taken from a hastily opened jar for dessert. He kissed her smooth forehead, and touched the children's cheeks and went away.

In the long dining room at Malvern, Pierce sat at the head of his table and ate silently. He was aware of the

children's voices chattering about him and now and again
he forced himself to listen and to answer a question, while
Lucinda's smooth voice rippled in and out of the children's
talk. He was thoroughly dissatisfied with what he had done.
As usual, he told himself, he had been too hasty after too
long delay. He put off a distasteful task endlessly and then
when it could be put off no longer he did it badly. Now
he had to talk with Tom tonight, when he would be tired
and less patient than he ought to be.

He put down his fork and knife, aware that he was eating
too much. When he was upset about something he ate without knowing what he was doing. He had consumed two help-
ings of the braised breast of guinea hen and too much sweet
corn and mashed potatoes. Green stuff he could not abide.
Lucinda's salads he called rabbit food.

"What's dessert?" he asked Marcus, the old butler, superintending the two young black boys who were waiting.

"Frozen raspberry custard, suh," Marcus said in his politely
gentle voice.

Pierce sighed. It was his favorite sweet. He wondered
irritably if he were greedy. Sometimes, surveying his naked
body in the mirror in the new bathroom, he saw unwillingly
that he was growing heavy. Good food was an attribute of
Malvern and its rich life. Not to have set a good table was
unthinkable, not to have eaten would have been folly. If
he were greedy it was not for food alone, but for all that
meant life. He ate the frozen custard slowly, savoring it. He
must remember not to eat hastily without tasting to the full
what was in his mouth. There was no use in merely filling
his belly.

Lucinda rose. "Come, my dears," she said to the girls. "We
will leave Papa and John. Pierce, I feel tired and shall make
my siesta longer than usual."

"I'll be out in the stables," he replied.

He reached out his arm and Sally stepped into its curve
and he gave her a squeeze and brushed her cheek with his
moustaches. "I have something for you," he whispered. "Tonight when you're in bed I'll come up and give it to you."

Her eyes shone and she nodded and skipped away, her skirts swinging above her ankles. He was left alone with John, and the boy, to his annoyance, began to talk about Tom.

"Uncle Tom says doubtless I shall make a better scholar than either Martin or Carey."

Pierce poured himself a glass of French wine. Some day he planned to make better wine than this from his own grapes. He had fine grapes and he made wines, but he declared often that he had not yet learned the secret of the transubstantiation of their water into wine. Each year he tasted his product and threatened to import a French wine maker. Lucinda did not care for wine and protested at this further complication of their household. He poured half a glass of wine for John.

"But I don't like wine, Papa," the boy protested.

"Learn to drink like a man," Pierce commanded him, "and don't set yourself above your brothers. Books are a very little part in a man's life. Your brother Martin has the best seat I ever saw on a horse and Carey is very clever."

He had pricked John's pride, for the boy had an instinctive and uncontrollable fear of horses. He said nothing but his face flushed as he touched the glass to his lips and set it down again.

"Even Sally rides much better than you do," Pierce went on. He was always stern to his sons and now he realized unwillingly, for he wanted to be a just man, that he was sterner toward John than any of them.

"Sally likes to ride and I don't," John murmured.

"A man ought to ride well whether he likes it or not," Pierce retorted.

"Uncle Tom doesn't," John murmured again.

"I hope you do not intend to model yourself entirely on your Uncle Tom," Pierce said. He was aware again of his injustice, for he recognized that the boy hurt him by admiring his uncle too much.

"Drink your wine," he said abruptly. John's face hardened but he lifted the glass and drank the wine down like medicine and took up his goblet and gulped down water after it. Pierce flung out his hand and knocked the goblet aside and it fell to the floor in a silvery crash of broken crystal.

"Don't let me see you do such a thing again!" he shouted. "When I say learn to drink wine I mean learn to like wine!"

"That I cannot do!" John cried at him.

Pierce glared at his son an instant and was suddenly pleased to see that the boy was glaring back at him. He burst into laughter. "Well, never mind," he said amiably. "Just get out of my sight for a bit."

"Yes, Papa," John rose, pushed in his chair and went out of the room slowly, his narrow shoulders held very straight. Pierce watched him, his eyes twinkling under his heavy brows. He might have expected rebellion from the two elder lads, but it was the first he had ever had from John. His own blood told, after all. He felt better.

Then he remembered Tom's mulatto boy he had seen this morning in Bettina's yard and he sobered again and got up, sighing noisily, and threw his napkin on the floor. He stalked up to his room and put on his riding clothes and went out into the hot afternoon sun which he loved.

As always when he did not know how to solve a problem, he went to his stables. There at least life was simple and uncomplicated, for horses were better than people. One could control their propagation, at least, he thought, and grinned at himself. Inside the cool and aromatic stable the stalls were empty, except for the one where his mare had foaled a week before. She had her foal with her, and he could hear Jake mumbling over it.

"What have you got them inside for, a day like this?" he called sharply. He belonged to the school of horse breeders who believed in the open.

"She was layin' down and I brung her in to see was she snake bit or somethin'," Jake replied. Snakes had become Jake's obsession, ever since the young mare's mother, Beauty, had died from the bite of a copperhead by the river where she had gone to drink.

Pierce himself was more nervous than he let himself

acknowledge and he hastened to the stall and looked at the mare. She was standing with her colt beside her, and Phelan, Jake's son, was rubbing her down.

"She looks all right," Pierce said.

The mare turned her beautiful head and whinnied at him and he fished out a lump of sugar from his pocket and fed it to her. The colt came up and smelled his hand and licked the sweet tentatively with its pink tongue. Phelan sat back on his haunches, a thin wisp of a boy, so black that his big mouth was in startling contrast.

"This yere colt is awful smart, Mas' Pierce," he said. "He ain' just anybody's business—he's somebody, yassuh."

Pierce surveyed this first colt of his young mare. It was not large, but it controlled its long legs with unusual skill. The color was chestnut without a mark, and the eyes were large and intelligent.

"We'll watch him," Pierce said. "Maybe there is something in him. Get him out in the open and let him learn to take care of himself and get his hoofs tough. We'll see how much nerve he has and whether he likes to race. That's the first thing. He's got to like it."

He had won races with Beauty and he was always looking for the perfect race horse. Malvern had everything for producing it. The blue grass of this river valley was good for horses as well as for cattle. He had exhibited one of his bulls in the second fair the county had held and it had weighed nearly four thousand pounds and was the second largest bull in the world. He had just as good a one to show next year. This colt would not be old enough to race then, but by the year after—

He stooped and examined the small exquisite body and ran his hands over its firm haunches and straight legs. "Its body is good enough, I do believe," he said in some excitement.

They looked at one another solemnly. Was this to be known in history as the first moment that a great horse was recognized?

"Watch him, you two," Pierce ordered. "And saddle Rex for me."

"Yassuh," Jake said gravely.

Pierce rode away in a few minutes on the horse he had bought for Tom, who so seldom used it that he had forgotten it was not his own. He was still thinking of the colt. So much more than a fine body was needed to make the perfect race horse, he reminded himself. Even good blood was not enough. There was the imponderable, unknowable character of the creature that had to be discovered. He had bred colts as fine as this one who had nevertheless no greatness in them. Beauty had had greatness, but she had had an own sister, sired as she had been by the famous Whirling Dervish, the dam for both of them Mary Malabar, and Beauty was a great horse and Silver Girl, though more exquisite to look upon, had been only a placid mare. He had not named this colt and he would not do so until he could discover more of its nature. If it had the intelligence for training, if it had the pride to win, he would give it a good name and as he watched the colt he'd watch Phelan for its jockey. There would be, of course, the question of who should be the trainer. He frowned over this, and decided on Henry Shulter in Charlestown. He'd send the colt to him to be looked at as soon as it was weaned.

He was quite happy again and restored to his usual mood of hearty good humor. There was nothing like horses, he thought—nothing, indeed, like going around and seeing Malvern for himself. He lifted his head and saw on the hillside meadow his shorthorn cattle, bred from the early stock brought here by his father fifty years before. Now he shipped hundreds of head abroad. Englishmen across the ocean were at this moment doubtless eating beefsteaks and roasts from Malvern cattle. But he was proudest of all of his bulls. He was wont to bet that his bulls, bred even to the common cattle of the mountains, would produce within a few generations the finest herds in the country. He wanted to share his pride with someone and he turned and rode back to the stable doors and shouted into its depths.

"You Jake—get Lilly ready for Miss Sally! We're going to

ride around. Tell Phelan to take the horse and tell her I'll meet her under the big oak."

A quarter of an hour later he waited, his horse reined in sharply, under the big oak which his great-grandfather had brought as a sapling from Sussex and his eyes caught the first glimpse of his daughter, cantering over the grassy pathway from the house. She wore her skyblue riding habit, and his heart beat when he saw her, graceful and erect upon the small bay horse. How lovely she was, how strong and proud! Where would he ever find a mate good enough for her? Somewhere, he supposed, a boy was growing up, God knew how or what! But if he were not good enough for Sally, he'd thrash him with his own hands and boot him out of the house.

She came up to him, her bright hair flying and her cheeks flushed. "Oh, Papa, you saved me!" she called. "Mama had just told me to take out my sewing."

"That's what I'm for," he answered, "to save you always, my pet."

They rode off together, and profound peace welled up from his heart. There was nothing in the world that could go wrong with him.

Nothing that Tom could say would rouse his anger, he told himself in the library late that evening. A distant thunderstorm skirted the mountain tops at sunset and the long room, scented with old leather, was cool and quiet. The children had gone to bed. He enjoyed the hour with them after dinner. John had read aloud for a quarter of an hour from Hamlet, and Sally had played the spinet charmingly. She did everything well, he had told himself, watching her proudly. Her little figure in the long white muslin dress tied with blue ribbons had sat slender and straight at the keyboard, and her curls had not hidden her pretty profile. He felt the music drift like fragrant incense through his dreaming mind, as he watched her. And little Lucie had recited a long poem that she had learned while they were away. He and Lucinda had exchanged amused looks after the careful curtsey she made at its end. When Georgia came to take them upstairs he had sat silent for a moment, unwilling to let the day go. There was the evening to face.

Then he remembered the ring he had bought for Sally, and he went upstairs. She was in her room and Georgia was brushing her hair with firm strokes. Lucinda was exacting about the girls' hair, it must shine as though it were polished or she complained that Georgia was lazy. Sally's hair was silvery blonde and it flew out from beneath the brush. He went into his room and found the small box and went back again.

"Hold out your hand, my sweet," he said with tenderness and she put out her little left hand. He slipped the ring on her third finger and the sapphire glowed on her white skin.

"That's your ring finger, Sally," he said playfully. "You must keep my ring on it until a handsome young man comes by, whom you'll love better than me."

If he thought to hear her protest that she would always love him best, he was to be disappointed. She held out her hand the better to admire her ring. "When will he come, Papa?" she asked.

He laughed and looked involuntarily at Georgia to share his amusement. She was smiling, too.

"I might not let him come," he said, teasingly. "I might sit on the porch with my gun—I shot a lot of Yankees with that gun!"

"I wouldn't marry a Yankee, Papa," Sally declared.

"Of course not," Pierce agreed. He looked at Georgia again and his smile faded. He remembered the evening that lay ahead. He did not want to tell her what he had said to Bettina. What if she asked? He decided to go downstairs.

"Goodnight, Sally, honey. Sapphires bring happiness—they brought me you."

He kissed her and went back to the drawing room where Lucinda sat by a lamp crocheting a cobweb of lace.

"Tom is coming in to talk to me," he told her abruptly.

"Where has he been all day?" Lucinda asked. "He's usually here for dinner, at least."

"We had a little set-to this morning," Pierce replied. "Tonight I'm going to have it out with him in the library."

"I shall stay here, unless you want me," Lucinda replied calmly.

"I think Tom and I had better be alone," he replied. "But you might ask Marcus to bring in some sherry and a couple of glasses. I'll make Tom drink in spite of himself."

He moved away lazily out of profound unwillingness and crossed the hall into the library. A few minutes later Marcus came in with a silver tray and the wine.

"When Tom comes, bring him straight in here," Pierce ordered.

"Yassuh," the old butler murmured.

He was about to leave the room when Pierce stopped him. Marcus had been in this house when he and Tom were born. His father had bought him in New Orleans, the year before, a young and slender man, trained in a famous plantation household that had been dispersed on the death of the master. Who knew Tom and himself so well as old Marcus?

"Marcus!" he called.

The man stood waiting, his hands hanging at his sides. "Yassuh?"

"Marcus, what do people say about my brother—and Bettina?"

Marcus let his underlip hang. "I don't listen to talk, Mas' Pierce."

"They do talk?"

"Some folks always talk."

"And others listen?"

"Some folks always got their y'ears stickin' out like umbrellas."

"Tom ought to marry—"

"Yassuh."

"Do you think Bettina—will—would—go away—?" He could not go on.

"I don't know these yere young folks nowadays, sir," Marcus said sadly. "But one thing I does believe in and it's stickin' to your own kind. I believe in lettin' othah folks alone, man and woman, and lookin' for your own skin coloh. Yassuh, then they's no trouble, high or low."

"You're right, Marcus."

"Yassuh." The old man went out and Pierce poured himself wine. Black folk didn't like mixture any better than white folk. He was not going to be easy with Tom, "so help me God," he muttered to himself. He lifted his glass and across the golden rim of the wine he saw his brother at the door, and put it down again.

"Come in, Tom," he said drily.

Tom came in, very tall and inclined to lounge. He sat down in one of the old leather arm chairs and slid to the small of his back. All afternoon in the school he had worked intensely, but not for one moment had he forgotten that this hour loomed ahead of him. He had passed through various moods, mingled and complex, wherein one emotion and then another rose above the others. Fear and love of his older brother, distaste for Lucinda, anger at himself for having let the years slip by without doing anything definite about Bettina, remorse for the three children—and underneath, a growing determination to be himself and do what he liked. What that was he did not actually know. When he thought of leaving Malvern and his brother he was torn in two. He did not want to live anywhere but here. He groaned aloud that he could not bring his children into this house where he had been born. Leslie was as brilliant as John and more beautiful, but he could never cross the threshold of this door except as a servant. Nothing that he could do for his son would change his inexorable destiny. He had fought to make such children free but they were not free, and for him the war was lost. The victors had been vanquished by the stubbornness of the persisting enemy. There was no victory and no peace because the hearts of men and women had not changed. Futile war and futile suffering and death!

"Sherry?" Pierce asked.

"Thanks," Tom said. He reached out his narrow white hand and took the glass by its thin stem and sipped the wine. He never drank, because Bettina hated the smell of it. Somewhere in her childhood her father had drunk increasingly of wine until he had stupefied his conscience. But tonight he would drink. He felt his nerves as tight as violin strings inside his body. The wine would relax him and help him to listen to Pierce reasonably and then to answer without passion. Above everything he did not want to quarrel with the brother he loved. He raised his eyes to Pierce's face and waited for him to begin.

Meeting those troubled grey eyes, Pierce saw in a flicker of memory the brother whom he had protected and fought for through years of their common boyhood. He had been the favorite son of his father and Tom had always been the one wrong in any quarrel. The old instinct rose in him.

"I want to get you out of this trouble, Tom," he said in his kindliest voice. "Let's talk about it sensibly. I reckon Bettina told you about this morning."

"She didn't tell me anything," Tom said calmly. "But after you went she cried a bit. That's unusual for her."

"I did wrong to go to her," Pierce said honestly. "I don't know what made me do it—something on the spur of the moment. Well, I should have waited to talk with you." He paused and then went on with effort. "I suppose men never like to mess around in affairs like this. Of course I've known all these years that you and Bettina have—stayed together. Well, you and I had that out when it first began and I haven't wanted to—speak again. But now Lucinda feels . . ."

"I thought it was Lucinda," Tom said, and was instantly angry.

Pierce shot up his black eyebrows. "Lucinda naturally thinks further ahead for the children than I do," he said. He was putting the restraint of patience upon himself, and Tom's heart melted again. Pierce was so good!

"Forgive me, Pierce," he said.

"Granted," Pierce replied a little heavily. He tried to go on with what he was saying, but now Lucinda was clearly between them. He felt he must defend her. "I think Lucinda is right, Tom, and I must say so. When the children were little, it didn't matter so much to the family. But now it's

different. John worships you, and I live in dread of his questions. It would be easy enough for me to explain it in a man-
to-man fashion—he's got to understand such things some
day—but what I can't explain is that this affair goes on and
on, and that there are children in that house right on the
road."

Tom's anger suddenly burst, white hot. "It is easy to explain—you can just tell him that Bettina and I love one
another and that the children are ours as he is yours and
his mother's."

"Tom, don't be a fool—you know I can't just say that—"
Pierce's voice was a groan.

"But it's so," Tom insisted.

"It isn't really so," Pierce retorted. "You can't just act like
Bettina was—was—"

"I can and do act as though Bettina were white," Tom
said with fury so vast that his voice was low and cold. "That
is what you have to understand, Pierce—I feel to Bettina as
my wife. I will take no other." Thus he declared himself.
His anger, rising out of old rebellion in this house, crystallized
his love and clarified his conscience.

Pierce rose half out of his chair. "Tom, do you mean to
say that you will not marry a decent woman that we can
be proud of as part of the family?"

"I mean I will never marry any other woman than Bettina.
I've begged Bettina to marry me. She won't—because of you
and Lucinda. She knows how you feel, you two. She says
our marriage would drag me down, out of this family where
I was born. She won't do it. God have mercy, she's so good—
she's—she'd beg me to marry a white woman, I believe, if
I would do it! Why, why she's better than any woman in the
world, and if this precious family of ours doesn't know
enough to know it—God help us all, what did we fight the
war for? It's worse now than it was before." He was beside
himself with pain. He got up out of his chair and thrusting
his hands into his pockets he began to walk in distraction
about the room.

Pierce stared at him. "Tom, what has come over you? You

talk like a crazy man! Never in all my days have I heard
such talk come from anybody. Why, the country would go
to pieces if—if—why, damn you, Tom, I've a mind to shove
you out of the house!" He got to his feet and clenched his
fists.

"Pierce, I want to come in," Lucinda stood at the door,
a slender figure in her white poplin frock, her head held
high. Both men turned at the sound of her voice. Tom sank
into his chair, and Pierce turned to her.

"Come in, my dear—" He was glad for her help. He began
to see that something very deep indeed separated him from
Tom, something that went back into their childhood, that
had sent them to opposite sides in the war, something perhaps
that even Malvern could not heal. He did not want to lose his
brother, and yet how could he keep him?

"I can't help hearing what you two are saying when you
talk so loudly," Lucinda said in her cool high voice. She sat
down and put her feet on a needlepoint footstool and crossed
her hands on her lap. On her fingers were the diamond rings
Pierce had given her when the two older boys were born and
the sapphire brooch was on her breast. She turned her head
with its piled blonde hair toward Tom. "Tom, I have never
said anything to you. I don't believe in inquiring into gentlemen's affairs, but I do have to think of my children. Sally has
already begun to ask questions and the niggras talk and she
hears them, of course. I don't intend to say anything now,
either, but only to ask that whatever it is that is going on
could be—put somewhere that it doesn't show."

Her manner, her appearance, were so pure and so impec-
cable that both men felt gross and uncomfortable. Lucinda
was the good woman, protecting her children. Pierce who
loved her felt himself humbled. But Tom did not love her.

"As long as there are women like you, Lucinda," he
drawled, restraining his fury, "there will be no justice on this
earth. You will keep your foot on the neck of any woman who
threatens your sacred position in the home."

It was Lucinda who understood first what he meant. The
quick red of her blonde coloring flowed up her slender white

neck into her cheeks. "I certainly don't feel myself threatened in my home by a niggra wench," she said.

"Yes, you do," Tom said, ruthlessly. "Why else do you care so much, you white women?"

"I don't care—" she cried.

"You care," he repeated, "because you're afraid of losing your men and you keep the other women down under your feet, because if you don't they'll be your equals and they will invade your sacred homes and rival you and excel you because men love them and escape you."

Lucinda screamed. "Tom, you stop—Pierce, make him stop that foul dirty talk—"

From sheer anger she began suddenly to cry and Tom clamped his jaws shut. "Sorry," he said abruptly to Pierce. "I reckon that's been shut up in me a long time. I'd better go."

Lucinda took the handkerchief from her eyes. "Yes, go!" she cried, "go and never come back!"

Tom rose. "Very well, madam—"

Pierce woke from his daze. "Now Tom—now Luce—look, we're one family! Luce didn't mean that, Tom."

Lucinda stabbed at her eyes with her handkerchief. "Don't call me Luce!" she sobbed.

"Lucinda doesn't mean that, Tom," Pierce began again. "Please, Tom, try to be reasonable. Try to see our side of it— the family side."

He went over to Lucinda and took her right hand and held it. "Lucinda, honey, we're going to fix things—don't worry. Tom isn't going to be unreasonable, honey—"

But Tom was walking to the door. He passed through it, and then paused in the hall. He lifted his head, and stood in one of those moments he knew so well, when the love and pain of living overwhelmed him. He had so nearly given up life once, in the prison, he had fought so hard for it again in this mighty old house which had sheltered him since his birth. Here he had found Bettina and without her he would have surely died. Even Pierce could not have stayed with him night and day through all the lonely hours of his weakness. The house had given him his life, but Bettina had saved that life. His eyes roamed over the hall, the stairs, which he and Pierce had climbed as children, the heavy walnut balustrade down which they had slid as little boys, Pierce always first and fearless and he coming after, terrified, but following Pierce. He could not bear to go.

And then in the midst of his pain and his longing he heard Lucinda's voice lifted in wild reproach.

"Oh, Pierce, you're standing up for him, you beast! You're a beast like all the others—men are beasts—beasts—beasts—"

"I'm not!" Pierce roared. "Look here, Luce—if—if it were before the war and I could do it—I'd—I'd sell Bettina and her brats down the river and get rid of them all—"

"I wish it were before the war!" Lucinda sobbed.

"God dammit, so do I!" Pierce cried.

Tom heard his brother's voice and hastened away. The house could shelter him no more.

# *Five*

---

BETTINA lay asleep in the moonlight. Summer and winter she had her bed by the window where she could look out into the shrub-enclosed back yard. The lawn and the narrow flower-beds which she tended so carefully by day were enchanting to her by night. When there was no moon she could smell the sweetness of the dark and the fragrance of dew. In winter the frost was fragrant. Like all women whose lives must be lived within boundaries, she had grown deeply and she had learned to make every small part of her life as large as the universe. Thus at night to single out a star and to lie in her bed gazing at it, to imagine its existence, enlarged her as a journey might enlarge a traveler. To dream of the one man she knew who possessed her, to ponder upon his qualities, his strength and his weakness, was enough for her whole life. Early in her life with Tom she had made up her mind to demand nothing of him. If he came it was her joy, but if he did not come, her life must go on. Sometimes he reproached her for this in one way or another. "I don't believe you miss me, Bettina. You are just as happy when I am not here—you and the children."

To which she answered out of her profound simplicity. "When you come it's like the sun breaking through and taking hold of a day I thought was going to be dark. But if the sun don't break through you have to get the dinner and clean the house just the same. I have to go on living, Tom. Besides, I know you will come—sometime. So do the children."

He had come to understand that reproach was folly. She was as fathomless as the sea and the sky, and as essential.

Now he hastened to her through the gathering night. Pierce's words were a spur to his feet and with every step he took he swore that the path on which he walked would know him no more. Never again would he go to Malvern. He renounced his birthright.

He could see the low outlines of Bettina's roof and the gate was still whiter than the darkness. He opened it and shut it loudly and then guided by the light of the candle that Bettina always kept in the window, he went into the house. If he came, he blew the candle out. If he did not come, it burned down into its pewter holder. Now, however, he lit the lamp in the living room and taking the candle with him he went upstairs into the room where she slept.

She lay on the wide bed by the window. He held the candle high and she opened her eyes and he was struck again by her extravagant beauty. Her pale face was set in the dark hair outspread on the pillow and her slender right arm was thrown above it. She made her nightgowns dainty and fine, and lace lay upon her bosom. She was fastidious even after all these years and she had her small reserves from him. Thus when the candlelight fell upon her she drew the sheet instinctively over her breasts. Then she smiled her slow and lovely smile. "Tom—I'd given you up tonight."

He set the candle down on the table and sat down on the bed and began to speak urgently. "Listen, Bettina—understand quickly what I say. I want us to get up and go away—now."

She sat up, instantly aware, and twisted her loose hair into a knot at her neck. She waited without speaking, her dark eyes wide.

Tom went on, "Pierce and I have quarreled. Lucinda came in. I don't want to stay here another day. You and I and the children are going away together. We're going now, because if I stay I might not be able to get away. And I want to go— I must go."

"Darling, could you tell me?" She had dreamed often of going away with him, and there was nothing but joy in the thought. But she would not let him go in haste. She had to be sure that there was no other way and that it was what he wanted most.

"I don't want to tell you," Tom said abruptly. "But I know as I know my own soul that if I stay they will not rest until I am parted from you. I can't part from you, Bettina."

His hand searched for hers but she did not yield it to him.

"Did they want you to send me away?" she asked.

"They want me to marry another woman—" he said harshly.

"You aren't married to me, Tom—"

"That's not my fault—I've wanted you to marry me."

"I can't marry you, darling. The ministers wouldn't marry us."

"We're going somewhere that I can marry you. Get up, Bettina, and get the children up. We're going to catch the four o'clock train north."

"Darling, I'll go if you promise me one thing."

"I can't make promises now, Bettina—"

"Only this one, that if you want to come back, you will come back. I can't take you away from Malvern forever, honey—you'll hate me."

"Malvern can burn down for all I care, and good riddance to all its old rubbish."

"But you were born there!"

She bent her head on her knees and he stroked the soft nape of her neck upward with the sweep of her hair. "If it makes you feel better about going, I'll promise," he said. "But I know I'll never want to come back. I've outgrown it. It's dead—in the past."

She lifted her head at his words. "You mean—"

"I mean you and I and our children are going to make our own world. It will be a good world, where everybody will be treated justly for what he is—even if it is only inside our own four walls."

A good world! With these words he took her by the soul and only thus could he have won her to follow him. She had to know that what she did was for good, and now she believed him. She got out of bed and silently they packed his roundbacked trunk and two carpetbags with clothes for the children and themselves.

"I shall want my books from Malvern," Tom said. "I don't care about anything else. I'll write Pierce that he can send them by railroad freight."

"I'll have to tell Georgia where we are, Tom."

"Of course."

He lit the lantern an hour later and walked down the road to the livery stable and roused Pete Calloway and asked for a vehicle. "I'll leave it at the railway station and you can fetch it tomorrow," he said.

Pete, in his long cotton nightshirt, leaned out of the window. "How come you ain't using your brother's vehicle?" he asked.

"I'm going away on my own business," Tom said, "and here's your money."

Pete came out scratching his head. "You ain't quarreled with him, have you?"

"Him" within fifty miles of Malvern meant only Pierce, and Tom smiled. "In a way," he said. "But never mind."

Pete was hitching up his second-best surrey. "Tell George I'll come around early to the station," he drawled. "Want me to meet you tomorrow night?"

"No, thanks—" Tom replied. Tomorrow Pete would tell over and over again how he had been roused in the night and how Tom had told him he had quarreled with his brother. But by tomorrow nothing that happened here would matter. He dropped two dollars into Pete's outstretched palm, saw how dirty that palm was, and climbed into the surrey and drove down the road again.

At the house Bettina and the children were dressed and waiting. Leslie was silent with astonishment and Georgy was ready to cry.

"Don't cry," Tom said. He picked her up and put her in the front seat beside him. "We are going to live where Papa can be at home with you always, like other people. Bettina, have you the money?"

He had long ago brought to her what he earned and she

kept it for him, using it when she needed it. At Malvern he had needed nothing except an occasional book.

"I have it all," she said. She turned her head to look at the little house that had sheltered her for so long. Within it she had been safe enough, but she knew that it could not shelter her children. She turned her head away again and climbed into the surrey, holding her baby in her arms. Leslie climbed in after her, and thus they drove away into the night, their faces set toward the north.

Pierce woke feeling tired. At his side Lucinda lay still asleep and he got out of the wide bed and went into the room next hers, which he called his own. Sometimes he slept here when Lucinda did not want him with her. He hesitated a few minutes at his window. The dawn was just beginning to break. It was an hour he loved. The mountains in the distance were purple and the grass on the lawns was silvery with small dew-sprinkled cobwebs. Had he not felt tired he would have put on his riding things and gone out. Instead he turned and slid his big body between the clean fresh sheets of his own bed. The quarrel with Tom was still to be mended but he did not want to think about it. He burrowed his head into the pillows and went to sleep again.

From this sleep he was wakened two hours later by Lucinda herself. It was so unusual an occurrence that at first he could not bring himself to believe it was she who stood over him.

"Wh-wha-what—" he muttered thickly, staring at her with sleep-bleared eyes. He was at the bottom of an ocean and she was hauling him up, calling his name over and over again.

"Pray tell!" she now said sharply. "I never did see anyone so stupefied! Anyone would think you had gone to bed drunk. Pierce, wake up—Tom's gone!"

She flung this at him like a spear and he sat up in bed and gaped at her.

"Gone where?" he asked out of confusion.

"Nobody knows—just gone! Pete Calloway came to say so. They've all gone."

"Who?"

"Bettina—everybody! I sent Jake down to see. The house is empty. Pete said that George told him they all came to the station and Tom bought tickets for Philadelphia."

"Oh, my God!" He was awake now and he leaped out of bed. Lucinda sat down.

"You get out of here, Lucinda," he ordered her. "You know I can dress faster if you're not here."

"Oh, Pierce—you're so silly—as if I hadn't seen you naked thousands of times—"

It was an old quarrel between them, petty and inexplicable and yet profound. Pierce had the excessive modesty of the big man, and Lucinda had no modesty at all. Lucinda's brazenness about her own body had secretly troubled and astonished Pierce through all the years of their marriage. There had been times when he found it exciting, but when these times were over, he disliked it. A truly good woman ought to cover herself. Yet he would not allow himself to think that Lucinda was not good. Her lack of natural modesty made his own increase. He did not like her in the room with him when he washed himself and dressed. To shave in her presence was ignoble and to scrub himself with soap and sponge before her was humiliation. He wanted to appear, even before her—ah, perhaps especially before her—as always himself and whole. There was nothing childish in his love of her.

She sauntered out of the room, half scornfully. Married people surely need not be so foolish, she thought. But in a strange and unconscious fashion it was more than foolishness to her. She was jealous of everything in Pierce. She wanted no reserves in him. Full possession must be hers, his body hers, in jealousy rather than passion.

But she went into her own room, for it was quite true that he could not or would not dress as quickly if she were with him and this morning he must be quick. She was not sure what it would mean to have Tom gone. There could be no school, of course. That meant the children would be underfoot all day. Well, Georgia must look after them then and teach them. What would she do with John? John would grieve, she thought with irritation. But he must get over it. She sat down before her mirror and examined the details of her hair and her eyelashes and skin, the silver hand mirror flashing a reflected sunlight upon her head. On the whole, it was good that Tom had gone for a while. She put down the mirror. Of course, she thought, that was it—he had simply taken Bettina away. Then he would come back again. It was not likely that he would leave Malvern and all its benefits.

Pierce came into the room a few minutes later shaved and dressed. "Where's Georgia?" he demanded.

"I sent her to get the children up," Lucinda replied.

"She may know something," Pierce said and went off to find her.

But Georgia did not know. He did not doubt the truth of her troubled eyes. She was curling Sally's hair about her finger. The child knelt before her and cried out when he came in, "Uncle Tom's run away!"

Everyone knew it, of course. There was no keeping things from the children in a huge household like this. Someone always told them.

"Georgia, you know anything about this?" he demanded.

She went on brushing the golden coils of Sally's hair about her finger.

"No, sir," she said. "Bettina didn't tell me anything. It's come as a—shock."

She lifted her eyes to his and he saw them full of tears.

"Didn't she tell you anything ever of such a possibility—if something went wrong?" he asked.

"No, sir," she said simply.

He had an uncomfortable conviction that he ought to tell her about yesterday, Bettina was all she had.

"Go away, Sally," he ordered. "I want to talk to Georgia."

"But why can't I hear?" Sally objected. "I know everything, anyway."

Pierce was appalled. "What do you mean by everything?" he demanded.

"I know Uncle Tom and Bettina have children together," she said.

"Oh, my God," Pierce groaned, "go on away, will you? Go and find your mother."

Then his heart twinged. It was his own fault that he had not put a stop to the mess long ago. But who could have foreseen that Tom would be so serious? He ought to have remembered that Tom had always been serious. He seized Sally and kissed her loudly, sighed, then let her go. He faced Georgia.

"Georgia, I did talk to Bettina yesterday, but she didn't give me a hint of what's happened. Now Bettina surely must have said sometime or other to you that she might go away," he argued.

Georgia stood up. "No, sir, we didn't talk much any more about things."

"What do you mean—any more?"

"We did talk a lot—at first," Georgia replied. "I mean—we used to try to think what was to become of us. I think she thought we'd never marry, of course."

"What's the 'of course' about it?" Pierce demanded.

"She didn't want us to marry—just anybody," Georgia said delicately.

"And do you think Bettina did well to allow Tom—to—to—"

"No, sir, I never thought so," Georgia said. "I told her from the first that it would be an embarrassment to the family—and to us. She understood that. But to be fair to Bettina, I think I ought to tell you, sir, that Master Tom certainly did persuade her."

"I am sure he did," Pierce said drily. He sighed again and stood up. "Well, I don't know what has happened to me," he said unhappily. "I don't know if I've lost a brother or not. I reckon we'll find out where they've gone. If she writes you, you must tell me at once."

He was too upset to notice that she was silent. She stood motionless while he walked heavily out of the room. Going down the stairs to his breakfast, it occurred to him that Georgia had spoken for herself his one thought of yesterday. If Bettina had properly married before Tom had come home none of this would have happened. Georgia ought to be married. Trouble came from unmarried females in a house—females that were young and beautiful and low enough in position to be at the mercy of men. He stood indecisive and then tramped back upstairs again. She was standing just where he had left her, her head drooping, her hands clasped behind her, as though in meditation. When he came in she looked up.

"Georgia, something you said made me think."

"Yes, sir?"

"You ought to get married yourself. We haven't any right just to absorb your life the way we do in this house."

She blushed and lifted her head still higher. "I don't want to marry, thank you, sir."

"Haven't you ever seen any man you wanted to marry?" he persisted.

"No, sir," she said quietly. She hesitated a moment and then went on. "And it wouldn't be any good if I did, I don't intend to marry, sir—ever."

"Georgia, every woman ought to marry," he declared.

"I don't want to bring another human being into the world —as I was brought here," she said in a strange quiet voice.

"But—but—" he stammered, "if you married a man—of your own race—"

"What is my race?" she asked him.

"Well—" he began, "well—"

"Yes, I know," she said in the same strange still voice. "Colored is where I belong—outside. But inside—I don't."

He was completely miserable in the presence of her soul thus bared before him and he retreated in haste. "You know, Georgia, if there was anything I could do—any single thing. My God, when I was fighting in the war I never dreamed of all it couldn't settle! But what can I do, Georgia?"

"Not a thing, Master Pierce, except just go on being—kind."

She was suddenly her usual self again and she turned to the bureau, opened the top drawer and began to sort Sally's ribbons. He stared at her back and at her reflected face in the mirror. Her lashes were downcast and her soft mouth firm, and feeling that he was where he should not be, he turned and went downstairs again, confused and unhappy.

Tom and Bettina had grown silent as the night wore on. The children curled into the red plush seat and were asleep and Bettina held the baby in her arms. Tom sat beside her, his arm touching hers to the shoulder. At first they had talked much in the excitement of what they had done, but as dawn broke over the fleeing landscape they ceased. They were tired and Bettina was bewildered with doubt. They had acted in such haste. Could she make it up to him if some day he was sorry?

But Tom would allow himself no doubts. He wanted to build the foundations of his new life carefully and he meant first to find a decent place for his family to live. "My family," he thought, and felt an unspeakable tenderness for this little group of human beings who depended upon him so wholly because he had created them. He had no worry about money. Bettina had enough of his savings for their immediate needs and he would write to Pierce and ask for his share of their inheritance. He had a respectable amount of money left him by his mother, besides, if he wanted to use it. He was fortunate. Not every man could start a new life with such confidence.

Forgetting the constant, irritating motion of the train he pondered on what it was he wanted most for his children. It was simple enough—a place where they could grow up as other children did in this country of theirs—his children's country. He had fought and nearly died to make it so. His jaw grew grim at the memories that crowded into his mind. Not he alone had died to make the children free. He remembered and would remember forever the young men's bodies, carted out of the prison camps, dying and dead, and shoveled into shallow graves. These, too, had died for his children. God helping him, he would try to find a place where what they had done would count at last.

He turned to Bettina. "We shall live in Philadelphia," he said.

"Oh, I would like that," Bettina exclaimed.

"The City of Brotherly Love," he said with a dry smile. "The variety may be better in the north."

"If a slave got to Philadelphia, he was safe," Bettina said simply.

The city became home to them from then on, although neither of them had ever seen it. When they stopped at the station the next afternoon it was home. Tom refused to notice the stares of the people around him as he marched through the waiting room. He carried the baby and the two older children clung to Bettina's hands. A porter took their bags, his eyes bulging, too. It was to this porter that Bettina turned in private inquiry.

"Can we folks put up at the hotels here?" she whispered.

He caught the whisper and exchanged secret looks with her. He shook his head. "You can't, nor the children," he mumbled. "You gotta go to a boardinghouse—downtown—"

How could she convey this to Tom? She caught step with him and looked up to him pleadingly. "Honey, let's sit down and rest a minute."

They sat down on the nearest bench. She took a startled glance to see if she would be forbidden and was reassured by the sight of an old black woman in a creased grey cotton frock, drowsing at the end of the seat and clutching a worn carpetbag to her lean stomach.

"Tom, where are you going to take us, dear?"

"To a hotel," he replied.

"Honey, they won't let us in—me and the children."

He stared at her and suddenly flushed. "They'd better."

"No, Tom, honey—wait! Let's not begin quarreling with folks here. Let's find a quiet boardinghouse for me and the children, and you go to a hotel for a few days. Then we can look around and find the house we want. It would make me much happier that way. I don't want to go where I'm not wanted—please, Tom!"

He yielded because he was tired and in spite of all, a stranger here. "Very well," he said.

They started again, the porter following with the bags and he found them a horse cab outside on the street driven by a ragged black man. The porter leaned to whisper to him as he turned and stared at Tom. What he was saying was plain enough to Bettina, and she pressed a coin into his hand after Tom had paid him. "Thank you for helping me and my children," she whispered.

"Woman, you shore needs help!" the porter whispered back.

It was the beginning of their new life.

# Six

---

PERFORCE, Pierce was compelled in the next years to put aside thinking of his family. The railroad stocks upon which Malvern still depended for the capital to expand its acres and to build the barns needed for housing greater crops suddenly weakened. In the last ten years the nation had gone wild over railroads. Little towns and villages had seen themselves swollen into cities and railroad centers, whirlpools of trade and commerce. In the years since Pierce had bought his first railroad shares, new roads had been incorporated almost every month. Railroad promoters rode east and west in palatial private cars, and dined and got drunk with promoters of stores and shops and locomotive works, and enthusiastic men sat far into the night mapping new cities which were never to exist except upon paper.

Pierce heard vaguely of these doings, but Malvern lay around him, so peaceful and so eternal, he could not believe that beneath Malvern, in banks and railroads, the foundations of his life were shaking. John MacBain had spoken out his fears and warnings half a dozen times, but Pierce, with the hearty good humor of a man who lives upon fertile lands, had taken them as manifestations of John's old tendency toward secret despair.

One morning after mid-December, when Lucinda was superintending the making of the yards of holly wreath to hang along the halls for Christmas, Jake brought him a telegram from John. It contained few words. "Things are bad. Come quick. John."

He took the telegram to Lucinda as she sat enthroned in a huge oak chair on the stair landing. At her feet Georgia crouched, weaving the holly twigs in and out with scarlet cord. Along the balustrade two or three young servants crawled, twining the wreath in and out of the banisters.

Lucinda read the telegram, her pretty brows knit in a frown. "Oh Pierce, of all things, just at Christmas!" she cried.

"Christmas is a week off," he said gravely. "I've got to go."

"I always count that Christmas begins when the boys come home," she protested.

"John wouldn't send for me unless he really needed me," he replied.

"Probably Molly has been playing the fool," she said sharply. Never before had she remarked on Molly's escapades.

He lifted his eyebrows at her. "I don't think it's Molly," he replied. "John can handle her. No, it's the railroad. Things haven't been going too well—"

Now she was alarmed. "Why, Pierce—"

"Too much expansion," he said briefly. Then he bent and kissed her hair. "Never mind, Luce—go on with Christmas— whatever it is we'll have Christmas as usual."

She nodded. Whatever it was, it was not her business.

Georgia stood up and red holly berries fell from her frock. "Shall I go and help pack, ma'am?" she asked in her gentle voice.

"Yes—well, I suppose so," Lucinda said, vexed.

"Minnie can take my place," Georgia suggested.

Pierce turned and went upstairs and behind him he heard Georgia's soft footfall. He had come to take her presence so much for granted in his house that she was scarcely a creature apart now from its life. He went into his rooms and she followed. To his own bedroom in the last five years he had added a booklined sitting room, so that if he were wakeful he could get up and read. He did not sleep well since Tom had gone away. It would take years to convince him that Tom was never coming back. When once in six months he had one of Tom's long letters he slept very badly indeed. Tom was perfectly happy as the headmaster of his own small private school. None of the retribution which should have fallen on his head had come. Pierce dared not show the letters to Lucinda, lest such happiness infuriate her. He locked them into a small strong box in his desk.

"I can pack your things, sir," Georgia was saying. "Why don't you sit down and rest yourself?"

He looked at her and yielded. "Well, maybe I will. I ought to look up some of my papers before I go."

"Yes, sir."

She went into his bedroom, leaving the door open between, he heard drawers open and shut, and the latch of his closet sounded once or twice. She knew where everything was, for it was she who kept his things in order. Joe was his valet, but Georgia kept his things neat. He was aware of a mild friendship between her and Joe. Joe had never married—

He got up and went into his bedroom. Georgia was folding his white evening shirts carefully. She looked up.

"I didn't tell Joe I was going," he said abruptly. "I'll want him along, of course."

"I'll tell him, sir," Georgia replied.

"I don't even know where he is," Pierce grumbled.

"I know," she said. Her cheeks dimpled. "It's safe enough that if he thinks you're busy he's in the kitchen."

She lifted the speaking tube from its hook near his bed and called into it, "Joe?"

She looked at Pierce, still smiling. "He's there," she said. "I knew he wouldn't be working on the holly. He's afraid of thorns."

"Joe lazy?" he inquired. He enjoyed dimples in any woman's cheeks.

"Oh, I don't know," she replied.

The dimples were still there and he kept looking at them. Then he felt his old uneasiness toward her. "Why don't you and Joe get married, Georgia?" he asked abruptly.

The dimples disappeared instantly. She hung up the speaking tube and flushed a deep rose. "I couldn't marry—him," she said in a low voice.

"It would be a good thing," he argued, still looking at her. "I'd give you the stone tenant house to live in."

She gazed back at him, her eyes suffering. "I—can't," she

whispered. Her face, open and quivering before his gaze, was like a magnolia flower. Her eyes were enormous and wet with sudden tears. The moment grew long, too long, then suddenly seeing the look upon his face she yielded to herself. She ran across the room and knelt before him and bent her head to his feet.

He was horrified and shaken. He looked down into her face and despised himself because he could not keep from seeing how beautiful she was. "I ought to send you away," he said in a strange hard voice.

"I have no home in the world but here," she whispered.

"Get up!" he commanded her. He stepped back and turned and strode toward the door. He looked back and she was there, on her knees still, her delicate hands clasped, looking at him with her dark and sorrowful eyes.

"I must leave in half an hour," he told her, and heard his own voice dry and harsh.

"Yes, sir." The words were a sigh.

He hastened downstairs to find Lucinda. She had left the landing and was in the library, still surrounded by holly wreaths and servants. She was standing by the mantelpiece, directing the placing of the decorations behind the portrait of his mother. He went and stood beside her silently, and looked at his mother's face.

"Do you think that wreath is too heavy?" Lucinda inquired.

"Perhaps," he said absently. He wanted to feel his mother's presence and Lucinda's. He put his arm about Lucinda's waist and took her right hand and pressed it to his lips. She let him caress her and then pulled her hand away, lifting her eyebrows at the servants who were stealing looks at them.

"Come to the door with me, Luce," he begged. "I shan't be seeing you maybe for a week."

"A week!" she echoed. "Pierce—that's Christmas Eve!"

"I'll try to get home sooner," he said.

"Has Georgia got your things ready?" she asked.

"Yes," he said shortly. The enormous complexity of his life suddenly appalled him. If he did not send Georgia away, how would he hide from Lucinda what he knew? And if he did send her away, what reason would he give? He heartily longed to tell Lucinda exactly what had happened and let her deal with Georgia as she would. But prudence forbade this. Lucinda would never believe that he had not done something to bring Georgia to her knees before him. Lucinda would never believe in his innocence—nor in any man's where a woman was concerned. He felt sweat stir at the roots of his hair and along his upper lip under his moustache and he dared not put himself at her mercy. She was his wife and she knew the secret weaknesses of his being and his life was with her and must be with her through the years until old age and death, and he could not be at her mercy.

"Goodbye, honey," he said. "Don't bother to come to the door, after all. The house looks lovely. And I'll be back before Christmas Eve, for sure."

Lucinda kissed him gratefully. "If you can get some champagne in Wheeling bring home a dozen bottles, Pierce. The boys won't think it's a real party without it."

"I will, my dear," he promised her.

He dreaded to go into the hall lest Georgia were there. But she was not. Joe was getting the bags into the carriage, and he grinned at Pierce.

"I shore did hustle myself," he panted. Pierce climbed into the carriage and Joe arranged the fur robe over his knees and jumped on the driving seat and the coachman pricked the twin black carriage horses with his whip and they set off down the long avenue of oaks.

"We've been through trouble before," John said. There had been no pretense at festivity this time when Pierce arrived at the great mansion set on a hill outside Wheeling, nor at any time during the days he had been here. On the fourth day, after an almost silent dinner, the three of them at one end of the huge oval dining table in an enormous dining room, Molly had gone upstairs and John had brought him to the dark paneled library. A fire burned in an English iron grate under a white marble mantelpiece where a wreath of marble was upheld by naked cupids. It was near midnight and they were

still talking, and the burden of their talk was what it had been
for hours on each of the days he had been here in John's
house. Financial depression threatened the country. Men had
seen it coming in vague and inexplicable fashion, a storm on
the horizon, a wind on the sea. Pierce had not felt it at Malvern, and soundly rooted in his lands, he had taken the
warnings he read in newspapers as the nervousness of business men whose fortunes were in flexible money instead of in
farms and cattle.

But John had told him that the depression had already
fallen upon the railroads. Passenger traffic was growing so
light that it scarcely paid to run the trains on short journeys,
and freight was falling off alarmingly fast. Something had to
be done to check the downward spiral of the times.

"I should have thought that the expansion before the war
would have taught you railroad fellows something," Pierce
said sourly.

John looked at him and grinned. "You ought to understand.
You've done a little expanding yourself at Malvern."

"Only for myself and my family," Pierce grumbled. "I
haven't taken the savings of widows and orphans."

"You've used the savings of widows and orphans," John retorted. "What would you have been if you hadn't? Not the
Squire of Malvern!"

Pierce avoided the thought. "After all you've told me,
there's only one thing to be done. Depression has hit the
whole country and we know it. Then wages have got to
come down."

"Easier said than done," John reminded him. "The men will
go on strike."

"Let them," Pierce said.

"You don't keep up with the times down there in the
country, Pierce," John complained. "Don't you read any
newspapers? Have you ever heard of a fellow called Marx?"

"No," Pierce said, "who is he?"

"Oh, my God," John groaned. "Did you ever hear of a
communist, Pierce?"

"No," Pierce said.

John leaned on the mantelpiece and shook a long forefinger at him. "You listen to me, Pierce," he said in the sharp high voice with which he harangued directors at dinner tables and gangs at the works. "A strike isn't a local nuisance nowadays. It's something more, by Gawd!"

"What?" asked Pierce.

"That's what I don't know," John's forefinger dropped. "That's what I'm trying to find out. When we have a strike here, in West Virginia, I don't feel the roots are here."

"Where are they?" Pierce asked, smiling incredulously.

"Over in Europe somewhere," John said solemnly.

Pierce yawned. "You always were a gloomy fellow, John. Come on to bed. A night's sleep will bring back your common-sense. What's Europe got to do with us?"

John shook his head and poured two small glasses of whiskey from the big cut glass decanter on the table. They lifted their glasses and drank to one another, and marched up the broad stairs side by side. Behind them a silent liveried servant put out the lamps and set the screen across the fireplace.

In the wide upstairs hall John opened a heavy mahogany door and Pierce stood on the threshold of his room. Then they heard Molly's voice. Her maid had opened the door opposite, and over the low footboard of her enormous bed, they saw Molly enthroned among silken pillows.

"Come in here, you two!" she called. "Pierce, you needn't mind me—you're just like a brother to me, damn you!"

They laughed, Pierce awkward for a moment. And then they went and stood at the foot of Molly's bed. She looked very pretty indeed, in her blue satin nightgown and lace cap tied with blue ribbons. Her ruddy hair was braided and hung in plaits over her shoulders. Her white arms were bare and she threw down her book.

"I couldn't sleep," she said frankly. "I'm worried to death. Pierce, are you afraid?"

"Of what?" he asked cautiously. He did not believe in talking about business with any woman.

"Those awful communists!" she wailed. "They want to take everything away from us!"

"Nonsense," he said smiling. "We're a civilized country, thank God."

"Think of what the rabble did in France!" she cried.

"Think of what they didn't," he reminded her. "The palaces are still there and yours will be too, my dear—don't worry!"

She was looking at him with bold bright eyes, and Pierce involuntarily glanced at John. He was staring at the rose-flowered carpet, the lines of his mouth saturnine.

"Goodnight, Molly—" Pierce said.

"Goodnight, Pierce," she replied, and made a face at him.

They went back to Pierce's room and Pierce laughed a little when he entered it. It was enormous, paneled in black walnut and curtained with red velvet.

"Napoleon might have slept in that," he said cheerfully, staring at the tented, triple-sized bed.

John smiled drily. "I believe he did," he remarked. "Though how these fellows get around to sleep in so many beds—"

Pierce laughed again. "I wouldn't have it at Malvern for a pretty penny," he said frankly.

Out of the darkness a huge brass lamp shone in a circle of yellow light and a coal fire burned and crackled in the black iron grate. John stood before it, warming his coat tails and Pierce stood facing him.

"You remember what I asked you, once?" John inquired.

Pierce nodded, unbuttoning his satin waistcoat.

"I ask you again," John said firmly. "There's a fellow hanging around Molly these days—you know Henry Mallows?"

"Yes," Pierce said.

"I don't want him to father any child of mine," John said with feeling. "A sissy, if I ever saw one!"

Pierce took off his coat and hung it over a chair.

"Doesn't his wife—"

"His wife," John said with bitterness, "is used to loose ways on her own account, from all I hear. Those lords and ladies!

Pierce, I'm fond of you. I could love any child of yours—as I'd love my own."

"I've had all the children I'm going to have, John." He spoke lightly, but his head swam. A woman's face sprang before his eyes, and he was shocked to discover that it was Georgia's as she had knelt before him. He turned away abruptly. Joe had unpacked his bags and his nightshirt lay on the big bed.

"I reckon I'll turn in, John." He faced his friend, smiled, and walked toward him and clasped John's long bony hand.

"Is that final?" John asked.

"Final," Pierce said.

"Then I won't ask you again."

"No, John."

Long into the night Pierce lay thinking and arranging his life. He was used to himself. Since he had been sixteen years old he had suffered from wild and brief flashes of interest in pretty women. He had never taken these feelings seriously, knowing them the common lot of most men. Nor had he ever spoken of them to Lucinda. They were no more significant than a wayward dream to be forgotten in the morning. Now carefully he relegated Georgia to such dreams. She was a servant in his house and nothing was more despicable than a man's folly with his wife's maid. It was a degradation entirely beneath him. He felt a boyish superiority in refusing to engage himself with Molly, the wife of his friend, and a renewal of devotion to John—good old John, who trusted him so much! He determined that if he had a chance, he would, for John's sake, talk to Molly and tell her not to destroy her husband's happiness. Upon the calm of moral rectitude he fell asleep in Napoleon's bed and did not dream.

The next morning, waked by Joe's footsteps creeping around the room, he lay in lazy comfort. At Malvern there was always the weather to rouse him early. As soon as the dawn broke he had the landsman's curiosity to know what the sky was and whether the sun would shine. Once out of bed he could not go back to it. But here in the city it did not matter what the weather was. It was simply inconvenient or convenient. Today it was convenient for home-going. A broad bar of bright winter sunshine lay across the floor and paled the flames leaping in the grate. Joe, holding up his master's trousers critically, met his eyes across them.

"You better change to your good grey pants today, Master Pierce," he said gravely. "Theseyere creases didn't set with all the pressin' I did."

"All right," Pierce yawned and stretched mightily. "We're going home so I might as well look pretty."

He felt gay and relieved of his problems. Today he would talk to Molly and clear his debt of friendship to John. Alone with Joe it suddenly occurred to him that he would speak of Georgia, and tell him he must marry her. He piled his pillows and lay back on them. Joe was lifting the grey trousers from the hanger in the big mahogany wardrobe.

"Joe!" he said suddenly.

Joe jumped and clutched the trousers. "Lordamighty, Marse Pierce, why you yell at me like that?" he asked reproachfully.

Pierce laughed. "I didn't mean to yell—I just thought of something. Joe, I told Georgia that if you and she would get married I'd let you have the little stone tenant house."

"It's a mighty nice house," Joe said thoughtfully, smoothing the creases of the trousers.

"Well?" Pierce asked.

"Georgia's a mighty nice girl," Joe said still more thoughtfully. "But I reckon she won't marry no colored man."

"She can't marry anybody else," Pierce said positively.

"No, sir—reckon she cain't," Joe agreed.

"Have you asked her?" Pierce inquired.

"I mention it, yes, sir—about a thousand times, I reckon. She always says the same thing. 'You go 'way fum me, Joe'—that's all she say—don't say nothin' else but just that. So I goes away."

"You try her again," Pierce commanded.

"Kin I tell her you said I was to?" Joe looked at him with a gleam of hope in his small dark eyes.

Pierce considered, staring into the canopy of the bed.

"Yes," he said finally, "tell her I said so. Tell her I want you two to get married and have children—right away."

"Yes, sir," Joe said doubtfully. "Thank you kindly, Marster Pierce."

He went away and Pierce got up and made a great splash of cold water in the flowered porcelain basin on the wash-stand. Then he dried himself before the fire. There was a mirror above the mantel and he saw his tall firm white body reflected in it. He would have been less than a man had he not felt complacently that he did not look his age by ten years.

He went down to breakfast half an hour later dressed in his grey suit and a new satin tie that Lucinda had ordered from New York for him. His dark hair, barely silvered at the temples, was smoothly brushed and he had trimmed the ends of his moustache. Molly was alone in the dining room, when he came in.

"John's gone to the office—he said to tell you," she told him. "I came down to have breakfast with you—you vain and handsome man!"

"Thank you, Molly," he said. He did not touch her hand but he smiled at her as the butler pulled out his chair for him. Kidneys and bacon and eggs were set before him and his coffee was poured. Then the servants went away and he was left alone with her.

"I'll breakfast with you, my dear," he said, "and then I'll go and see if John has any more news for me before I take the train south."

"I'll miss you, Pierce—I always miss you—" she said. She leaned her arms on the table and the white lace of her elbow sleeves fell away from them. She wore a blue satin thing—a peignoir of some sort, he supposed. He did not look at her beyond a glance.

"You know what a fuss we make over Christmas," he said, buttering a muffin. "Lucinda scolded me for leaving at all."

"Has Lucinda changed?"

"Not a bit—a dash of silver over her right temple that makes her more beautiful than ever."

Molly took her coffee cup in both hands and sipped from it, her eyes contemplating him over the edge. He looked up, caught their gaze and looked at his plate again.

"I suppose she's very much the mistress of the manor?" She put an edge of malice to the words, but he refused to hear it.

"Lucinda has always been that," he said cheerfully, "even when I came back from the war and found half the servants gone and the house threadbare and nothing but cornbread in the pantry. Of course, now, Malvern's all that we've dreamed —almost!"

"You've stayed in love with her, Pierce?"

"How could I help it?" he retorted.

"My Gawd, she's had a very good thing in you, Pierce," Molly said flatly. "Jewels and children—and a great fine house —and acres of prosperous land—and racing horses—"

He lifted his head. "Molly, you should have seen Beauty's foal win the Darby! Lord, it made me think of music! Phelan's turned into a great little jockey. Of course Beauty is living on the best of the pasture, retired, honorably discharged."

"How many foals have you had from her that were first-rate?"

"Four good racing horses—"

They both loved horses, and they forgot themselves, as he meant they should.

"I wish John cared about horses," Molly said with discontentment.

"His horses are all iron," Pierce said lightly.

"John and I don't have anything in common," she said in a low voice.

He cut through a rasher of bacon firmly. "Yes, you do, Molly. You have this fine house together and you have big parties and you have your trips to Europe and you have damn near everything a woman needs—"

"Except the one thing—"

"Lots of women don't want children," he countered.

"Don't be silly," she retorted. "You know what I want . . . Pierce, are we going to grow old like this?"

He met her squarely. "Yes, Molly—just like this, my dear. I love you but I love John better." He put half a well-buttered muffin into his mouth.

"You don't care what I do?" she demanded.

"I don't want John hurt," he replied.

"You don't care if I'm hurt?"

"Molly, I've made it a rule never to care about any woman except Lucinda. But if you hurt John, then—"

"Then what, Pierce?"

"I reckon I don't want to see you again as long as we live."

"If you don't care what I do, what does that matter to me?"

"Henry Mallows," he began.

"You know I don't care about Henry!" she broke in.

"Then why—"

She interrupted him passionately. "Because you won't look at me—and every morning I look at myself in the mirror and see myself growing older, and I think—"

He burst into loud laughter. "You see yourself looking like the rose of Sharon," he said briskly, "and you think what mischief you can do this day. Ah, Molly, I know you! Even if I— gave in to you—which I never will, my red-haired darling— you will still look in your mirror in the morning and think of what mischief you can do."

"Pierce, I wouldn't—I promise you—Oh, Pierce, dearest—"

She was half out of her chair and he threw down his napkin. He was sick with disgust at himself. For the fraction of a second when he looked at her smooth pink skin he had thought of Georgia's cream-pale face again—not Lucinda—

"I swear I think there's something wrong with my insides," he groaned. "I keep seeing things." He got up and pushed in his chair. "I've been eating and drinking too well here, Molly. It's time I left."

Let her do what she would, he thought. John would have to bear his own burden. He smiled at her as she stood staring at him and then he turned quickly and left the room. Upstairs in his own room he sent for Joe. They took an early train and went away without telling Molly or John goodbye. He wanted to get home.

Christmas Eve at Malvern had never been so magnificent. Pierce gave himself up to the joy of his children. Martin was at the University, and Carey was beginning his first year. Both of them were tall and handsome and he was certain that neither was virgin. But it was none of his business. They were men and must lead men's lives. He had wondered uneasily if he ought to warn them.

He discussed it with Lucinda after the big dance on Christmas Eve. They lay side by side in her spacious bed, enjoying together every detail of the evening's scene. The house was subsiding into stillness about them. Guests were gone and they could hear the servants downstairs moving about, sweeping and straightening and putting away dishes. Then the stillness of the country night covered them. But the house was still awake. Beams cracked and the wind echoed in the chimneys. He loved the sound of the great old house settling for the night, with mild groans and wistful sighs and creaks.

"What would you tell the boys, pray?" Lucinda asked crisply out of the darkness.

"I don't know," he pondered, "just warn them, maybe—"

"I've warned them about nasty diseases," she said.

"I wasn't thinking of that," he replied. "Boys pick up that sort of knowledge from one another easily enough."

"What then, pray?" Lucinda inquired. "You don't know a thing about women, Pierce!"

"Oh, I don't, eh?" he growled.

"No," she said flatly and yawned.

"I know you," he maintained.

"Oh, nonsense!" she cried.

"I certainly know you," he insisted. "I can almost tell what you're going to say."

"That's why I say it," she replied. "But it's not what I think."

He was confounded by this mischief. "Then why don't you say what you think?" he demanded of her.

"Because it's not what you want me to say." Her voice was pert and he was infuriated.

"Oh rubbish!" he said loudly.

"Oh rubbish," she echoed. "There—didn't I say you wouldn't like it?"

He felt pinpricked without knowing where to find the pin. "Don't think I take you seriously," he told her with majesty from his pillow.

"No, dear—I know you don't." Her voice was dangerous.

"Why should I?" he inquired.

"I can't imagine." She yawned again pretentiously and he turned his back for a moment. Then he flounced over again.

"See here, Luce, we can't go to sleep like this!"

"I can go to sleep anyhow—I'm dead," she retorted.

"You know I have to feel things are all right between us—"

"Aren't they? I didn't know they weren't."

He was silent a moment. Then he put his hand through the darkness and touched her soft breast.

She shook his hand off. "Please, Pierce—not tonight, for mercy's sake!"

"You're cold as stone these days—" he accused her.

"No, I'm not," she denied. "But you've grown—careless."

"I want another child, Luce!"

"Diamonds and sapphires couldn't tempt me," she replied firmly.

He leaped out of bed at that and went stamping into his own room and banged the door. He was not given to self-pity, but he allowed himself a measure of it now. What was the use of a man's being faithful to his wife? If Lucinda only knew, he thought savagely, that twice in the fortnight he had refused other women—but he could not tell her. She would laugh aloud and then turn on him with malice and suspicion. He could hear her voice. "And what, pray tell, made her think you were—willing?"

No denials could be valid. Truth itself was not valid to Lucinda where the maleness of a man was concerned. He got into his solitary bed, and in a temper he pulled the covers strongly and left his feet bare. In fury he wrapped them about his feet and lay in a snarl of sheets and blankets and dug his head into the pillows. Lucinda was not a comfortable woman. She did not appreciate him nor the strength of his self-denials. Then he grinned at himself ruefully in the darkness. Self-denial? He was in love with Lucinda still, and she alone could stir his passion. But she was not comfortable, he maintained against this too severe honesty. He loved her more than she loved him. He sighed gustily into the night. It would be pleasant to be loved, for once, more than he loved. He fell asleep, still warming himself with self-pity.

In the midst of the peace of the next summer, after the spring crops had been sown and the winter wheat harvested, at the time of year when Malvern was at the height of its glory, Pierce one day picked up the county newspaper after his ample noon meal. He lay on a long wicker chair on the terrace, preparing for his usual afternoon nap.

At the sight of the headlines all thought of sleep left him abruptly. He sat up, reading avidly, then groaned and threw the paper on the stone flags. Then he seized it to read again the shocking news. Two days ago, in Martinsburg, a sensible city of his own state, the railroad crews had struck in protest to the third cut in their wages.

All during the spring Pierce had followed with approval the news of the recurring wage cuts for the railroad employees. It was only fair, he told himself and Lucinda and anyone else who was near him, that workingmen should share the growing disaster of the times. He himself was suffering enough by not getting any dividends. Martin and Carey, home for holidays, had listened to him in their separate ways, Martin without interest and Carey with shrewd, smiling attention. The only dissenting voice in his house was his third son John, who out of perversity and contrariness to himself, Pierce felt, took the side of workingmen. But he shouted John down easily.

"Don't talk about what you can't understand!" he had ordered.

The last time John had muttered something. Pierce could not hear it.

"What did you say, sir?" he demanded.

John had lifted his head. "I said that I don't think you understand things yourself, Father—"

Pierce had been shocked at such impudence. "Understand what?" he had demanded of this gangling boy.

"What it's like to be a workingman," John said sturdily.

Pierce had snorted laughter. "And you think you do?" he had inquired.

"I have more imagination than you have, Father," John had replied fearlessly.

Pierce's anger melted. He liked his sons to be fearless even toward himself. "Get along with you and your imagination," he said, his eyes twinkling. Then out of respect for the boy he had added honestly, "And I like you to stand up to me, John—it's manly of you."

He had been comforted by the warm look in the boy's grey eyes—Tom's eyes, they were.

But there was no doubt that depression was sweeping over the country like a hurricane. No one understood why these storms recurred in a country where enterprise was free and where every man got what he deserved if he worked hard. Pierce believed that it was a man's own fault if he did not prosper, and with his feet firm upon his own soil, he took the depression as an act of God, inexplicable and irritating as acts of God were apt to be.

He had been pleased when in May the other railroads had begun to cut wages drastically and had complained loudly to John MacBain and his own directors because their railroad did not do so. A few weeks ago he had been delighted to receive from the president of the company a notice that at last wages had been reduced, in despair over the continuing depression. In a brief note to John MacBain, for Pierce hated letterwriting, he had expressed his pleasure and his confidence that dividends could be restored soon.

"We are on the right track at last," he had written John. "Labor has got out of hand and must be controlled. People who have put their money into the railroads must get it back." This letter John had not answered, but John also hated to write letters and never did so unless there was a crisis.

Only yesterday, in church, Pierce had given thanks to God sincerely for all good things, including health and peace in his time. The glorious summer sunshine had slanted down through the stained glass windows of the Presbyterian church of his fathers. Here he and Tom had sat as small boys, sighing and wriggling. Here his children had been christened. He had thanked God frankly for wealth—well, why not for wealth?

And even while he was giving thanks to God this thing had already happened! He felt cheated and he got up impulsively to find Lucinda and complain to her. Then he sat down again and stared across his fields to the mountains. Lucinda would not be interested. She had always divided life firmly into what was men's business and what was hers. Whatever the difficulties he had, she did not consider them her affair. Money might be hard to get, but what else had men to do but to get it? He missed Tom, as he often did, in swift short spasms of needing to talk to a man. Malvern had good neighbors. Nobody could be more fun than the Raleighs and the Bentons and the Carters and the Hulmes and a dozen other families, when it came to fox-hunting and horse-racing. Pierce took pride in the fact that on any weekend he could gather twenty families at Malvern and on any day in hunting season. But his sons were still young and he had no man in the house to quarrel with and argue with and be knit to, as he had been knit to Tom.

What would Tom think of such news? He got up again and began to pace the sunlit flags of the long terrace. Philadelphia was near Baltimore. He could go to the company offices at Baltimore and find out for himself exactly what was happening and what might be expected to happen. He could reinforce company policies with his own advice. Then he'd run over to Philadelphia and see Tom.

"I might as well own up that I want to see the fellow again," he thought sentimentally. He had not seen Tom once in all these years, although they had written regularly if not often. He wouldn't tell Lucinda—they had not mentioned Tom for a long while. He had stopped telling her even when he had a letter, because she closed her lips firmly at the very sound of Tom's name.

But he went to find her to tell her of his plan to go to Baltimore. He found her surrounded by their daughters, to whom she was teaching sewing. That is, she was sitting in her rose-satin chair, in her own sitting room upstairs, taking dainty stitches in a bit of linen, and Sally and Lucie were sitting beside her. Lucie was absorbed but Sally was frowning and pausing every moment to look out of the open window. Between the two girls Georgia came and went, examining stitches and correcting mistakes. She looked at him when he came in and away again. Since that strange day when she had knelt at his feet, she had spoken no word to him beyond what was absolutely necessary in the communication of servant to master. His own behavior had been as careful, and between them, like scar tissue over a wound, they had constructed a surface.

"Luce," he began abruptly. "There's a railroad strike. I've got to go to the head offices at Baltimore. I'm going to telegraph John MacBain to meet me there."

Lucinda looked up from her sewing and raised her delicate eyebrows. "What can you accomplish, Pierce? You're not an executive."

"I'm one of the Board of Directors, nevertheless," he said firmly. "I'm going to see for myself what the men are thinking of and what's to be done. If necessary, I'll ask for a special meeting of the directors on behalf of the stockholders. We can't let the railroad get into the hands of labor. It'll be the end of the country. Socialism—communism—whatever you want to call it—"

He was halted by a swift look from Georgia's suddenly upraised eyes. Then she looked down again. She was at Sally's side now, and she began to rip out a line of stitches.

"Oh dear—" Sally cried, "don't tell me I've got them wrong again! Georgia, you are mean—"

"You pay no mind to what you're doing, Miss Sally," Georgia said quietly.

Sally turned to him. "Papa, if you're going to Baltimore— let me go with you!"

"Pray tell—" Lucinda cried at her daughter. "Why should

you go to Baltimore? I've a mind to go myself though, Pierce. While you're busy at meetings I could get myself and the girls some new frocks."

He was horrified at this onslaught of women and struggled against it but in vain. By the time he left the room a few minutes later not only Lucinda and Sally were going with him but Lucie as well and Georgia to look after the girls and serve Lucinda. He groaned in mock anguish. "I thought I was going to do business instead of squiring a lot of women!"

"We'll look after ourselves," Lucinda said sweetly. "You don't need to pay us any mind. I shall take the girls to Washington maybe—or even New York."

He could think of no good reason to forbid it. The boys were safe enough at home. If Lucinda had made up her mind to come with him the girls might as well come too. He telegraphed John MacBain and Lucinda included an invitation to Molly and what he had planned as a severe business trip now became a holiday. In the secret part of his mind he said that he would nevertheless escape his women and go and see Tom. The next day in the midst of much packing Georgia stopped him in the upper hall, her arms full of frocks.

"Master Pierce, if you think of a way, I'd like to go and see Bettina."

"Of course," he said. "I'll speak to your mistress." He had long ago forgotten that once he had not wanted to be called master in his house nor to have Lucinda called mistress.

By the time they set out for Baltimore the shadow over the country had darkened still more. Pierce studied the newspapers for hours every day. To his disgust, some of the western railroads had avoided trouble by raising wages as quickly as the men demanded. He was angry because he was frightened. His dividends had been so deeply cut this year that he was hard put to it to know how to pay the costs of his racing stable. It was unthinkable that Malvern should suffer because a horde of ignorant and dirty workingmen were dissatisfied with steady wages and good jobs.

Yet it was not just Malvern, he told himself honestly, that was his concern. Malvern was symbol of all that was sound and good in the nation. Family life, the land, healthy amusements, educated children, civilized ways of living—all were threatened. He wrote a letter of commendation to a magazine that printed a cartoon showing a skeleton disguised as a union rabble rouser, wearing a ribbon on which was printed "Communist." He was so angry one day that he could not eat his dinner because the foreigner named Marx, of whom John MacBain had spoken, was quoted in a northern newspaper as gloating over the rising strikes and dissensions and proclaiming them the beginning of a real revolution.

He had thrown the paper down and got to his feet and paced the dining room floor. "In God's name what have Americans to make a revolution about?" he bellowed to Lucinda and their children. "We aren't a lot of dirty starving peasants. We've got democracy here—a government, by God—"

"Pierce, stop cursing before the girls," Lucinda commanded him. "Sit down and eat your beef before it's cold."

He had obeyed, but he could not eat as much as usual and he spent the rainy afternoon gloomily in his library, drinking too much with a savage satisfaction that if the world was going to hell he might as well go with it.

When they met John MacBain and Molly in Baltimore, at the great old-fashioned hotel which they had made their rendezvous, Pierce got rid of the womenfolk as fast as he could. He seized John by the arm and took him into the bar. It was mid-afternoon, and the place was empty but the two men sat down to drink, each comforted by the sight of the other's grim looks.

"John, what the hell—" Pierce began. "It's this stinking European fellow that's behind everything!" By now Pierce had read enough to feel that he had found the source of evil. The man Marx was a threat to all that Malvern was.

John nodded and then said somberly, "All the same, Pierce, no foreigner could make headway here if we didn't have four million unemployed. By Gawd, man, that's a tenth of our population, pretty nearly! What's happening at Martinsburg—" he broke off, shaking his head again.

"What's happening now?" Pierce demanded. "I thought the police had—"

John snorted. "Police! They gave up. The mob was something awful. Why, Pierce, man, where have you been? The President of the United States has ordered out the government artillery!"

"Good God," Pierce gasped. "But where are the state troops?"

"They wouldn't fire on the strikers," John said glumly. "Rotten with communism—the lot of them!"

Pierce felt dizzy with alarm. What he had seen as a dissatisfaction localized to a single industry, inspired by a single man, now grew into a danger as wide as the nation. He looked about the strange room and wished himself back at Malvern. The confidence with which he had left his own state, had crossed Virginia and Maryland, was gone. He was a stranger here, and who would listen to him? He dreaded meeting the executives whom he had been so sure he could guide. Then he pushed aside fear.

"John, we've got to be a beacon to the nation," he said. "We've got to lead the railroads so wisely and so firmly that what we do will be a light to other industries. Everything depends on the railroads—we're basic! If we can keep running and whip our men into reason, the nation will keep steady."

"Amen, Pierce—if we can do it," John replied.

They lifted their glasses simultaneously and looked at one another.

"Damn it, John," Pierce said, "I can't think of a thing in this world that's worth proposing!"

"Nor I, by Gawd," John agreed with unutterable gloom.

They drank their whiskey down in silence and for the comfort of their own bodies.

Pierce was awakened the next morning by his arm being shaken and then by the sound of shots. He looked up into Lucinda's terrified eyes.

"Pierce—Pierce," she was crying, "wake up—there's some sort of a battle going on outside!"

He opened his dazed eyes wide and heard a roar like that of the sea beating against cliffs. He leaped out of bed, his nightshirt flying around him, and rushed to the window. A mob of people filled the street, milling, pushing, surging, yelling. "It's here," he cried, "the strike!"

"Let's get out of this town, Pierce!" Lucinda cried back.

"You and the girls," he amended. 'You'd better go right to Washington as quick as you can before all the trains stop. Get out of the room, Luce, so that I can get dressed."

She ran into the next room, obedient for once. Then the hall door opened and Joe came in. The white showed around the pupils of his eyes. "Lordy, lordy, what we goin' to do?" he groaned. "The war's bust out again—what the Yankees want now, marster?"

Before Pierce could answer, there was a loud knock and John MacBain came in, fully dressed. He had a telegram in his hand.

"I've got to get to Pittsburgh, Pierce," he announced abruptly. "The Pennsylvania militia has been ordered out— they're fighting mobs in the streets, there, too, by Gawd!"

"Pittsburgh!" Pierce groaned. "The whole country has gone mad."

"They're burning rolling stock there," John said heavily. "You've got to meet the directors without me, Pierce."

"If I have to, I have to," Pierce said doggedly.

They clasped hands firmly and John was gone. Pierce turned. Behind him Joe stood waiting to shave him, mug in one hand and razor in the other. Pierce saw his hand shaking like an aspen.

"Give the razor to me. If you're as scared as that, you'll cut my throat," he said sharply. All this nonsense, he thought angrily. What was the matter with him?

He dipped the brush in the soapy water briskly, swabbed his chin, and began to shave himself with long even strokes.

Behind him Joe moaned, "We all be killed, I reckon!"

"Nonsense," Pierce replied. Now that action was necessary he felt strong and competent. He had been an officer in the army, and he felt his blood grow cool again. He was not afraid of battle, now that he knew who the enemy was. He had sworn never again to enter a war against his fellow men but these communists were not fellow men. They were devils of destruction.

"You tell Georgia to help your mistress and the girls pack up right away," he commanded Joe. "After breakfast I'll get them into the private car and off to Washington."

"You and me—" Joe faltered.

"We're going to stay right here," Pierce said grimly.

"Oh my—oh my!" Joe whispered under his breath.

He tiptoed out of the room and Pierce dressed himself. He had just buttoned his collar when the door opened smartly and he saw Sally mirrored over his shoulder. She was dressed for travel in her blue suit and hat. Her cheeks were flaming and her blue eyes were bright.

"Papa—" She came in and shut the door. "I'm not going to Washington—"

Pierce felt enormous irritation. "Oh yes, you are," he retorted to her reflection in the mirror. "I'm going to be too busy to look after women—"

"Papa, I want to stay with you—"

"You can't stay with me—you must stay out of my way."

"Papa—" she began again, but he snapped at her.

"Now, Sally, you can't have your wish this time! The whole country is in danger. I've got to get to the company offices as fast as I can get rid of you girls."

"But, Papa—why are they fighting?"

"It's a strike—you know that—" He was trying to fasten his tie.

"But why, Papa?"

"Well—they don't want their wages cut."

"Why do you cut them, Papa?"

"It's not I—it's the company."

"But you told the company to do it—"

"I simply gave my opinion—the company is losing money— why, our profits are cut in half! The men have to share in the loss, that's all. Management can't take it all—"

"But, Papa, did you lose money or only just not make so much?"

"It's the same thing," Pierce declared.

"No, it isn't," Sally maintained.

Pierce turned on his beloved child with wrath and fury. "Now Sally, you don't know what you're talking about. If I expect to make five thousand dollars on a horse and I don't make but twenty-five hundred, I've lost twenty-five hundred dollars."

"No, you haven't, Papa—you haven't lost anything. You have the twenty-five hundred."

She made such a picture of beauty as she stood there, her pretty face serious, her cheeks flaming, her red-gold hair curling under her blue hat, that his heart was smitten in the midst of his anger, and he softened.

"Honey, don't you try to tell a man he hasn't lost money when he knows his pocket is lighter than it ought to be. You get along—have you had your breakfast?"

Sally shook her head.

"Well, then, eat fast—I'm going straight to the station to see about a train to pull the car out—a freight or anything—"

"Papa, I warn you—" His daughter flung up her head and faced him. "If you make me go to Washington—I'll—I'll run away!"

"Sally—Sally!" he groaned.

From the street the roar came beating through the closed windows into the room. "There's no time, child!"

"I will run away," she repeated.

"What shall I do with her?" he asked loudly, lifting his eyes to the ceiling.

He wheeled and crossed the room and opened Lucinda's door. She was in the next room with Georgia and Lucie, and all of them were packing the bags.

"Lucinda!" he shouted. "Sally is playing the fool—"

"I sent her to you," Lucinda said briefly. 'I can do nothing with her. She insists on staying with you. You've spoiled her, Pierce, though I've warned you again and again."

In the doorway Sally stood smiling, triumphant. "Neither of

you can do anything with me," she said pleasantly. "So—I'm not going!"

Her parents looked at her, Lucinda coldly, Pierce savagely. "I've a good mind to give you a beating," he muttered through his teeth.

"It's too late," Lucinda reminded him. "You wouldn't lay a finger on her when she was little."

Georgia looked up. "If you are willing, ma'am—sir—could I take Miss Sally to Philadelphia? Joe can go in my place to Washington, ma'am."

They turned to her, grasping at the straw of escape.

"I've been thinking I would ask you to let me visit Bettina, please," Georgia said. "If you're willing, ma'am—Miss Sally can come, too."

"No," Lucinda said.

"Yes!" Sally cried. "Yes—yes—Papa, I've always wanted to see Uncle Tom again—"

"Sally!" Lucie's prim whisper, horror-struck, hissed across the room.

"I don't care—I do," Sally insisted.

"Sally can stay at a hotel," Pierce reasoned to Lucinda. "Georgia can be with her and look after her and Tom can come and see her."

A volley of shots struck in the street and a window pane shattered.

Lucinda put her hands to her ears. "We've got to get away before we're all killed—"

An hour later Pierce stood alone on the platform of the railroad station. His private car had gone, the last in a line of passage cars headed for the south. No one knew when the next train would leave, if ever. Trains were still leaving irregularly for the north, and on one of them he had put Sally and Georgia into a day coach, jammed with frightened people trying to leave Baltimore. He had held Sally close for a moment, exasperated with love for this wilful child of his. But Sally had been gay and excited.

"Mind you stay at a hotel," he had commanded. "Your mama will never let me hear the end of it if you don't."

"Of course," she had promised, without, he felt, in the least meaning it. He saw them on the train, squeezed against the window, and through the open window he had continued to talk.

"If things quiet down," he said, "I may run up myself for a day or so, tell Tom. If I find you've been disobedient, Sally—"

"Oh, *no!*" she trilled.

The whistle blew and she waved and laughed. He saw Georgia's face, softly alight, behind her.

"I hold you responsible for your young mistress, Georgia!" he shouted. The train was moving and he did not hear her answer, whatever it was. He caught her smile, and had a pang of foreboding.

But there was no time to think of what he felt. Across the platform a group of guardsmen were carrying the body of a young man. They laid him down and Pierce saw that he was dead. He drew near and looked down at him. He was bleeding from a gunwound and his face was mangled to a pulp, the features wiped away.

"A brick bat out of the damned mob," one of the men muttered.

Before Pierce could speak the mob surged into the station.

"Get out of here, sir!" the guardsmen begged him—"They'll tear you to pieces—in that silk hat!"

They surrounded him and hurried him across the tracks, and he made his way alone by back streets to the offices where the directors awaited him.

Pierce had never before faced the Board without John. Now as he looked down the long mahogany table, lined with grim faces, he felt his resolution fade. The power was in the hands of these men. He had been all for wielding that power while he was in Malvern. What threatened Malvern threatened the world. But now in the great dim board room, hung with red velvet from ceiling to floor at every window and paneled with the portraits of dead directors, he was confused. Feelings that he had forgotten came crowding back into his mind, memories so distant that he would have said they had ceased to exist.

He remembered again the young men who had died under his command in the war. They had fought with heartbreaking bravery, the pure bravery of the young, who alone are unselfish enough to die for a cause. The young man whom he had just seen in the street had died, too. How uselessly! A brick flung at random had crushed him. He had been ordered out this morning to do his duty and now he was dead.

He was distracted by his memories, confused and mingled with the news in telegrams and messages which lay before him.

"Military action must be taken all along the railroad," Henry Mallows was saying in his high clear cold voice. "Nothing else will suffice."

"The mob has command," Jim McCagney said. He had aged greatly in the years that he had sat on the Board. His bitter grey eyes were set deep under eyebrows like bunches of dry heather.

Daniel Rutherford, the youngest of them all, turned at the sound of an open door, and took an envelope from a messenger boy. He tore it open and read it. "The Mayor has sworn in three thousand citizens as special police," he cried. "He promises that the ringleaders of the mob will be in jail tonight."

"Tut!" Jim McCagney growled, "don't give a hoot for citizens in a case like this. Mallows is right. Guns are what's wanted."

"A detachment of one hundred marines is expected this evening," Baird Hancock said drily.

"It's the shops I'm thinking of," Jonathan Yates put in. He was the one man in the room who had come up from the ranks, a thin, tired-looking man in a broadcloth suit too large for him. The heavy, velvet-lined collar rode up the back of his head and now and again he struggled with it.

Pierce was staring at the despatches before him. "Pittsburgh, Reading, Harrisburg, Shamokin, Hornellsville, Chicago, Cincinnati, Zanesville, Columbus, Fort Wayne, St. Louis, Kansas City," he read the names aloud solemnly.

Murmurs of anger rose from the men around the table. Pierce lifted his head. "I came into this room as fixed as any of you in my determination to put down these strikes," he said slowly. "Now as I see these fires catching from one place to another clear across the country, I ask myself—what have we done that was wrong?"

"Man, it's not us—it's the Reds!" McCagney shouted. "Our men alone wouldn't have dared! The foreign communists have used our honest working folk as a pretext for their infamous machinations to overthrow the government of the United States!" He leaped to his feet, towering six foot six, his white hair flying, his beard a tangle. He banged the table with his fists. "Ne'er-do-wells!" he bellowed. "Rascals—robbers—internationalists!" He ground out the last word between his teeth with special hatred.

Silence followed, and in the silence Pierce drove away his memories. What had the past to do with today? "If we have proof that these strikes are inspired by foreigners," he said slowly, "then it is time to put on our uniforms again and fight."

"Amen, amen—" The word roared around the table from mouth to mouth.

They sat far into the night, while messages continued to pour in from the four corners of the nation. At midnight a last message was sent by the mayor. Two hundred and fifty rebels had been imprisoned. "Upon inquiry," the mayor reported, "it was found that not one of them had been a worker on the railroad."

"If we needed any further proof of foreign machination," Henry Mallows said looking about triumphantly, "here it is."

Pierce looked back at him, and wished that he need not agree with him. He had disliked Henry Mallows increasingly throughout the evening. Mallows had grown more handsome and distinguished looking with the years. Worldliness became him. His smooth cheeks and well-cut mouth were still young. What had seemed timid and foreign in his youth

had become hard and self-assured as he had become a native
and a patriot in his own country. His foreign wife had grown
into a silent and delicate creature, finicking and invalid.
There had been no children.

Pierce turned away from this man of whom John MacBain
had spoken so bitterly, and looked at the other listening,
stubborn faces. "We must remember that the sympathies of
the press and of the people, however, are with the workingmen," he said. "If we act too severely or even too swiftly we
may find ourselves condemned, though unjustly. We must
distinguish between our own men and the communists."

Silence fell about him as the directors digested this common sense.

"I move we adjourn," Jim McCagney said abruptly.

"To meet again on Monday morning," Henry Mallows
amended.

Pierce seconded the amended motion and it was carried
and the endless meeting was over.

Pierce slept deep in exhaustion through the night and was
awakened just before dawn by a fire alarm. He got out of
bed and without lighting the lamp he went to the window and
looked down. The streets were swarming again with people.
Trouble had begun again. Toward the west the sky blazed
almost to the zenith.

The railroad shops!

He dressed himself hurriedly and went out bareheaded,
fearing that his silk hat would betray him. The streets were
so crowded that he could barely force his way westward. It
was an hour before he reached the railroad shops and found
that they had not yet caught fire. A train of oil cars was
burning. The firemen had isolated the cars and so far had
saved the shops. While they worked the mob turned to a
lumberyard and planing mill a few blocks away and set it
afire. In a few minutes the air was filled with smoke and the
flames roared black-edged toward the sky.

Pierce stood back among the crowd, watching and helpless.
He looked at the faces around him. Some were silent and

grave, some were wild, some were drunken. He recognized no one and with a strange feeling that the whole world was burning to destruction he went back to the hotel. Downstairs the clerk gave him his door key and noted his return.

"Terrible, ain't it, sir?" he murmured.

"Yes," Pierce said.

He felt chilled although the night had been warm. But there was no hot water with which to warm himself. He was grimed with smoke and he washed himself in cold water and then put on his nightshirt again and got back into bed.

He lay shivering and strangely lonely, but for no one. He did not want Lucinda or the children. He was glad that they were not with him. His mood was old and he recognized it as the mood of many nights in the war when battle loomed in the morning. Then as though to carry the illusion to reality he heard the sudden sharpness of guns firing in the streets. He listened, lying tense and ready to spring out of bed. Then the sounds were stilled and he fell asleep at last for an hour.

All through the next day he came and went, restless and yet exhausted. The streets were milling with people again, the crowds falling back only before the marines who had arrived early in the morning. It was a war which he did not understand. What was the cause and what the end?

By afternoon eight marines and eight policemen were dead. How many other dead there were no one knew, for the mob hid their own dead. At midnight the mayor reported again. The armed men had won and the city was safe once more. Trains would run within the hour. Pierce went back to the hotel and found a telegram from John MacBain.

"Change in company policy absolutely necessary. Postpone meeting until I come. John."

Pierce rang for a messenger and sent the telegram to Henry Mallows. Crisis in Baltimore was over, but would arms suffice for final victory? He sat down in his room, grimed and exhausted and this night too tired to go to sleep. Suddenly he knew what he wanted. He wanted to go and see Tom. Maybe Tom could tell him what the war was about.

# Seven

PIERCE knew from Tom's letters that what he would see was a decent house on a quiet street in Philadelphia. He hired a hansom cab at the disordered railroad station and arrived at Tom's house in the middle of the afternoon. The heat of the day had been ended by a sharp swift thunderstorm, which had beaten against the windows of the train. Now the sycamore trees that lined both sides of the street were wet and the air was clean. The cab drew up in front of a whitewashed stone house. He compared the number on the door with that of the figures set at the top of Tom's last letter, got out and paid the driver. For a moment he had a strange feeling of isolation as the cab drove away. Then he crossed the street and knocked on the oak door. White marble steps shone beneath his feet and the knocker was polished brass. Bettina had always been a good worker.

Bettina herself opened the door. At the sight of him she stood rigid for a moment. Then a deep flush spread over her face. She controlled her surprise.

"Come in," she said quietly. "We are glad to see you."

He stepped into the hall. "Tom home?" he asked.

She made no move to take his hat and stick and he put them on a settee. "I expect him in a very few minutes," she replied.

She avoided the use of his name. He noticed it and did not care. Had Lucinda been with him, he would have been uncomfortable at such namelessness, but Lucinda could not possibly have been with him.

"Come into the parlor, please," Bettina said. She opened the door into a cool dim room.

172

He hesitated. "Now, Bettina, you know I don't care much for parlors." He gave her his frank smile. "Why don't you take me into Tom's study? I'd relish a good cold drink, too."

Bettina dimpled suddenly. The dimples which became Georgia's soft oval cheeks were odd in her handsome and angular face. "How good you are!" she exclaimed under her breath.

"Nonsense," he said, but he was set at ease by his own goodness. He followed her into a large room whose three windows, placed side by side, faced upon a garden. It looked comfortable to him. He sank down in Tom's big leather chair and gave a great sigh. "Bettina, I'm so tired—so damned tired and confused—I've got to rest."

"Then rest here," she replied. She stood before him and they looked at each other.

He smiled suddenly. "I know why you look different—you haven't got an apron on."

"Tom won't let me wear aprons any more," she told him.

"Sally staying at the hotel?" he asked abruptly.

"Yes," Bettina said. Then after a second, she added, "This is a colored street."

"It is? Looks mighty nice!"

"Nice people live here."

"Where's Georgia?"

"She's with Miss Sally. They and Tom went to the museum with the school children. But she has a room here."

"Tom doesn't have school in summer, surely," he said.

"No—but he does have some work going on in the building for the neighborhood children. The summer's long and they get into mischief."

"Where are yours?"

"Leslie has a summer job in the store down the street. Georgy went with Georgia. The other two are out there—" She lifted her eyes to the garden and he saw a girl playing with a little boy. The girl's hair was softly curled down her back and it was a copper color. The sun shone on it. The little boy was very dark.

"That's Lettice, she was the baby when we left—and we have small Tom—that's all."

"Why don't you sit down?" Pierce asked.

"Because I am going to fetch you a cool drink," Bettina replied. She went away and he sat on, motionless. Their talk had been nothing but commonplace and yet that was extraordinary. He had talked to her as casually as though she were his real sister-in-law—as casually but not as intimately. He felt dazed and shaken. The world was completely upset. Here was where his own brother lived! But the house was a home. The garden was pretty and well kept and the walls were lined with flower beds. This room was clean and pleasant—a man's room, full of books. Through the open windows a scent drifted in which he could not recognize. He lay back in Tom's chair and closed his eyes and smelled the scent, a clean spiced odor. No one knew where he was. He could rest here. Tom's world—not his world—but so quiet and clean—

He must have dropped asleep. When he came back to himself Bettina was standing there again, looking at him with pitying soft eyes. She held a silver tray and on it a slender glass, frosted cold. She set the tray upon the table beside him.

"Indeed you are tired," she said in her rich voice. "When you have drunk this let me take you upstairs to Tom's room. You can stretch yourself on his bed and sleep."

"Don't tell Sally I'm here," he begged. "I'm too tired."

"I won't tell her," she promised.

"What's that sweet smell?" he asked.

"White clematis," she replied.

He drank the cool sharp drink thirstily in a few gulps and rose to his feet and followed her upstairs. Tom's room—then he did not share a room with Bettina. Yes, he could recognize Tom's room. It was a big room, with little furniture but that little solid and good. The windows were open, but the shutters were drawn, and the late afternoon breeze fluttered the white curtains. Bettina drew back the covers of the bed and he saw smooth white linen sheets. He wanted to sleep and sleep.

"Tom has a bathroom right there," she pointed to a door.

"He has rigged himself up a shower bath, he calls it. It's really wonderful. It will refresh you. Sleep and don't wake until you wake yourself. No one will call you."

She went away, and he stood looking about the dim, cool room. It had every small comfort that could be devised. Cold water stood in a pitcher by Tom's bed, books on the table, a bed lamp, a fire place for winter, a soft woven rag rug under his feet, a handwoven coverlet on the bed of delft blue and white. Bettina's work everywhere! He opened the door of the bathroom, and saw Tom's shower bath. He had heard of such things but had never seen one. He undressed, stood under something that looked like a flower sprinkler, pulled a chain and felt a rain of cool water descend upon him from a hidden tank above his head. He wiped himself dry with a handwoven towel, and opened drawers in Tom's bureaus until he found a nightshirt. Everything was in order, the clothes smelled clean and fresh with green lavender.

He dropped upon the bed and was instantly asleep.

Some time in the night he awoke. The chime of a clock in the house was still ringing in his ears. He could not tell the hour because he did not know how many times it had struck before he woke. But the moonlight was lying across the floor in stripes of gold. He sat up and listened. The house was still. Everyone was asleep. No, he heard voices, muted, floating upward from under his window, Tom's voice, then Bettina's. He got up and put on his shirt and trousers and opened his door. A hanging oil lamp lit the stairs and he went down, guided by the voices, to the end of the downstairs hall. He opened a door and there on a narrow brick terrace facing the garden, he saw Tom.

He was shocked to see the moonlight silver upon Tom's head. Tom greyhaired already, ahead of him!

"Tom!" he called softly, and Tom turned his head. His face was the same, thinner, but kind and severe together.

"Pierce!"

The two men ran into each other's arms without shame.

"How good of you to come!" Tom murmured.

"Nonsense!" Pierce said. He looked at Tom with wet eyes. "I don't know why I didn't come before."

"Sit down, Pierce. He's hungry, Bettina," Tom declared.

"Maybe I am," Pierce admitted.

"I have your supper waiting," Bettina said.

They went into the house, into the dining room, and at the table two places were laid.

"You two sit down, please," Bettina said. "Tom, you have a bite, too?"

"Only a little of your cold chicken broth, my dear," Tom said.

Bettina went away, and the two brothers looked at each other by the light of the candles Bettina had placed on the table.

"I want to ask you a thousand things," Pierce said abruptly.

"I want to answer them all," Tom said steadily.

"I don't know how long I can stay," Pierce went on. "The railroad is in a mess."

"But now you will come back again and again," Tom replied.

Pierce smiled and Bettina came in with food. It was delicious food and he was ravenous. While they ate Bettina came and went silently. He did not know where to begin with Tom. He wanted to tell him everything at once and he wanted to hear everything at once, and yet he did not know where to begin. And Tom sat in his easy quiet, without haste, in a relaxed peace. When Bettina had brought the iced lemon custard he looked up at her.

"Sit down now, Bettina," he said.

She sat down naturally at the end of the table, and Pierce could not but see her beauty. She had kept her slender figure. Tonight she wore a gown of soft green stuff—muslin, perhaps or silk—he did not know stuffs. But it was not rustling or stiff. White lace lay on her shoulders and in a knot on her bosom. Her dark hair sparkled with a few threads of silver, and she had put a white jasmine in the big coil at her nape. The old fire and anger of her youth had gone from her dark eyes. They were full of peace, tinged with sadness. Bettina, Tom's wife—

if ever he saw a woman who looked a wife it was she. He was surprised at his acceptance of her.

"We had a very interesting afternoon," Tom was saying, half lightly. "Sally's mind is keen. She wants to see everything—know everything. That's remarkable, Pierce."

"Has she been here?" Pierce asked.

"Every day," Tom said.

They hesitated. Then Pierce asked bluntly, "How does she take it, Tom?"

"Without a sign," Tom answered. He drank his tumbler of water and Bettina filled it again. "I've wanted to ask you something," Tom went on.

Pierce had finished his custard. "Why not?" he replied. He was beginning to feel wonderfully comfortable, rested and fed.

"Your son John writes to me, Pierce," Tom went on. "He wants to come and visit us. I said he had to ask you. He says that you wouldn't understand."

Pierce grinned. "I don't know why children always think their parents are nitwits."

"He's afraid of his mother," Tom said.

"Then he is the nitwit," Pierce said robustly. "Of course, Lucinda would object. But what of it?"

"Then shall I tell him—"

"You tell him to give me a chance," Pierce said, pushing back his chair.

They went back to the moonlit terrace. Bettina poured their coffee and then rose. "I think I shall retire, Tom, if you don't mind." She put out her hand and he took it and kissed it. He looked at her searchingly. "Only if you're tired," he said. "I'd rather you stayed with us."

"There's tomorrow," she said gently and went away.

In the silent garden, the moonlight outlining the shrubs in shadows and silvering the flowers, the two men sat on, smoking. The silence continued. But it was not heavy upon them now nor uneasy. It was peace, deep peace.

"This seems another world," Pierce said abruptly.

"It's our world," Tom said. "Mine, Bettina's, our children's."

"Are you lonely, Tom?"

"No, Pierce. I have everything."

"If Bettina should die—"

"I would live on here."

Pierce stirred in his chair. "But, Tom," he protested. "It's damned selfish, isn't it? You ought to be helping to clear up the mess we've got ourselves into—these strikes—the communism—the whole country's threatened."

"No," Tom said gently. "I don't have to help in those things. They're all parts of the struggle. I've made my struggle—so has Bettina. We've won through."

"To what?" Pierce asked.

"To our own peace," Tom answered in tranquillity.

The dreamlike calm of his spirit persisted. He woke the next morning and Tom's room was familiar to him and yet strange, as though he had waked in his own room but in a strange house. He lay on the pillows, not caring what the hour. The house was full of small pleasant sounds. Children's voices came up from the garden and he heard quiet footsteps pass his door. Then a clear but muted voice rose through the silence. He listened and heard not a hymn nor a spiritual but an old English lullaby which his own mother used to sing to him and to Tom. It must be one of Tom's children and it must be Georgy. He knew Georgia's voice and it was not hers. Hers was deep and tender but this voice was high and clear, a bright rich soprano. It broke off suddenly as though someone had hushed it and he knew it had been stopped for him. He got up, lazily conscience-smitten, and curious, too, to see Tom's children.

When he went downstairs Tom heard his footsteps and came to the door of the study. By the light of the morning Tom looked calm and poised, his fair skin ruddy and his blue eyes clear. He was as slender as ever, his shoulders as straight. The youngest child whom Pierce had seen only in the garden came toddling through a door and Tom picked him up and held him. He saw the love in Tom's eyes and felt his own heart shaken.

"This fellow I haven't seen," he said, trying to speak lightly. He took the child's fat brown hand.

"Small Tom, this is your uncle," Tom said. The boy did not speak, but he gazed at Pierce with large eyes full of serene interest.

"Can't you say good morning?" Tom inquired of his son.

Small Tom shook his head and the men laughed to ease their emotion.

"Come and have your breakfast," Tom said. He put the child down and they walked together to the dining room. Georgy was there, arranging a silver bowl of roses. She looked up gravely. Pierce realized that yesterday the children had been kept from him, but today he would see them as they were in this house.

"My daughter," Tom said formally. "Georgy, this is your uncle."

Georgy put out a narrow smooth hand, and Pierce, somewhat to his own astonishment, took it.

"How do you do," he said.

"Mother asks, how will you have your eggs?" she inquired, in a soft clear voice.

"Scrambled, please," Pierce said. Tom's daughter was an exceedingly pretty girl, and he smiled at her as he sat down. "Did I hear you singing?" he demanded.

She flushed. "I forgot," she said. "Mother had told me to be quiet."

"It was a pleasant way to wake," Pierce said. He began to eat the sliced oranges in front of him.

"Bring the coffee, my dear," Tom said gently. He who knew Pierce so well could feel the trembling of foundations within his brother. Pierce was behaving wonderfully, out of the natural goodness of his nature, but change must not come too fast.

"You had your breakfast?" Pierce shot up his dark eyebrows.

"We have our family breakfast early," Tom replied. "Leslie has to go to work at seven, and the children like to play in the garden in the cool of the morning."

"I haven't seen Leslie—this time," Pierce said.

"He'll be home for lunch," Tom replied.

The door opened and his second daughter stood there, a plate of toast in her hand.

"Come in, Lettice, while the toast's hot," he said.

She came tiptoeing in, trying to take great care, her fringed eyes wide, and her tongue between her lips.

Pierce could not keep back his smile for children. "That's wonderful toast," he said heartily. "I want a piece right now."

Something in her shy and dewy look made him think of Georgia. She had Georgia's softness of contour. He watched her while she tiptoed away again, not speaking a word.

"Handsome children, Tom," he said.

"I think so," Tom agreed.

Both brothers knew that the dam they were building with their scanty commonplace words must break. They must open their hearts to each other. Pierce must know Tom's life, and he must tell Tom everything. They were too close, strangely closer than ever after these years of separation.

"Sally here?" Pierce muttered.

Tom shook his head. "Not yet this morning."

"Hold her off, will you?" Pierce did not look at him. "I have to get things straight myself, Tom."

"I know," Tom said gently. His voice, always deep, had taken on a still deeper quality. The harshness of youth had disappeared from it. No, there was something else. Pierce recognized it. Tom had so long heard Bettina's voice and the soft voices of her people that his own voice had grown slow and deep.

"Georgia knew you and I would have to talk," Tom went on. "She is taking Sally to shop this morning."

"She's staying with Sally at the hotel, isn't she?" Pierce asked.

"Of course," Tom replied. He hesitated and then went on resolutely. "Pierce, Georgia wants to leave Malvern. We've always told her we had a room for her when she wanted to come. Now she does."

To save himself Pierce could not answer naturally. "I don't

know what Lucinda will say," he murmured. He took a fourth slice of toast which he did not want.

"Georgia is afraid of that," Tom said. "But I told her I knew you would wish her to do as she likes."

"Did she tell you to talk to me?" Pierce inquired.

"No, as a matter of fact she asked me not to," Tom replied. frankly. "I do it on my own responsibility. Let her stay, Pierce. She's never been a servant."

"I know that," Pierce said. The toast grew dry in his mouth and he swallowed coffee to wash it down. Then he touched his lips with his napkin and got up.

"Let's get away together, Tom," he said. "Somehow my heart feels ready to break over you."

"You must not feel so," Tom said quickly. "I am happy, Pierce. You'll see—"

They went out in silence to the study and Tom closed the door and turned the key.

As though the whole house knew the door had been closed and the key turned a new silence surrounded them. The garden was full of sunshine, but there was not a voice in it of child or of bird. It was a hot and windless morning. The shades had been partly drawn and the room was darkened. A jug of water stood on the table, frosted and cool and beside it was a bowl of early grapes.

"Bettina knew we'd want to shut ourselves up," Tom said with a smile. "She knows everything without being told." He sat down opposite Pierce on an easy chair. "It is a great experience to live with someone like Bettina," he said, looking straight at Pierce. "Uncanny sometimes, when I feel the thoughts being plucked out of my brain, almost before I've thought them!"

"I suppose so," Pierce mumbled.

Tom held the lead. He filled his pipe and lit it, and went on, his words slow and clear. "It comes, I think, from an inheritance of having to divine what men and women who hold the power over them are thinking and feeling. When I remember that, I am angry. But as a gift, it's subtle and profound. Bettina is subtle and profound—and deep and clear and honest as a child."

Pierce could not answer. Let Tom pour himself out! He sat looking at his brother.

Tom looked back with his fearless blue gaze. "What I want to make clear to you, Pierce, before we begin any talk at all is that never, for one second, not in the day nor in the depths of the night, do I regret what I have done. The life I live is the one life I can live—anything else would have been meaningless for me. . . . I am *happy*, I tell you, to the bottom of my being."

"I will believe that," Pierce said, "but don't pretend to me that it has been easy, Tom, for that I won't believe."

"It wasn't easy when I was trying to live in two worlds," Tom said. "But I have to thank Lucinda for showing me," he added.

"Lucinda?"

"Yes, Lucinda threw me out of your house that night, more or less—remember?"

"No," Pierce said.

"Yes, you do, Pierce," Tom said. "Be honest, man! If I had wanted to live at Malvern I'd have had to give up Bettina."

"I don't think Lucinda is unreasonable," Pierce answered. "She wouldn't have said anything—if Bettina hadn't lived there by the side of the road—and the children—"

"She wouldn't have said anything if I had kept Bettina hidden, and the children illegitimate," Tom said harshly.

"Well," Pierce said hesitating—"You know how she—how we all, for that matter—were brought up."

"The war—those long hours in prison," Tom said abruptly. "I had the chance to think myself through. If I had done what Lucinda wanted—it would have meant that I had—lost the war—so far as I was concerned. Don't you see, Pierce, when I knew I loved Bettina—I had to love her openly? The children are ours, hers and mine, could I be ashamed of that? If so, then what was all the shooting for?"

Pierce felt Lucinda's hands on his heart. "Still and all,

Tom, you have to acknowledge—that if all the white men who have—have—had children by—by—"

"Go on," Tom said coldly.

Pierce went on doggedly. The sweat sprang under the roots of his hair—"If they insisted on—on making the whole thing legal—where would women like Lucinda be? Tom—you can't just think of yourself. You've got to think of our race."

Tom bit the end of his pipe. The two brothers stared at each other. Then Tom spoke. "I do think only of myself and I shall think only of myself. What any race does is not my business. I am one man—Tom Delaney. If I act with what I consider honor, if that honor gives me satisfaction, if I am happy and my children are happy, then I consider that I have done my duty by the race to which I belong."

"All right, Tom," Pierce said steadily. "You've been wanting to say it this long time to me, I reckon. Now you've said it."

Tom drew a deep breath. "Yes!" he cried. "I've said it."

"All right, Tom," Pierce repeated. "What next?"

Tom laughed. "It's your turn," he retorted.

"There's nothing much I have to tell," Pierce said mildly. "Malvern is about what I'd planned, you know. Martin is finishing this year at the University and then he thinks he'll take up farming with me. He wants to go into cattle in a big way. Carey wants to be a lawyer, I reckon. John will enter in the fall. I don't understand him very well. He doesn't like horses. Sally—you've seen Sally! Lucie is Lucinda in small type. That's all my children."

He spoke half sadly and Tom leaned on the arms of his chair. "Where's your heart, Pierce?" he inquired softly.

"Well, Tom, I don't know," Pierce answered. He wanted to open his heart and he did not know how. He had not for so long opened it even to himself. He smiled wryly at his brother. "Sometimes I wonder if being so busy about farming and horses and building and all the hundred and one things that go on around a place like Malvern haven't pretty well dried up my heart."

He considered telling Tom about John MacBain and Molly

and decided he would not. It was not important enough to him. He remembered with sour sweet discomfort the day that Georgia had knelt before him—and this he could not tell. He did not know what it meant and he preferred not to know.

"I'm glad Georgia is going to live here," he said with such seeming irrelevance that Tom looked surprised. "I mean," Pierce said, "I feel she's very lonely now at Malvern, and while I can't help it and it's none of my business, I know it's not the place for her. Joe wants to marry her—but I know that's impossible."

"I should think so," Tom said with indignation.

Pierce hastened away from smouldering coals. He had no wish to see them blaze into the atmosphere of this room. The air of freedom in which Tom lived made him at once envious and afraid. He veered away from himself. "I suppose if I were to say what concerns me most, it is the state of the nation. Tom, sometimes I wonder why we fought the war. Things are in a worse mess than ever."

Tom looked at him with calm, waiting eyes. So would he view any turmoil from now until eternity, Pierce thought ruefully. Only out of complete personal satisfaction could a man so look at the struggles of others.

"These strikes," he went on gloomily. "They've broken out all over the country. Tom, what does it mean? I've been so busy at Malvern I haven't kept up. My dividends came in as steady as sunrise until a year or two ago. The depression has hit everybody—wouldn't you think the railroad workers would see it reasonable that their wages have to be cut?"

"They don't see why business is bad," Tom returned.

"Who does?" Pierce retorted irritably. He felt on his own ground again. "Who on earth knows why business goes up and down like this? We have to take the bad with the good."

"Their good is so small—their bad so nearly—nothing." Tom observed.

Pierce looked at his brother with deep suspicion. "Tom, you aren't a communist!"

"What makes you think I am?" Tom countered.

"It would explain a lot of things," Pierce said.

"You mean it would explain my marriage," Tom said.

"Well—" Pierce muttered.

Tom broke in. "No, I'm not a communist. I'm a school-master, and outside my home and my children that's all I'm interested in. I've made my revolution, Pierce. Let other men make theirs."

"People talk about revolution," Pierce said. "What does it get anybody?"

"Mine brought me everything I wanted," Tom said, smiling.

"I wish you'd speak sensibly," Pierce cried. "What I want to know is—do you think these strikes are being fomented by foreigners over in Europe?"

Tom replied mildly, "I don't know, Pierce. But I do know that when men are frightened and discontented they gather around any man who is not afraid."

He was pressing fresh tobacco into his pipe and he did not look up. "I know that because in a small way people gather around me here in this street. Nobody even in this town knows or cares about—people like Bettina and Georgia—men and women of intelligence—children of slaves wanting to be free—"

"Niggras?" Pierce interposed cruelly.

"Yes," Tom said.

Pierce looked at him curiously. "Tom, you mix around with niggras all the time?"

"Inside this town," Tom said in his deep steady voice, "there is a little secret world. Men and women and children inhabit it. They have their homes. They are friends, they make music, they listen to music. Some of the theaters here let them come in, some don't. We all went to hear Eric Tyne." He looked at Pierce and smiled. "He sat in that very chair where you're sitting. He came into our world—world-sized people do. Edwin Booth—" Tom broke off, and smiled again.

Pierce stared at him in silence.

"The people in this secret world know all the places that

let them come in," Tom went on. "They go where they can be free and they stay away from the places—and the people— who want to push them down again. It's a world within a world you might call it—but I call it the world of tomorrow —the pilot world. We're bringing our children up in it— they'll be ready—"

"Ready for what?" Pierce asked abruptly.

"Ready for tomorrow," Tom said. Tears came into his eyes but he looked through them steadfastly at his brother.

After Tom had left him Pierce sat on in the study alone for awhile. Noon came and in the hall he heard Sally's voice, and then Georgia's. He dreaded to go out and meet them. Could he be natural and himself in this house? And was his child, Sally, at home here? He grew solemn at the thought. Sally mixing with such people! What if one of them wanted to marry her? Lucinda would never forgive him. But could he forgive himself? His gorge rose and he got up and paced the floor. He'd take her home with him, of course—tomorrow, anyway. And he would not allow her to come here again. The horror of his thinking impelled him to the door and he went out into the hall and followed the voices across into the sitting room. There Sally sat, Tom's baby in her arms, holding him as she had held her dolls. She looked up at her father and met his troubled eyes.

"Papa, did you ever see such an adorable baby?"

Thus she postponed his questions and thus she brought him into the circle of the house. Georgy was at her side and Lettice was staring at her, forefinger in her mouth. The children were brushed and clean for their midday meal. The door opened and a tall lad came in. It was Leslie. He stood still, gazing with wary shyness at Pierce.

"Leslie?" Pierce asked. This was Tom's son! He looked unsmiling at the grave boy. Intelligent eyes—too sad—clever thin face, delicate lips—only the extravagant curling eye-lashes and the waving hair—but the boy was three-fourths white—

"Yes," Leslie said.

Pierce put out his hand and Leslie smiled, and put his own narrow dark hand into it. A good boy, Pierce told himself, a fine boy—own cousin to his sons! But Martin would never acknowledge that.

Then the door opened and Georgia came in.

"Luncheon is ready, please," she said, as though at Malvern. She looked at Pierce frankly, smiled slightly, and closed the door again.

But nothing else was at all like Malvern. Tom sat at the head of the long table and Bettina at the foot, and Georgia at Tom's right and Sally at his left, and Pierce at Bettina's right. He kept saying to himself, "This is Tom's house—this is Tom's family." He ate his food, finding it difficult to speak. Once he asked Leslie what he did, and listened to his reply that he clerked in the store for the summer but that in the autumn he would go back to school.

"What are you going to make of yourself?" he inquired.

"I don't know yet," Leslie replied. His young voice was quiet and courteous and without hint of subservience.

A colored maid served the meal well, and once an elderly woman came in from the kitchen with a hot dish. Pierce ate with appreciation, in spite of the strangeness, for the food was good and delicately flavored. The children were gay. Once Small Tom cried in his high chair and once Georgy fell into an argument with Lettice. Tom corrected them firmly.

Pierce sat in a dream, seeing everything. Again and again his eyes came back to Georgia. She was removed from him by the length of the table and she did not once speak to him. She spoke very little to anyone. His eyes caught hers once and both looked away quickly. Only Sally was herself.

The meal was over and suddenly he knew he could stand no more of Tom's house. He must get away into his own world again, for here he was confused to the depths of his being.

He motioned to Sally and she came tripping to his side. "Come out in the garden with me," he ordered. They stepped out of the open French windows upon the narrow brick terrace and from it into the garden path. She clung to his arm.

"Sally, I want you to come away with me," he said.

"Oh, Papa!" she wailed. "I'm having a lovely time."

"I need you," he said sternly. "I'm lonely and all mixed up in my mind. Let's you and I go back together to Malvern, honey. I want to be alone there for a bit, before your mama and Lucie come back."

She looked up at him and saw with alarm that his lips were trembling and at once she melted. "Of course, Papa," she said and squeezed his arm. They walked up and down the length of the garden a few times. "But, Papa—just one thing—"

"Yes?" He did not know what she would ask now after these days.

"Georgia doesn't want to come back to us."

"I know," he said.

"Did she tell you?"

"Tom did."

"You've got to let her stay."

"Of course—"

"And help Mama not to mind!"

"You and I'll do that—" He pressed her clasped hands against his side.

When they turned again Georgia was standing in the door and Sally called her.

"Georgia, come here—"

She came down the terrace steps, the sunshine bright upon her white dress. Pierce looked at her with revulsion and admiration. He was afraid of her beauty. The sun revealed her flawless creamy skin, the golden depths of her dark eyes, and he looked down at the path as they paused before her.

"Papa says you may stay, Georgia, and we will make it right with Mama."

"Thank you very much, Mr. Delaney," Georgia said.

He looked up and met her eyes. "I know you haven't been very happy at Malvern."

"Yes—I have been happy," Georgia answered. "But it is better now for me to leave it—and find my own place."

He bowed his head, and kept Sally's hand tight under his arm, and drew her with him into the house, and Georgia stood alone in the garden.

"Poor Papa," Sally said.

They were back at Malvern again and he and Sally were riding along the familiar woodland paths. His horse was Beauty's great-grandchild, and Sally rode her own golden bay that he had bought for her once in Kentucky.

"Explain your pity," he said gaily. It was good to be safe at home.

"You're living before the war, Papa," Sally said smartly.

"You mean I'm old," he said.

"No—because Martin is just like you. It's Malvern that does it—all this—"

She waved her riding crop at the rolling green of the hills and blue of mountains beyond. "You made this and Martin inherits it, and neither of you can bear to give it up."

"Who's asking us to give it up?" Pierce demanded.

"Nobody, darling—but you're afraid somebody might!"

"You and Carey and John—you're more enlightened, I suppose?" he said with heavy pretense at sarcasm.

She shook her head. "I don't like Carey—he'll just be a sharp lawyer. Carey has no principle—did you know that, Papa? But John—oh, well, one of these days you'll quarrel with John and maybe throw him out of the house and he knows it. He's getting ready for it."

He was aghast at her intuition. It corroborated his own. He was afraid of his third son. The boy did not reveal himself.

"And you?" he asked, avoiding his fears.

"Oh, Lucie and I—we don't belong in Malvern anyway—we'll have to be married off and go somewhere else. It doesn't matter about women."

He looked at her lovely face. She held her head high, and he saw only her sweet profile, the red gold hair piled under the little black derby hat. "Sally, I wish you wouldn't talk like that—you'll always be my daughter, whomever you marry—"

"Unless I marry someone you don't like," she amended and flashed him a smile lit by intense blue eyes.

"I can't imagine that," he said gravely.

"You mustn't imagine what I can or can't do," she said willfully.

He felt he must strike now upon this hot iron. "Sally, I sincerely hope the visit to Tom's house has not upset you."

She did not answer and he went on. "I confess it upset me very much. Tom has done something, which if many men did it, could destroy our whole nation—our civilization, indeed—"

Sally interrupted him. "I haven't seen anybody I want to marry yet, if that's what you mean, Papa."

He was so relieved that he was impelled to hide it. "I am not thinking only of your marriage, Sally. I am thinking of—of—of the foundations of our country." He went on reluctantly. "We are a white nation—and we must stay white—"

His eyes met hers, and he was shocked by the brilliant, mocking mischief hers revealed. She burst into laughter.

"Oh, Papa, how funny men are!"

He stared at her, and she took out a tiny lace handkerchief from the breast pocket of her coat and wiped her eyes. "As if Uncle Tom had really done anything unusual! He's only owned up to it, that's all." She was laughing again—high laughter, with an edge of heartbreak in it. "But that is very unusual—I grant you, Papa—and maybe such honesty does threaten the—the nation!"

"Sally!" he cried.

But she shook her head and smiling too brightly she struck her horse hard and galloped ahead of him and disappeared down the long green lane. He let her go. He was frightened at the glimpse she had shown him into herself, and he wanted to see no more.

When he got home there was a telegram from John Mac-Bain asking him to come at once to Chicago. He left, thankfully, without seeing Sally. Lucinda would be home by the time he came back, and the house would be itself again.

He met John in the red plush parlor of the bridal suite of the railroad hotel, and was shocked by his haggard looks. John sat at a small round table drinking whiskey from a cloudy glass tumbler. He had not shaved or washed, and he did not get up when Pierce came in.

"Thank God you've come," he groaned. "I haven't slept in I don't know how many nights, Pierce—I got here yesterday from Pittsburgh—there's only four hundred police here—they can't handle the mob."

"That means more war," Pierce exclaimed.

John nodded. "Want some whiskey?"

"No," Pierce said.

John poured half a tumbler and drank it down. He got up and wiped his hand across his beard. "You come with me and see what we're up against—but you better leave that silk hat here—it'll only be a target for pot shots—"

Pierce took off his hat and followed John into the street. They hailed a horse cab lurking in an alley.

"Market Street," John ordered the driver.

"You don't want to go there," the driver remonstrated. "Why, there must be ten thousand people now in that mob."

"That's why I want to go," John said grimly. "Put us down a block away and we'll walk—"

They took the ride in silence, unwilling to reveal to the driver who they were. A block away he set them down and John paid the fare. They could hear the roar of the mob and the loud, shrieking harangue of voices. They turned the corner of Market Street and saw a sea of heads. "Good God, John," Pierce muttered, "where have they come from?"

"By Gawd, the communists have forced everybody to stop work," John said sternly. "We'll wedge our way in—then you listen for yourself—and tell me what we ought to do, Pierce —if you can."

They edged their way through the crowd. No one noticed them. The eyes of men and women alike were glazed and

unseeing. There were six platforms along the street, a man
haranguing on each, and to his astonishment Pierce heard
German as well as English. He stood almost directly beneath
a young man with blond uncombed hair and frenzied face.

"Better for a thousand of us to be shot in the streets
than ten thousand of us to starve!" the young man screamed,
and a deep roar rose from the mob.

He felt the mob respond to the wild words that were being
thrown to them. They began to surge about him, to move
in a terrible rhythm. He felt himself caught upon the waves,
twisted and pressed upon. Yet no one knew him or cared
who he was. The movement was bestial and mad, and he
grew frightened.

"Let's get out of this," he muttered to John.

John nodded, and hooking arms they began to work their
way out doggedly, breaking across the rhythm, silent in the
midst of the roar, until they were free at last, staggering out
of the mob as though a sea had thrown them upon a beach.

They went back to the hotel and Pierce stripped himself
of his clothes. They stank of the mob. He bathed himself
and dressed clean from head to foot.

"Go and wash and shave yourself, John," he commanded.
"You and I have got to get hold of things."

An hour later they had eaten and Pierce was planning
resolutely what must be done.

"This isn't going to be finished within a day," he told
John. "You come with me and we'll go and see the mayor."

"You going to wear that hat?" John asked. Pierce had put
on his silk top hat again.

"I am," Pierce said with determination. "I don't belong
to the mob and I want everybody to know it."

It was two o'clock in the afternoon and the mob had taken
possession of the railroad yards. They had the news from a
terrified clerk as they stepped from the hotel door.

"Half of them are drunk!" the fellow wailed to John.

"Get out of my way," Pierce said contemptuously, and
pushed him aside.

They drove to the mayor's offices and found that he was

at home. They were ushered into a great parlor where the mayor was staring out of the long windows, his hands in his pockets, his hat on the back of his head. About the room were his aides and secretaries.

"I have come to demand that the property of the railroad be protected by the Grand Army of the Republic," Pierce said formally, when a doorman had announced them.

"Great guns!" the mayor replied, "I am thinking of the whole city! Why, sir, that mob will reach twenty thousand by night!"

"Why don't you get the whole police force armed?" Pierce demanded.

"We haven't guns enough," the mayor groaned.

"There must be guns—" Pierce retorted. "Guns hidden in attics or hung on walls—relics from the war, if nothing else."

His tall upright frame, his harsh voice, his bold blue eyes took command of the wavering and frightened men. The mayor yelled at his henchmen and they began to scurry from the room.

Pierce sat down by a rosewood table and banged it with his fist. "And now," he said loudly, "send for the Army!"

The mayor hesitated and bit his nails.

"It isn't of Chicago alone I'm thinking," Pierce said, "nor of the railroad—it's the nation we have to save. If this mob is unchecked, mobs will rise in a dozen other big cities."

"I'll do what I can," the mayor promised. In an hour the order had gone and they waited for reply. It came before midnight. The Grand Army of the Republic was on its way. Meantime messengers brought more news of the mob. There had been a battle on Market Street, but the mob was dispersed. Four policemen were wounded, one dead. The railroad roundhouse had been taken back and the fires in the engines put out. An hour later there were five more dead. Again no one knew the number of the dead among the mob. Whenever a man fell, he was hidden.

Pierce and John slept in the mayor's house that night. No meals were served in the great dining room but servants brought platters of sandwiches and cold meats into the parlor which had become the center of the city's control, and the men ate little and drank much. Pierce went to bed in a stupor of weariness and was awakened again by gun shots in the morning. When he had dressed and hastened downstairs he found that the first contingents of the Army had arrived, had met the overflow of the mob in an open space near a hall, and had dispersed them. Meantime the meeting in the hall had gone on behind locked doors.

By noon six more policemen were wounded. Still no one knew or counted the number of wounded in the unarmed mob. The rioters continued to take their dead away as soon as they fell.

In the disordered parlor Pierce sat all day listening, suggesting, conferring, but underneath activity he was aware of a deep empty silence. What did this war mean, here in the heart of his country? Who were the enemies—and for whom did he fight? He left his own questions unanswered.

The strange war ended the next day in a foolish way which only confused him the more. A crowd of Bohemian women, angered because two of their lads had been killed the night before, gathered together from the small Bohemian villages on the outskirts of the city. They fought fiercely, out of outraged motherhood, until in the middle of the evening the hardbitten Regulars appeared and dispersed them. By the middle of the next day the rioters had been overcome and the city took stock of its wounds. Shops had been looted and men robbed. A farmer coming into the city with his vegetables had been waylaid and beaten and his little store of money taken away. To the unrest of the working people had been added the selfishness of petty thieves and the lawlessness of gangsters.

"We've licked them," the mayor sighed, and wiped his bald head with a handkerchief so dirty that it left a smear of black across his face.

"Wait," Pierce said and opened a telegram that a boy held at his elbow.

It announced the attack of a mob in San Francisco upon Chinatown.

"I'm going," John said. "I'll drive these communists into the Pacific Ocean and hold 'em under!"

"I am going home," Pierce said heavily.

The strikes subsided and the war ended slowly as the weeks passed. Everywhere the mob was put down by Regulars from the Federal Army. In his library Pierce studied the newspapers and approved, but with deep disquiet. Of course the mob must be put down. Order must be upheld. He could not hide from himself that he was profoundly relieved when Malvern stood safe once more upon a subdued working class. But, out of his disquiet, he now recommended and worked for substantial wage increases. He wrote long, detailed letters to every member of the Board of Directors. To Henry Mallows he wrote with peculiar insistence: "I tell you, I have seen the faces of these men and women—yes, women, too. They are savage with despair. In the interests of our own security we must grant them enough for life, even if our own dividends shrink for a while."

To Jim McCagney he wrote: "We overbuilt. Let's face our own mistake. We went too fast for the country. But the country will catch up with us if we can be willing to make less profit for the next few years. It's a great country, and we haven't begun to produce what we can. I'm a farmer and I know."

At Malvern he steadily set himself to bigger crops and finer animals, as his duty to the nation.

But underneath all his efforts he still knew secret terror. He woke at night in a sweat, seeing the faces of the mob. In his dreams they were mixed up strangely with Tom and Tom's house and the faces of Tom's children—yes, and of Georgia's. He woke frightened even on the clear bright mornings of autumn and harvest and the peace which followed the summer's storms.

"We've got to do something about the poor," he told Lucinda again and again and at the next Board meeting in a restored Baltimore he argued his fellow members into setting up a relief department in the company for the benefit of the sick and aged and those who had suffered from accident in their work.

He met the solid opposition of everyone, even of John Mac-Bain.

"We licked them with the help of the Army, and that's how we'll have to lick them always," John declared.

But Pierce argued his case stubbornly. "For our own safety it is better to have contented workingmen than discontented ones."

"You can't satisfy workingmen," Jonathan Yates said with his thin tired smile. He was more relentless than any of them, now that he had risen above his fellows.

"We've got to be realistic," Henry Mallows said. His narrow face hardened. He tore the gold band from a slender cigar and lit it. Perfume spread in the air with the smoke. "Anything that doesn't bring in returns to the stockholders—" he went on.

John MacBain looked at him with the repulsion he would have showed a snake. "Oh hell," he said suddenly. "I'm with Pierce Delaney, after all."

"And I," Pierce said quietly, "consider it the height of realism and self-interest for the rich to be generous to the poor. There is a point, Mallows, where it is good business to keep workingmen alive."

But it was not until the next year, when the new decade began and the depression was over, that Pierce succeeded in establishing his relief department. Six thousand dollars were laid aside, and within the first five months almost six hundred people were aided in one way or another.

In his library at Malvern, Pierce read the reports and approved them and felt that with his own hands he was building a dam against the disaster of the future.

# Eight

THE DANGEROUS DECADE passed, and the inexplicable tides of prosperity rolled over the country again. At Malvern, Pierce put up new greenhouses and stables. When John MacBain came in January his land hunger grew beyond control.

Pierce had made the library into his business office, and was dreaming of a new south wing which would be the formal library for the house. The plans lay on the great oak able in the middle of the room. Less and less often now did Pierce leave home and more and more men came to Malvern to see him. They were glad to come for the house was famous. Secretly Pierce was somewhat ashamed of the new livery which Lucinda had designed for the men servants. The crimson and yellow seemed to him absurd. But he humored her in all things and laughed with his friends gently behind her back. Lucinda was still pretty enough to be excused for follies.

Pierce stood before the great window and surveyed his lands, now white under a foot of soft snow. "John, you might as well sell me your place—I've rented all these years."

John, sitting in a wing chair by the roaring fire, was studying a sheet of paper. "I'll leave the house as a summer place for you and Mollie," Pierce went on.

John did not look up. "I don't want that house," he said drily. "I haven't been in it for a handful of years and you know it."

"Then I'll let Carey have it some day," Pierce said promptly. "I've been wanting to settle a house on him when he marries. Martin's to have this one, of course."

"You going to let him come here after he's married?" John inquired. Martin's engagement to Mary Louise Wyeth had been announced at the great Christmas party.

"The place is big enough for us all," Pierce replied. He had been pleased with the small demure girl whom Martin had brought to Malvern for inspection. Martin had grown up handsome and strong and comfortably average as a young man. He had been graduated from the University decently but without honors. He danced beautifully and rode well. Lucinda was enormously proud of him. Carey was a shrewd thin young chap, already a skilled debater. It was useful to have a lawyer in the family—a good second son, prudent and contented with his place.

"What are you going to provide for your third son, you lord of the manor?" John inquired with affectionate sarcasm.

"So far John doesn't seem to want anything of me," Pierce replied. He sat down in the great chair opposite his friend.

"Every family has to have a radical," John said absently. He pursed his lips over his papers. "You're going to get a pretty piece of money this year, Pierce."

"That's why I want to buy your land," Pierce retorted.

John grinned, and looked at him over his spectacles. "You've a lust for land. If I weren't an honest man I could bleed you white!"

Pierce smiled. They were very close, he and John. He had learned to love this man as his own brother. John knew him through and through, all his softness as well as his ruthlessness. There was no softness in John. He was as hard and driving as his own beloved locomotives.

"Though some sons-of-guns are talking about laying down a strike road next to ours, by Gawd," John said.

"I suppose we can buy them out," Pierce said mildly.

"Hell no," John said briskly. "Let them lay it and spend their money! Then we'll run them out of business—make cars better than theirs and our engines faster. When they're busted we'll buy them out cheap."

Pierce gazed into the flaming logs. When he built the new library he was going to make an even bigger chimney piece. He yielded to the meditative reflective mood which became more and more natural to him as he grew older. Had Malvern not belonged to him—and he to Malvern—what would he have been? A very different man! He did not deceive himself. In the night when he woke and lay alone with himself he remembered his youth and the troubled ideals and dreams that had stirred in him after the war. His heart still moved when he thought of the young men who had died under his command. As clearly as he saw the faces of his own sons he could see young Barnstable's face as he lay dead, his left arm and shoulder torn away. Pierce had sworn in those days that he would make a better world. It had been a better world for him and for his children, but he was not sure of anything else. He had made Malvern fulfill only his own dreams for himself.

"You and Lucinda going to Baltimore in October for the big shindig?" John asked. He put down the papers and began to fill his pipe.

"Lucinda won't want to miss it, I am sure." Pierce replied. "But I confess, John, I hate more and more to leave Malvern."

"I can't blame you for that," John said. "But you ought to go, Pierce. Not many American cities can celebrate a hundred and fifty years—and they're going to give the railroad a fine place in the parade."

"You don't expect me to join the parade, I hope," Pierce said smiling.

The door opened and a man servant came in with fresh logs. He scarcely knew his own servants any more since Lucinda had hired an English housekeeper. He had only stipulated that the people on the place be kept in the house. But the children grew up fast. He had an idea that this young fellow was one of Joe's younger brothers. Joe had married a pot-black young Negress the year after Georgia left. At the thought of Georgia he felt an old confusion, almost shy. But he did not allow himself to think of her.

"I'm going to try out that new engine in May," John went on. "I expect it to make a mile in two minutes, maybe in one."

Pierce got up restlessly. He paced the room, around the table, passed the window, and came back again to stand before the leaping flames that were roaring up the wide chimney. He said absently, "Strange that the last time we went to Baltimore the country looked as though it were going to pieces! Now we're all riding high again—I'll never understand the one or the other." No, he would not see Georgia again when he went to Tom's. It was too dangerous. Last time Lucinda—

"We are selling more abroad than we're buying. That's why," John said confidently, "money is coming into the country."

"It's not as simple as that," Pierce mused.

He stood gazing into the fire. At one end of a pine log a narrow blue flame darted out like a sword and licked its way through the mass of coals, twice as hot and twice as fierce as ordinary flame.

What had become of the surging mobs of people who had risen to burn the roundhouses and the stations and the houses of the rich in the decade through which they had passed? They were silent now, but for how long? For his lifetime, perhaps—but would Martin be strong enough for the next generation? Nothing had been really solved. Nobody knew, nobody understood, why there had been a crisis or why now the crisis had passed, and until people understood causes—

"There has to be a topdog," John was saying confidently. "If men like you and me don't stay on top, Pierce, these radicals and socialists will ride us. And with that lot go the professional reformers and the internationalists—all enemies of the republic, I say."

"I suppose so," Pierce said absently. Had he been as single-minded as John MacBain he would have been able to enjoy even Malvern more than he had. His love for Malvern was terrifying, and he knew it was because he felt it always possible that he might lose it. The life he had built up so carefully in beauty and richness and success might collapse. It was more than the danger in the nation. The possibility of weakness was within himself. Lucinda never let him forget that he was Tom's brother.

Lucinda came in at this moment, black velvet trailing to her feet. She was still so beautiful that he could not fail to see it and to admire her for preserving her gift.

"Are you two men going to spend the evening here?" she demanded. "The guests will come at any moment, Pierce— and Molly is back from her ride, John."

As soon as Lucinda entered the room, doubt left it. She was sure of herself and of her right to enter and to stay. And then behind her the hall rose to life. The great front door opened with a swirl of snow, voices mingled with laughter, and at the same moment Molly came downstairs and into the library. Molly by heroism had kept her figure slim enough to ride her horse. Her full face was handsome and rosy and her red hair held no grey. She and John were still together but he had ceased to ask her what she did and she went away from him for weeks at a time. Pierce knew because he had found John alone at his Wheeling mansion, wintry and silent, one November day. They had talked business all evening and not once had he mentioned Molly until at midnight they had stood up to part.

"She's left me for a while, Pierce," John said with dry lips.

"On a visit," Pierce said gently.

"Yes—just a visit—" John said. He looked at Pierce with such shame and agony in his eyes that Pierce had looked away.

"The war changed all of us," he said. "I often wonder what I'd have been—without it. . . . And Tom, of course—"

"Yes, it wrecked Tom," John said. He considered Tom as one dead. Then he cleared his throat. "I feel such awful pity for—for Molly, Pierce. I want you to know I don't blame her. I'm only grateful—she'll never leave me for good. She's told me that—I didn't ask it—but she promised me."

"Molly's a good woman," Pierce had said gravely.

"Yes," John had replied. Then after a second, "The war wasn't her fault—nor mine."

"No," Pierce had said.

John had looked at him and a strange bewilderment came into his eyes. "Whose fault was it though, Pierce?"

"God knows, I don't, any more," Pierce had said. "All that we fought for seemed so clear when we were fighting—those fellows dying! But now—it's all a murk. Even the ones who were slaves aren't better off." He had spoken savagely at that moment. Had there never been a war Tom would have been at Malvern.

Molly came up to him now and slipped her arm through his. Lucinda met his eyes with smiling tolerance. Long ago she had ceased to have any jealousy toward Molly. He knew that. But now sudden perception came into his mind. Had her tolerance begun after that first time he had gone to see Georgia? Had she said to herself, "Let him have anyone except Georgia?" He felt Molly's plump shoulder pressing his arm and could barely keep himself from moving from her in repulsion at Lucinda's duplicity.

"Come!" he said, forcing himself to heartiness. "The guests are waiting."

"John was asking if you'd want to go to Baltimore in October," he said to Lucinda that night. He sat watching her while she performed the last rites upon her skin. Her maid had brushed and braided her hair and gone away. It was past midnight. The guests were in their rooms.

Lucinda did not look at him. At the mention of Baltimore she stiffened. It had been on a visit to Baltimore that she had discovered that he sometimes saw Georgia. Not that he had to this day acknowledged it—he maintained that he went only to see Tom, and upon that they had quarreled.

"I hope I have the right to see my own brother!" he had insisted coldly.

She had turned to him with dreadful acumen. "As if you could lie to me!" she had cried. "Pierce Delaney, I can see through you as though you were made of glass! You want to see Georgia!"

He had been staggered. She had discovered what he

himself had refused to know. Then she had spat out the words at him. "You and your brother Tom!"

He had stared at her, his blood frozen in his veins with terror. "How foul women are," he had muttered, and he had left the room instantly. They had never spoken of Georgia again.

She did not speak of her now. "Everything depends upon when Martin and Mary Louise decide to be married," she said lightly.

"I have no desire to go to Baltimore," he said. "I'm getting too old for such shindigs."

She laughed at this. "As if you didn't know you are handsomer than ever!" She came and sat on a footstool at his knee. The glow from the coals in the small brass decorated grate, which she had brought over from England shone upon her face. He felt an amazing tenderness for her and put his hand on her neck. But she slipped from under his touch. "Not tonight," she said firmly.

He withdrew his hand quickly and with anger. "You don't allow me even to show you affection, without thinking I—" he broke off.

Lucinda laughed. "I know you too well, my dear," she said— Then she yawned. "But I have nothing on my conscience. I am a very good wife to you, I'm sure—you are treated well, Pierce, and you know it."

"I don't want to be—treated well—as you call it—" he said.

"Now let's not begin on what you want—at this hour of the night," she said. She got up quickly and moved about, straightening one small object after another, a luster bowl on the table, a small French clock beside her bed, a Dresden china pair of figures on the mantel, the crystal-hung candlesticks on the mantel.

"I know it means nothing to you what I want," he said somberly. "You've made out a formula for me, damn you, Luce! You run me on a schedule—a timetable—you don't allow anything for my feelings—"

"Your feelings, my dear," she interposed, "always have the same common denominator."

He clasped his jaws shut and got up. "Good night," he said.

"Now you are angry," she said brightly. "You can't bear the truth, can you, Pierce! You never could . . . So you'll never get the truth from me . . . I promise you! Don't worry!"

She was angry, too, and this was rare enough to make him pause. "I am not angry," he said more mildly. "It's just that you—think you know everything—about everything."

"Only about you," she said.

She climbed into the high bed and lay back against her lace-edged pillows and yawned again.

"Good night, Pierce," she said. "Get up in a good mood tomorrow, please." She blew out the lamp and he had to stumble through the darkness as best he could.

He went into his own room prickling with rage. She had put him in the wrong again in her own inexplicable fashion. But he was not in the wrong. She had him in a cage of her own making, a cage whereby whatever he said she let him know that she had known already what he was going to say and how he was going to feel. He rebelled against her calm assumption that there was nothing in him which she did not know and yet he was hamstrung by the thought that even so she might be right. She had an uncanny way of ferreting out his most secret thought. Whether there was something in this of the telepathy out of which people were making parlor games nowadays—but he had gone to such absurd lengths as not to think in her presence of things which he wished to keep to himself. And yet he loved her more than ever, too, in a helpless fashion. She was in his being, his children's mother. He wished Sally were at home, but Sally was at school in Lewisburg . . . And Sally was growing away from him, too— he suspected her of it. Even last summer she was always off on some visit or other. He had never felt close to Lucie, the last child to be at home. Lucinda had hired an English governess for her.

He sighed and climbed into his great bed and blew out the lamp. Away from Malvern people looked up to him as a successful man. Even at Malvern they looked up to him.

Only Lucinda reduced him to an unreasonable, disgusting creature, always at the mercy of—of animal passion. He closed his eyes and waited fretfully for sleep.

In late May John asked him to go to Philadelphia to look at the site for a great new terminal building. He showed the letter to Lucinda. She read it, and raised her eyebrows.

"I suppose you think you have to go," she said.

"It is not a matter of what I think," Pierce returned with firmness. "When John asks me to do something for the business I must do it." She shrugged her shoulders at the word "business," and the talk was ended.

He approached Philadelphia with his usual calm. Many times now during the years he had come here to see Tom. Many times? Perhaps half a dozen times, all told, always with business as his honest purpose. Out of the half dozen times twice he saw only Tom, downtown at his hotel. They had exchanged brief news about the family on both sides. The other times he had gone to Tom's home.

Tom had had no more children. Leslie had grown up and had gone to New York to work on a newspaper. There he had married a young West Indian. Pierce had never seen her, but he had looked at the wedding photograph in the parlor of Tom's home. If he was surprised at the sight of the dark loveliness of the girl in the long white satin gown and cloudy white veil he had said nothing. Not by one word did he ever let Tom know such surprise. Leslie had grown into a handsome fellow, dismayingly like Pierce's own father. He was clever and quick and more and more he had cut himself off from his family and lived in the world of his own kind in New York.

Lettice wanted to be a trained nurse and Georgy was to be a teacher. Of all the children only Georgy was filled with the fierce flame of equality. She was going south, she said, as soon as she finished school, and work for the sharecroppers. Georgy was dark, so dark that she would have to move into the Jim Crow cars in Virginia. Pierce smothered the strange feeling it gave him when he thought of the slim brown creature who was his own niece having to declare herself. Some day, of course, he told himself in the secret recesses of his conscience, all such things would have to cease. His own niece, Jim Crowed on the railroad that enriched Malvern—but he could do nothing about it. . . . Small Tom no one knew. He was in the throes of boyhood, a tall, gangling, curly-haired boy whose lips were a trifle too full.

John MacBain met him at the station and together they got into a carriage and the black coachman drove them to the busiest part of downtown, where the new building was to stand. It would cover a whole block.

"It's a great expense even for a terminal," Pierce said.

"It won't just be a terminal," John retorted. "We are planning to push the road on north—to Newark, maybe, and Jersey City, or even to New York."

"I hope it is worth it to the stockholders," Pierce said somewhat bleakly.

He and John represented different elements in the business. Pierce considered himself and was considered the representative of the stockholders. John was president and represented management.

John said crisply, "You know our policy, Pierce—it's always been sound—management conservative and stockholders patient, labor responsible. Then we'll all win together."

"This is a damned politicians' town," Pierce growled. "You're going to have to line the pockets of a hundred or two of them."

"We never have played politics and we never will," John said firmly. "Once start bribing politicians and they'll drive you to bankruptcy with their greed."

Pierce looked doubtfully at the big square. It was hard to imagine the shops and houses torn down and a great high building reared in the midst of these pushing crowds of people.

"I'm afraid of expansion, John," he said. "Remember what expansion did to us in those other years."

"This isn't expansion," John retorted. "We are following trade this time—not going ahead of it. We're connecting the terminals that trade has already made—not building side lines."

"John, as long as the railroad is under your management I'll agree to anything," Pierce said at last. "But don't take your hands off the engine for one moment."

John gave his thin long smile. "I plan to live another thirty years, Pierce," he drawled. "And all I've got to live for is the railroad."

They parted, John having got his way, "as management always does," Pierce told him with a rueful smile, and then Pierce kept the carriage and drove across town into the quiet streets where Tom's world was. A peaceful world, Pierce always thought, aloof and untouched by rivalry or struggle. It had been a matter for secret surprise to him that Tom had lifted no banners and had led no crusade for the people into which he had married. "In your own way," he had once told Tom, "you have lived as selfish a life as I have myself at Malvern."

"There is a difference," Tom had retorted. "My life in itself has been a revolution—yours hasn't."

He thought of Tom's words now as he drove down the tree-lined street. Quietly, house by house, the well-to-do Negroes had moved into this fine and old section of the city. There was nothing external to tell of the change. Houses were spacious and lawns were neat, gardens were beautiful and the streets clean. A few well-dressed children played behind closed iron gates. One had to look closely to see that they were not white. Pierce had always the illusion when he came here that he was leaving one country and going into another, as in Europe one passed from Germany into France. He was uneasy in the illusion, for this was a country within a country.

He got out of the cab before the whitewashed stone house, paid the cabman and opened the white-painted gate. He walked down the path to the front door and rang the bell. A maid in a white frilled apron opened the door. She greeted him quietly and asked him to come in. At the same moment he heard light footsteps on the stair and Georgy

ran down. She stood still upon seeing him, uncertain, as all
Tom's children were still uncertain of him. He saw the doubt
in her dark eyes and felt compunction. After all, these children were not to blame for being born.

He held out his arms unexpectedly, and with a rush of
wonder she came into them. He felt her thin young arms hug
him. Then he stepped back. "You've grown, my child," he
said.

She smiled, her teeth very white. "I do grow," she said.
Her voice had a lovely musical lilt, and he noticed it for
the first time.

"Is my brother Tom at home?" he asked.

"We expect Father in about an hour," she replied. "He
and Mother went to see some pictures at the art gallery."

"Nobody home but you?" he asked.

"Aunt Georgia is upstairs," she replied.

There was the briefest pause. He put down his hat and
stick on a table.

"I wonder if you two could give me some tea?" he asked.

"Of course," she said. She skipped upstairs ahead of him,
and he heard her calling, "Aunt Georgia—someone's here—
I'm going to make tea!"

So she avoided the use of his name, as they all did. Even
Bettina in all these years had managed without speaking
his name. There was a delicacy in them that was too proud
to presume upon relationship. He appreciated the quality
but was somehow conscience-smitten because of it. Then he
went into the upstairs parlor which had become Georgia's
own.

There was no use in pretending that the sight of her
did not move him. But what it was that he felt he did not
know and would not discover. Something was released in
him, a tension broke. He wanted only to sit in her presence
and draw his breath in great sighs of relief.

She sat by the open window, dressed as usual in a full soft
white dress. She turned her face toward him and her dark
eyes were liquid and calm. She did not smile nor speak a
word. "Georgia," he said. He sat down in the chair opposite

her and gazed at her and she gazed back at him in silence.

He brought himself back with effort. "Well, how are you?"

"Quite well," she replied. "You look well," she added.

"I'm getting old," he said gently.

"It's good," she murmured.

"You don't change," he said.

She clasped her soft beautiful hands on her lap and he looked at them. He had never touched even her hand. Now he put out his own hand.

"After all these years I suppose I may?" he said abruptly.

Her creamy face flushed delicately. Then she put out her right hand and he took it between both his. The blood beat in his ears.

"I want to be honest with you," he said. "I don't know what it is that I feel when I am with you—but something very comforting. I wish you could live in my house again, Georgia. My house has not been the same without you. Even now I— we—miss you."

"I can't live there," she murmured.

"I know that," he said. "I don't ask it."

He pressed her hand and laid it softly on her knee and sat back in his chair. "You and I—we've never talked out to each other. Now—I want to, Georgia."

"Yes," she said, "it's time. I've always thought that when we began to get old—we could."

They heard the brisk footsteps of Georgy coming up the stair. "Tomorrow," he said. "Will you drive with me into the country? I'll tell Tom."

"Yes," she said, and bent her head. He saw the softly parted hair, and the downcast lashes, the turn of her lips.

"Here's the tea," Georgy cried at the door, "and I made cinnamon toast—"

He moved through the rest of the day in a strange lassitude of mind and body. In all these years he had not spoken to Georgia of himself nor of her. And yet he had known always that she waited unchanged. Tom and Bettina came home. He heard their voices and footsteps and the children's voices. Then he heard Tom's steps along the hall to the guest-room where he was sitting.

He had never slept under Tom's roof since his first visit. But he had said to Georgy as she cleared away the tea things, "I shall stay here, my child, if you have a room for me."

Her face lit with joy. "Oh—will you?" she breathed. "Of course—the guestroom—it's always ready—"

"Then I will go to it—I am tired." He had been touched by her joy.

She had brought him into this cool green and white room and had tiptoed away. He had closed the door, frightened and bewildered by the depths of his feeling and yet he was calm. He wanted to sleep—to sleep and rest, and yet he was not sleepy. He sat down in a deeply cushioned chair and leaned back and closed his eyes. Now he was face to face with something that he knew was inevitable, that he had always known was inevitable. Whatever was to come, he had at last met the unavoidable. Whatever it was he had forbidden himself he would forbid no longer.

Tom knocked at the door gently and he said, "Come in," and his brother came in.

"Are you ill?" Tom exclaimed.

"No," Pierce said.

"But you're white as a sheet!"

"Tom, I'm frightened and relieved—but I don't know what I am going to do—"

Tom sat down and gazed at him with anxiety. "What's happened?"

"I don't know," Pierce said. "But I am going to sleep here tonight, Tom. And I have asked Georgia to let me talk with her tomorrow—a long talk—such as I have never allowed myself."

Tom's face grew stern. "To what end, Pierce?"

"I don't know," Pierce said. "When I know I'll tell you honestly, Tom—or she will."

Pierce dismissed the driver and took the carriage himself. He was ashamed of his involuntary and yet surprised relief at the fact that no one would realize that Georgia was—not a white woman. He had driven along the empty side streets into the roads which led most quickly to the country.

"I don't know why I didn't want to talk inside the house," he said frankly. They had scarcely spoken at all as he drove. She had smiled once or twice. He had glanced at her and from her calm had grown calm himself.

"It's a beautiful day," she said.

The mild day was almost windless and the afternoon was bright. No one had been at the door to see them go. Tom had made an excuse of not being able to get back from school until late, and the children did not come back at noon. Bettina had gone to visit a friend. The house had been empty when they left it, and he knew it would be empty when they got back.

Outside the city limits he drove up a winding lane which was hidden by trees until it came to the top of a hill. There he stopped. "This looks like our hill," he said. He waved his whip at the view. "We can enjoy the world spread before us while we talk."

He fastened the horse to a tree and she put her hand in his and stepped out of the carriage. Even today she had worn her soft white muslin frock. The shawl around her shoulders was white wool, and her bonnet-shaped straw hat was white.

"Here's a log—and I'll put the robe down for us to sit on."

She let him serve her, and when he had made ready she sat down and put back her shawl from her shoulders. She did not look at him. It was impossible to tell from her face what she thought. She was submissive and gentle and full of dignity. He did not dare touch her hand. Indeed, he must not.

"You have been living far away all these years," he said. "I don't know how to begin."

She turned her soft eyes to him now. "We can begin where we are," she said. "We know everything about each other."

"Do I know everything about you?" he asked.

She smiled. "There is not much to know. I've lived in my sister's house, and helped her with the children."

She looked down as she spoke and at her feet she saw a violet and she stooped and plucked it and fastened it at her bosom and went on speaking in her placid sweet voice. "Now I am planning to take Georgy away—to Europe—to train her voice."

"To Europe!" he echoed and was stunned.

"I always wanted to sing," she went on, "but of course I hadn't the opportunity. I know Georgy can be a great singer and I'd like to have my share in that."

"I thought she wanted to be a teacher," he objected.

She shook her head. "I don't want her to get embroiled in all the sorrows of our race," she said quietly. "Of what use is that? We must wait until the time of wisdom comes to the world."

She spoke half dreamily and he felt her far away from him indeed.

"You have changed very much, Georgia," he said sharply.

She shook her head. "No, I have only had time to think— much time. I have had time to ask myself why it was that Bettina and I have had to live solitary. Oh yes—Bettina, too! You see, she is really quite alone—cut off from—everybody except—her husband. And I have been cut off—in quite the same way—except that I have never married—shall never marry."

"If you go to Europe there might be someone—" He felt jealousy and at the same time he thought of Lucinda.

She shook her head. "No, not for me."

He wanted to take her hand again as he had yesterday and could not. "I feel somehow a cur," he murmured.

She shook her head again, smiled and did not speak.

"Or a fool," he said. "Because I am so confused."

"We are born out of time," she said quietly.

He took her words and pondered them and could not reply to them. In silence he gazed out over the rolling hills and the shallow valleys. Among their vivid green the red barns and white farmhouses gleamed like jewels. A dove moaned in the trees near by. She began to speak again musingly. "I've missed Malvern, too. I loved to serve you—taking care of your clothes and tidying your room—all that—but I had to give it up, for fear—"

"Fear of me?"

"Fear of myself. It would have been easy to stay there at Malvern—lovely—"

"But you can't come back," he said sadly.

"Never!"

"I know that."

"And I know," she went on more firmly, "that it isn't me you need. You feel at ease with me—not just because of me—but because far back in you somewhere, you've mixed me up with Maum Tessie who wetnursed you and took care of you when you were little."

He flushed, but she raised her hand. "Yes, that's true. If your—wife—had been softer—you wouldn't have needed anybody else."

They fell into silence again. She was complete and untouchable. She had thought through everything as he had never dared to do, had reached the end of herself, had grown to the height of womanhood, and whatever his half-ashamed, unacknowledged yearnings had been he knew now that they would never be fulfilled. . . . He was amazed and perplexed that in the midst of his disappointment and stifled chagrin, he felt a strange relief.

She rose and drew her shawl about her shoulders and looked at the little gold watch that hung on a short chain from her ribbon belt. "We have been here nearly two hours—"

"Sitting quiet most of the time," he said, smiling, half sadly.

"But saying all that had to be said," she replied.

He got up then and they stood for a moment looking over the countryside. Then he turned and put his hands on her shoulders. They were soft under his grip. He looked deep into her dark eyes and she met his gaze faithfully.

"I have a queer contented feeling," he said.

She smiled back at him.

He went on, choosing his words carefully, one by one, as they distilled in pure essence out of the depths of his being. "For the first time in life, I think I know what the war was about—and I'm glad Tom's side won—because it made you free and what you are this day."

"Yes," she said.

He went away that night and when he was gone Georgia turned to Tom and Bettina.

"I feel it your due that you know what happened between him and me this day," she said simply.

The children had gone upstairs to bed and they sat in the big sitting room. The soft spring night, drifting in from the open window, was warm with the hint of summer soon to come. Georgia had said almost nothing all evening. Even when Pierce went away she had still said nothing. But she gave him her hand in parting. This was much. Never before had she put out her hand to him as though they were equals. Now they were, and she acknowledged it.

Bettina was sewing on some child's garment. She put it down. Tom had picked up the newspaper. He let it fall. Both waited.

"You have let me live here as though it were my home," Georgia went on.

"My home is your home—you know that," Bettina reminded her. She had aged in these years, and Georgia seemed much the younger in looks and in manner and she deferred to Bettina in everything. Now she looked at her sister and then at Tom. She touched her lips with her tongue. Shy and modest as she was, they could see how difficultly she spoke and they waited, always gentle toward this gentle creature.

"He's grown older and more thoughtful—as we all do. Whatever it was, he came here this time in need of comfort. And so he thought of me. Bettina," she turned to her sister. "It's not like you and Tom. Even if it were—it's too late. I told him—I want to take Georgy to Europe and get her voice trained."

"To Europe!" Tom cried.

"I want to go away," Georgia said. Her lips were trembling. "Very far away, and I would like to help Georgy to sing—the way I always wanted to myself and never could."

"But the money—" Tom began.

Bettina spoke suddenly. "Tom, I've never let you use your inheritance on us. I ask you to use it now."

He looked at Bettina. She was his wife, though he had been forced to compel her to marriage. When they had moved into this house, when he was headmaster at last of his own small school for boys, he had taken her with him one Sunday to an Amish meeting and by the rites of the Amishmen he had made her his wife and himself her husband. He had put upon her finger the narrow gold ring she had so steadfastly refused to wear. The rite was as much for himself as for her. He wanted to make final, for himself, the thing he had chosen to do. He wanted the sanction of church as well as of conscience. Never would he forget the strange silence of the people in the meeting house. Rigidly accepting his freedom to do what he felt was right, nevertheless he comprehended their conflict, their reluctance at what their own consciences, trained in the creed of non-resistance, insisted upon. But he was content. Bettina became his wife by the law of God. She felt it as he did. Whatever conflict had been between them ceased. They had lived in the peace of isolation from their kind, hers as well as his, dependent upon one another and deeply knit. And yet her fierce independence even of him had never allowed him to spend anything of his inheritance on her or her children until this moment.

"I'll be proud to use it so," he said gently.

Two weeks later his house seemed empty. He did not know which to miss more, the singing, fiery, laughing, easily angry girl who was his daughter, or Georgia's soft presence. Both were gone.

# Nine

Pierce was confronted with news as he stepped into the hall at Malvern. Martin was waiting for him, watching the front door through the open door of the library, and Lucinda had a servant posted to tell her of his arrival. She swept down the wide stairs, holding her skirts with both hands, and Martin leaped out of the chair where he had been reading the county newspaper. They greeted Pierce so affectionately and with such excitement that he smiled at them drily.

"What now?" he inquired.

"Father, Mary Louise has set the day of our wedding," Martin said solemnly. "The eighteenth of June!"

"And that means the girls and I must get our gowns," Lucinda interrupted her son, "and the porcelain service you've ordered from England— Oh, Pierce, it can't possibly get here in time!"

"Mary Lou and I won't need it for three months, Mother— we'll be in Europe—" Martin broke in.

"We have plenty of dishes, I hope," Pierce said. "They'll be coming here to Malvern to live, Luce—good news, Martin."

"Every bride should have her own porcelain and silver," Lucinda said firmly.

He was at the stairs, feeling weary and anxious for the quiet of his own room. Joe was ahead of him with the luggage.

"Pierce, do hurry—do!" Lucinda urged him. "There's so much to plan."

"I will," he promised—"but I'd like a bite to eat, my dear."

"I'll order a lunch for you on a tray—we finished an hour ago," Lucinda said.

He inclined his head, smiled at his son, and walked slowly upstairs. The weariness was more than that of not sleeping well on the train. He felt shaken and bewildered, his security threatened, and by himself. He felt that in some secret fashion he had betrayed Malvern and his family, although nothing that had passed between him and Georgia was shameful—actually, how little shameful, when compared to Lucinda's own father, who had taken mistresses as a matter of course, from among his slaves. But Lucinda had never considered her father's children by slaves as her kin, by the remotest drop of blood. Had she seen him, Pierce, her husband, talking with Georgia, as he had done, she could never have forgiven him. Therefore he would never tell her, lest peace be destroyed in his house.

His ancestors had built Malvern for the ages, and a war, unforeseen and terrible, had nearly wrecked what they had built. By chance Malvern had escaped and he had carried on the building, strengthening and improving the place until it had become a symbol of safety for himself and his children and their children. But he knew now that neither he nor they were safe. He perceived dimly the essential difference between himself and Tom. Tom had projected himself and his life into the future. He had built a house not made with hands. His love, the love which had grown so strangely under the very roofs of Malvern, had given him a home and security. "I've bolstered the past," Pierce thought. "Tom's built for the future." But he would never have understood this had it not been for Georgia.

In his own rooms he dismissed Joe and stood looking out of the long windows that faced the avenue of oaks winding to the gates. What a strange chance it had been that into Malvern had come the two women, gentle and beautiful, to serve and yet never to be servants! If Bettina and Georgia had not been here, if there had only been Jake and Joe and old Annie and Phelan, and all the crew of ignorant black folk, he and Tom would have been different men. Those black folk belonged to the past, but Georgia and Bettina did not.

He sat down and put his head in his hands and closed his eyes. He saw Georgia again as she had looked beside him on the hill, the sun on her faultless skin. Her eyes, so exquisitely shaped and colored, were lit with pure intelligence. That was her fascination for him, that within her golden beauty and clear simplicity there should dwell high intelligence and sensitive feeling.

Lucinda opened the door and saw him thus and cried out, "Pierce, are you ill?"

He let his hands fall and tried to smile. "No—only tired, my dear."

"Something is wrong!"

"Nothing except large vague general things," he replied.

"I insist that you tell me," she demanded.

"I'm troubled for the future, my dear—"

"You mean the railroad?"

"The railroad is only part of it—perhaps our whole nation is only part of it—" he said slowly.

She lost interest. "Oh, that—Pierce, really, we haven't time for such things." She came in and sat down. "I want to take the girls to New York. It's the only possible way to get our gowns in time. I have decided on a pale hyacinth blue for myself, with silver lace—very narrow. Sally and Lucie are bridesmaids and they will wear daffodil yellow—I want to show the Wyeths that we are quite as good as they—although Malvern is in West Virginia, it is only just over the border. If it hadn't been for the war—"

"Do as you like," he said absently.

She was suddenly angry. "Pierce, I don't believe you care at all that Martin is going to be married—our eldest son!"

He roused himself at this. "I do care, Luce. Maybe that's why I feel so troubled. I don't believe the world is going to get easier for the children. I don't know what's ahead—"

"Really, Pierce!" Lucinda cried. "Of all times to talk so! Why, you said yourself only a few days ago that things were better—the strikes put down, and the depression over—" Her prettiness suddenly disappeared in a sharp look. "You've been to visit Tom again," she said.

Her shrewdness confounded him. Then he recovered. "Yes, I have been to see Tom," he said.

She flushed swiftly from neck to hair, a deep and furious pink. "I suppose Georgia is there," she said.

He looked at her, not knowing how to answer her. She would never understand, however he tried to tell her, that she was not threatened by Georgia. He could never make her understand how he felt about Georgia, that it was not love—not love of a woman. He could never make her comprehend that Georgia was a revelation to him of a truth which he did not yet fully comprehend in himself. In his hesitation he was speechless. She stared at him, he saw the flush drain from her face until it was dead white and her eyes were the color of frost.

"Luce!" he cried in alarm.

But she did not answer. She went away and closed the door behind her.

He leaped to his feet to stride after her, to seize and compel her to listen to him. But what would he say? He did not know. He sat down again and so sat for a while, the house very silent about him. Would she tell Martin—whatever it was she feared? He pressed his lips together firmly, got up, washed, and changed his clothes. When he went downstairs he looked at himself—he made sure of himself before his mirror. At the bottom of the stairs he went into the dining room. A tray was on the table. Lucinda was there and with her Martin. He knew the moment he met his son's eyes that she had said nothing. He glanced at her but she looked away from him and took her seat at the table and poured his coffee.

"Well, Martin," he said gently. There was something tender and touching in the young man's joy. Nothing must spoil it.

"Father—" Martin began. "I reckon I'm too excited to talk," he said. He broke off, and their eyes met.

Pierce smiled. "I know, my son."

So had he felt on the day when Lucinda had set the day

for their marriage. He remembered her loveliness, slender
and delicate. He turned to her. "We remember, don't we?"
he murmured.

She looked back at him with eyes so cold and hard that
he all but gasped. Did she hate him? But for what? He
hastened to hide himself and her from their son.

He lifted his wine glass. "I hope you'll be happy, my son,"
he said.

But he was increasingly disturbed as the days drew nearer
to Martin's wedding day. Lucinda did not forgive him, and
yet there was nothing to forgive. He knew it and could not
explain to her the state of his own feelings and the con-
fusions and fears that filled his mind. A healthy rage might
have cured them, a vast upheaval of open anger, a quarrel
that would have cleansed them both of their secret thoughts.
But she gave him no chance for such healing. She was con-
stantly busy about the wedding, and she made her absorption into an icy covering for herself. Her voice was clear, her
eyes calm, her whole bearing as composed as usual. But
when he leaned to kiss her cheek it was cold beneath his
lips. Twice he seized her in his arms and bent her like a
reed to his body, and each time passion died out of him.
Her whole body was cold, slim and smooth and unyielding.
She knew it and she looked at him with malice that terrified
him.

"Don't look at me like that, Luce!" he implored her.

She turned her eyes away, lashes falling, and did not
answer him. He could not reach her, and at last he tried to
ignore her. Sometime, as soon as possible, he would have it
out with her. But nothing now must spoil Martin's wedding.

He was especially tender to his eldest son in all these days.
He wanted Martin to have the life he had dreamed of when
he came back from the war, which outwardly he had lived
and yet had not realized within himself. Whether it was his
fault or Lucinda's he did not know. But he knew that somehow between them, while Malvern had been perfected in
beauty, they who were its heart and its soul had not grown

together into fulfillment, and by that much Malvern was empty within.

Nevertheless he went to his son's wedding in state in his private car, and reproached himself for discontent. No man could have asked for a handsomer family than his. He saw them as his possession when one by one they stepped upon the platform at Wyeth. Lucinda was crisply composed, the mother of fine children. She looked as slender and almost as youthful as her daughters, her silver grey costume and her air of worldly wisdom were the chief signs of her being older than they. Sally was his darling, warm-skinned, bright-haired, taller and a little plumper than her mother. She wore a soft blue frock and coat and a wide blue hat with a rosy lining. Lucie was a thin shoot of girl, pretty and cool in a cream-colored frock and straw hat, and Carey and John were dressed alike in dark blue suits. Pierce took proud stock of their health and good color, of the soft smooth complexions of his daughters and of his sons' height. He had no ugly duckling.

The love he felt for them overflowed and he pressed Lucinda's hand inside his arm. "Thanks for handsome children, my dear," he murmured, smiling down at her.

She flashed an upward look at him from under the tilted grey hat brim. "They are handsome," she agreed, and softened toward him for the first time in all these days. "They have a handsome father," she said. He was absurdly grateful and his spirits rose. Perhaps he and Lucinda could renew themselves in this young marriage.

Martin had come the day before. Mrs. Wyeth had invited them to stay the week, but Lucinda had refused. It would be more dignified, she announced, if they came in their own private railroad car and only spent the day before the wedding with the Wyeth family. She did not want to stay on after the wedding was over. "There is nothing so melancholy as a house after a wedding," she declared.

Thus they proceeded in the middle of the bright summer afternoon to the long rambling white-painted house that stood conspicuously on a hill above the little town.

Two carriages had met them, driven by black coachmen in

smart new uniforms. Mary Lou was the eldest daughter and the first child to be married and everything was at its best. Pierce felt himself being carried back into the old world in which he had grown up, far from the seething possibilities of the future. Wyeth village had not changed at all. He had used to drive through its single street when he went to see Lucinda in the days when he was courting her. Together they had gone sometimes to a Christmas ball at the Wyeth mansion or to a garden party on its lawns, the lawns which old Mr. Wyeth had struggled so valiantly to make into smooth green slopes. But the red Virginia soil had refused to nourish grass seed from England, and the native crab grass had kept its voracious hold. Virginia could produce her own fabulous beauty of redbud and dogwood and applebloom, and Scotch heather flourished like a weed. But English lawns she would not grow.

The carriages rolled up the long avenue of beeches and approached the house he remembered. Nothing had changed but he had a strange sense of the passing years. He turned to Sally at his side.

"Sally, child, can you imagine your pa in a long-tailed blue coat, dancing with the prettiest girl in the world on that very porch?" He reached for Sally's little hand. She still wore his sapphire ring upon her third finger but any day now he must expect to see it supplanted by another. She looked up at him with her warm violet eyes.

"I know who was the handsomest man," she murmured. "I wish I could have seen my pa."

The warmth which he missed in Lucinda he found in Sally, he told himself, and why should he complain? But some day soon the warmth would be for another man and then he would feel very lonely indeed. He sighed and looked ahead. He and Lucinda must come together closely and more close as time went on. Old age was over the horizon and they must go through it knit together. He must find a way to win her trust.

Then there was no more time for thinking. Colonel Wyeth had flung open the door and stood, a tall dramatic figure, with welcoming arms. They got out of the carriages and black men sprang to fetch their bags and black women in spotless white aprons appeared with smiles and murmurs of pleasure to take them to hospitable rooms. The wide hall, the breezeway, open from front to back of the house, was fragrant with lilies. Colonel Wyeth clapped Pierce on the shoulder.

"Come and quench your thirst," he shouted. "We're one family now, Pierce. God, what a handsome son you're givin' me and Ma'y Lou—well, I say in all modesty that she is his match—pretty, though, the way a woman should be. But that's her mother. Man, I don't mind tellin' you now but I had a time makin' up my mind between my Dolly and your Lucinda in the old days—I don't know that I ever chose—I saw your eyes stealin' around to Lucinda and so I said, 'Dolly's my girl—' "

It was the old, comfortable, cheerful, ignorant, happy world. He felt it close about him. Gleaming polished silver, paneled walls, old portraits, velvet curtains and flowered carpets, good food, wonderful thirst-satisfying, thirst-stimulating drink, and everywhere obsequious smiling dark faces. He sank back into his childhood. Here it lived on unchanged. Had he said to Charles Wyeth that anything was changed or could be changed, the tall lean silvery haired Virginian would have laughed. Nobody could change Virginia, he would have declared.

He sat drinking a softly sharp, frosted, fragrant julep, in a great room whose windows were open upon a curving river, to which a meadow sloped. Wyeth was talking incessantly—

"It gives a man queer mixed feelin's, Pierce. A little gyurl, the little thing that's been runnin' round the house a few years, the joy of the home, and now I'm givin' my little joy away! Oh, don't misunderstand me—Martin's a credit to you—a sound young man without any of these hyeah radical notions that are comin' in from the no'th. I feel puffectly safe about my little Ma'y Lou. All the same—" He shook his head.

Pierce smiled. "I know—I was thinking the very same thing about my Sally. It won't be long—"

"Has she got herself a beau?"

"Six or eight or so," Pierce said, "but I notice she's beginning to concentrate."

"A mighty pretty gyurl," Wyeth said mournfully, and continuing in the same mournful tone. "How's cattle over your way? I hyeah you've come to be a mighty cattle man."

"I'm a fool," Pierce said ruefully. "I reckon I'm trying to buy all the cattle in the States."

"It's all right if the market holds," Wyeth said judicially. He spoke with authority on all subjects. "Though it's a mighty gamble, if you've got nothin' but cattle. But you were smart to go on for railroads, too. Thataway a man has two strings to his bow."

"If both strings don't break the same year," Pierce agreed.

"Well, I reckon they got the communists or socialists or whatever they are scotched for good," Wyeth said gaily. "We can't allow that sort of internationalism to get in here from foreign countries."

"No," Pierce agreed. He wondered what Wyeth would say if he knew about Tom. But nobody knew. It was as if Tom were dead and had been dead for years.

"Not that it ever could happen here," Wyeth went on heartily. His ruddy cheeks, his long moustache, his fine white hands holding the tall frosty glass were absurdly like the portrait of his own father hanging on the paneled wall behind him. "I'd rather see my daughter dead than married to one of those radicals who believe that black is as good as white." He held his glass to be refilled. "I like niggahs, don't I, Henry?" The elderly man servant standing at his side smiled faintly as he bent with the tray. "But I like 'em where they belong—and where they're happiest."

"Martin is no radical—so far as I know," Pierce said mildly.

He wondered if it were weakness that kept him from telling the truth as he saw it to this comfortable man, the truth about Tom, about the strikes, about his own vague fears. Wyeth was perhaps stupid. No, he was not stupid, he was surrounded and isolated by comfort. He had inherited wealth and home and friends as he had inherited his family and its blood. He could be destroyed but not changed.

Pierce allowed a waiting servant to replace his glass while he took in the meaning of these words. The quick and the dead—the wise old phrase came into his mind. The dead were those who would not comprehend and share in change. He thought of Lucinda with a strange foreboding. And she, his wife!

He drank long and deep of the smooth liquid in the silvery cold glass in his hand and quelled the monstrous fears in his mind.

The day passed in a dream of pleasure. The great and ancient house lent itself to the young marriage. Guests came and settled into its shelter, gentle handsome old people, young and beautiful men and women, children excited and gay. Friends whom he had forgotten and relatives he scarcely remembered. A web of kinship seemed to bind them together. Wyeths were related to Carters who were seventh cousins to Delaneys and Pages and Randolphs, and Lees were knit into the blood streams of all. The world grew secure and steady in kinship and common ancestry. In the evening he went with his sons to the stag dinner for Martin, and he sat in silent admiration of the young groom and in pride that the life from his own loins had borne this fruit that would bear again. He was fulfilled before other men. He had everything that a man could want. Had he not?

When at the end of the dinner they rose, glasses in hand to toast his son, he lifted his own glass high and his eyes met Martin's. The image of his son was dimmed in sudden smarting tears. More than he wanted happiness for himself he wanted Martin to be happy. He wanted Malvern to be the home of the next generation in peace and security. He must devote himself for the rest of his years to building that security.

He was very tender to Lucinda that night and he humbled himself before her.

"This day takes me back, my darling," he said.

They were alone at last, long after midnight. In the cool high-ceilinged bedroom a great double bed was set between long windows opening to a balcony. He led her out in the moonlight, his arm around her, and for a moment they had gazed over the gleaming landscape. Then they came in together and made ready for sleep. He was ready first and he climbed on the double step and got into the bed. She in her white nightgown was still brushing her hair. So she had done on their wedding night and he had imagined shyness in the long brushing. He knew now that Lucinda was never shy. Nevertheless, he would be gentle with her and win her back to him.

"Your lovely hair," he said. "I remember the first time I saw it down like that. You kept brushing it—"

She smiled, not looking at him, and put the brush down. Then she turned down the lamp and stepped up and into the bed beside him. The moonlight from the open doors lay across the floor like a bright carpet.

"I hope Mary Lou will be as beautiful as you are, after their son is grown and ready to be married," he murmured. He saw the endless vista of the generations ahead and he drew her into his arms. "We've made a great family, you and I," he said.

Still she was silent. He wondered for a moment if she could continue in anger. But her slender body was pliant in his arms. He stifled the impulse to cry out, "Forgive me," for he had done nothing to forgive. She had been very angry, but for no cause of his. In her own self there was something—what, he could not know, that kept her angry with him for what he was, a man and her husband. He sighed and loosened his arms. She lay for a moment as if surprised, and then of her own accord, firmly she put his hands upon her breasts.

Standing beside Lucinda next day in the little Episcopalian church which had been built by a Wyeth two hundred years before, Pierce listened to Martin declare his vows to the little lace-veiled figure at his side. He was beset by doubts. Why had he not taken more pains to discover what sort of a woman Mary Lou was? Why had he merely accepted her as another pretty girl, sweet-tempered, yielding, feminine, charming—

when actually she had the power to make his son happy or wretched?

It was too late—"I, Martin, take thee, Mary Louise, to be my wedded wife—"

It suddenly became more solemn, more portentous than his own marriage had been. For now he knew that marriage was heart and hearth in a man's life. When it went wrong nothing was right. But his marriage had been good. He loved Lucinda and would love her until he died. What folly to ask more than he had! She had been true to him, faithful to the letter and to the spirit. Poor John MacBain! Lucinda had fitted Malvern as the queen fits the castle. She had given him sons and daughters, superbly she had given him these. Then why was he ungrateful and why was he fearful for his son? Last night in bed, Lucinda had given herself—no, she had given her body. And he had taken her body. He had strained her in his arms, searching for what he did not have—her complete trust, her whole love.

And then he understood. These he would never have because he was man and she was woman. His maleness she would distrust until she died. His maleness was his weakness against which she would protect herself. Secretly, while she loved him, she hated him because he was a man. And yet as a man she needed him and depended upon him and must please him and sometimes serve him that she might be served, and for this she hated him. Above all men she preferred him —ah, there was no doubt of that—but she hated him.

The organ burst into triumphant music and he looked up, bewildered. While he had been mulling his bitter thoughts his son had been married. The young husband and wife turned and marched down the aisle, Martin's head high, Mary Lou's face downcast and tenderly smiling. She pressed her cheek for one brief second against Martin's arm and he turned his head quickly and looked down at her. Pierce could not bear the sight. His yearning rose to agony.

"Let it be a good marriage!" he prayed suddenly, and stared down at his hands gripped upon the rail of the seat in front of him.

"Come, Pierce!" Lucinda whispered. She slipped her hand in his arm and they mingled with the slowly moving crowd.

"A beautiful wedding," people said and looked at one another with wet eyes. "A lovely wedding!"

Wyeth met him at the door and seized his hand. "I can sleep nights," he said to Pierce. "I know she's going into a fine old Southern family—you never know, these days!"

"She is very welcome," Pierce said with dignity and lifted his head high.

# Ten

WHEN HE WAS at home again he felt the necessity to build. Building Malvern gave him the conviction of growth and increase and substance and permanence. He determined to begin the new library at once and he considered the enlargement of the dairy barns. Hitherto he had grown cattle for beef for sale beyond the family use of milk and cream. But milk was a coming industry. He read of a new bottling machine which had been patented the year before and he toyed with the idea of a huge retail milk business. That would need more land and he called his head farmer Mathews and together they reviewed the outlying farms and who might be willing to sell.

Mathews was a white man, a tenacious, hardworking, greedy fellow who knew how to get work out of the hands—a poor white from Virginia. He was obsequious to Pierce and his sons and flattering to Lucinda and her daughters and ruthless to everyone else. He was married to a fat white woman and they had a half-grown family of children who stared hungrily at everyone from the big house. They lived in the stone tenant house.

Now in the office, beyond which he never went, Mathews talked. "We can get Blake's farm cheap, Mr. Delaney. I know he can't meet the mortgage."

"What's the matter with him?" Pierce inquired.

"His sons are no good—they buy a lot of machinery and let it lay around outside."

"Machinery!" Pierce grunted. "Men think it will work for them but nothing takes the place of elbow grease."

229

His faint mist of pity for the Blakes disappeared. "Get it as cheaply as you can," he told Mathews.

He spent the next year in poring over plans and watching foundations rise. Martin came home from Europe with Mary Lou and they took their place in the house. When he could remember to do so, Pierce asked his son's opinion about such small things as the placing of a gable and the piping of water into the new barn. Most of the time he forgot to ask. The hunting season came and Martin and Mary Lou were away day after day. He saw them canter off in the morning over the lawns silvered with frost and took a moment's pride in their grace and bearing. Red coats on horseback were handsome on an autumn morning.

"Life can go peacefully if I only let it alone," he told himself. He talked little with Lucinda, and being tired at night he slept heavily. He took on weight because he ate too much, and unaware of it himself, he drank more than he had before. He was out all day and the fresh air made him hungry. Business was excellent. He scarcely heard from John MacBain any more and his railroad dividends were steady. Tom wrote his letters twice a year, long and careful. Georgy was developing a real voice. It looked as though she and Georgia would not be coming home for three or four years.

Pierce told Lucinda with what he hoped was carelessness that Tom's second daughter was going to be a singer.

"Pray tell," Lucinda remarked, examining the needlepoint piece upon which she was working.

"They're in Paris," he went on.

Lucinda laughed. "Oh, the French!" she said. She did not look up. He wanted to tell her that Georgia was there, too. But she refused to show any interest and he was afraid that if he mentioned Georgia's name she would revive her secret, undying anger.

"None of my family ever could sing," he said instead.

"Singing and play-acting don't come in good families," Lucinda replied.

He gave up and went away. There was no use in trying to talk to Lucinda. He wanted to forget all women. Then he

thought of Sally. Irritation mounted in him. Why didn't Sally
get married? She had beaux by the dozen, in and out of the
house, hanging around. She had stopped school suddenly, declaring that she was tired of it, and he had expected that of
course she would marry. Then she wanted him to travel with
her, but he did not feel like traveling. She had suggested to
him one evening when they were alone that he let her go to
Paris and join Georgy.

"I might study something in Paris," she said.

He looked at her grimly. Sally was now so pretty that she
was a menace and he so considered her. "If you can persuade
your mama to allow you to do that, I will say nothing," he
told her.

She made a face at him. "Coward!" she exclaimed.

"Call me any names you like," he had returned.

He had enjoyed the big ball at Christmas but he saw not
the slightest sign from Sally of interest in any of the young
men who flocked about her fondly. He reproached her for this
in the early hours of dawn when the last guest had gone
and she yawned and drooped her eyelids.

"Aren't you going to marry any of these poor young fellows?" he demanded.

"They're tasteless in my mouth," she complained.

"Sally, you can't be an old maid!" he had cried in alarm.
"Look here, honey, you pick yourself a pretty young man
and I'll settle twenty-five thousand dollars on you. Or you
can pick a piece of Malvern for your own, if you like, and
I'll build you a house."

She shook her head. "I don't know one pretty young man
from the other," she declared.

In May, Sally suddenly broke his heart. It came so quickly
that he was stricken before he knew it. In February she had
accepted an invitation to a houseparty in New York. He had
not wanted her to go. He himself had never been to New
York, and Lucinda for all her talk had never been there but
the once, before Martin was married, to get her frocks. She
came back declaring that she hated it. Nobody knew who

she was and they wouldn't wait on her in the shops even when she said "Mrs. Pierce Delaney." But Sally had friends who lived there, whom she had met when they all went to White Sulphur occasionally. People had strange friends nowadays. When he was young his friends were the children of his father's friends.

So he had let her go to New York for a week, and had been heartily relieved when she came home, unchanged except for a brown sealskin coat and hat which horrified him when she told him what they cost. Of the amusements she had enjoyed she said nothing—or almost nothing. There had been a young Brazilian, the second son of a Portuguese family in Rio de Janeiro, who had come to New York with his father to sell diamonds.

"Diamonds!" Pierce echoed. "What for?"

Sally shrugged her shoulders. "Why does anybody sell diamonds?" she countered.

"But the people in Brazil are savages," Pierce objected. "At least they're all mixed up with Indians and niggras."

"Alvarez Lopez de Pre' is no savage," she said, dimpling. She looked at her father sidewise with wicked eyes. "He's a very pretty young man," she had declared with emphasis.

He had thought nothing of it at the time. But when in May he got her letter, he remembered. He was alone at Malvern. Carey and John were still at the university and Lucinda, declaring she was rundown, had taken the girls to White Sulphur for two weeks.

"Dear Papa," Sally wrote in her pretty, slanting handwriting. "When you get this I shall be on the high seas with my husband. Papa, I am Mrs. Alvarez Lopez de Pre'—a pretty name, is it not? You must come and see me in my Brazilian home. Alvarez tells me that the house is handsome and that in the patio there is a fountain which rises thirty feet into the air. Dear Papa, when you have finished being cross with me, then write me. I couldn't marry any of the tasteless young men at home. Alvarez is tall and dark—his skin is quite brown. I adore his looks."

This letter he found among all the letters on his desk one

morning in August. He caught the next train out of the small
depot near Malvern, which had been put in especially for his
shipments of cattle to the coast. The road to White Sulphur
he himself had done much to build, a decade ago and more,
foreseeing that it would bring to the great watering place visitors from all over the world.

The spa had never looked more beautiful than it did this
day when he stepped from the train in sore anxiety. The sky
was cloudless, and the huge hotel sparkled under the sunshine, its paint as white as snow, its flags brilliant. Small guest
cottages shone among the green of the trees and up and down
the walk guests strolled, the women carrying bright parasols
and the men bareheaded or wearing wide straw hats. He himself had visited here not long before in order to inspect the
new game of golf which some Scotchmen had brought over.

But now he wanted only to find Lucinda quickly. He di-
rected the carriage he had hired at the station to go straight
to the cottage which he and Lucinda regularly used when
they came here to drink the waters. It was the hour before
the great afternoon dinner, and he knew that Lucinda would
be there. He found her on the small piazza, Lucie and Mary
Lou beside her. She was fanning herself with a silken Chinese
fan and looked the picture of idle pleasure as he stepped from
the carriage.

"Pierce!" she cried. "Of all things!"

But he could not greet her. "Lucinda, how could you let
Sally leave you?" he demanded.

He had tried to think how to break the dreadful news, but
when he saw her he forgot all he had planned.

"Mercy, Pierce," Lucinda cried. "How you scare me! Where
did you come from? Why didn't you write me you were coming?"

"When did Sally leave you?" Pierce demanded.

Mary Lou looked down at the embroidery she was doing,
and Lucie was silent with fright.

"Pray tell," Lucinda said impatiently, "what is the matter
with you, Pierce? Sally left two days ago to visit in New
York. She went with the Carrington Randolphs—you know

that Candace is her best friend. What is wrong with that?"

He held out Sally's letter then and she took it. He stood waiting, watching her face, and he saw the blood drain away from her cheeks. She read it and looked up at him and he could not have asked for more horror than he saw there.

"Oh, Pierce!" she whispered—"oh—how could she—"

The letter dropped to the floor. Lucie in her small secret way reached for it. She read it and Mary Lou glanced over her shoulder.

"There is nothing we can do, Luce," Pierce groaned. "Only, who is this fellow? The Randolphs? I shall go to them at once—"

"Here is a corner turned down and glued," Lucie announced. "It has 'For Mama' written on it very tiny."

"Give it to me," Lucinda cried. She snatched the letter and tore the corner open. Inside Sally had written in small and clear letters, "Tell Mama for her comfort that the Lopez de Pre' family is four hundred years old."

Lucinda's fair skin flushed rose-colored. "As if that matters!" she cried passionately—"when the man is black!"

She turned on Pierce in sudden fury. "This comes of you and your precious brother! Sally would never—never have done such a thing if it hadn't been for Tom!"

There was such hatred in her bright blue eyes that he stepped back involuntarily. "Take heed what you say, Lucinda," he said to her sternly.

"It's true, it's true!" she cried. "This is what happens when you treat niggras like white—they steal into your house—"

"Be silent!" he shouted, and taking her by the arm he pulled her into the house and shut the door and put down the open windows.

But Lucinda would not listen to him. She flung herself on her bed and wept aloud. "I shall have nothing left," she sobbed, "nothing—nothing—"

He accused her, "You think of yourself—only of yourself—"

She roused herself to shake her fists at him in her rage. "I do not think of myself, Pierce Delaney! I think of all—all of us white women fending off these niggras that men like you love so much—trying to keep them out of our homes—to keep them from robbing us of all we have left—"

She looked so absurd, so melodramatic in her anger and her weeping that he began to laugh loud, cruel laughter.

"Oh don't be so silly, Luce!" he shouted. He threw a look of disgust at her grimacing tear-stained face. "Good God, women like you—you drive us—to—to—"

"To what?" she screamed. "Go on—say it!"

"I won't!" he bellowed.

"Mama—Mama!" Lucie's frightened voice at the door re-called them both. "People can hear you and Papa!"

Lucinda got up from the bed and went to the washstand and poured water into the china basin and began to wash her face.

Pierce sat down. "I shall go straight after that fellow," he muttered. "I shall fetch Sally home."

Lucinda shouted. "It's too late, you fool—I won't have a black grandchild—I can tell you."

"Brazilians aren't black," he retorted.

But he was not sure what they were, and he did not go. When he reached New York two days later, Carrington Randolph met him and took him to the hotel. There in the vast quiet parlor of a Waldorf suite he met Mrs. Randolph and Candace, who waited for them.

"I know how you feel," Mrs. Randolph said gently. She was a tall thin Virginian with a pretty face too small and delicate for her long body. "Of course we'd all rawtheh have had our deah Sally mah'y a Virginia gentleman, and indeed I thought she was going to fancy our own son—he's so in love with her. But she didn't tell anybody—not even Candy, did she, honey?"

Candace shook her dark head. She was a year older than Sally, a rebellious, spoiled, secretly intelligent girl. "Sally didn't tell anybody very much," she said guardedly. She smiled. "But he is very rich," she added.

"That would make no difference to Sally," Pierce declared.

"Well, then he's good-looking," Candace said wilfully.

"Only so dark," Mrs. Randolph mourned.

Carrington Randolph cleared his throat. "The tragic thing

about it is that the fellow is Catholic, and so I suppose Sally's tied for life. I assure you, if we had known—but we didn't. She simply left us a note, saying she'd written you—"

Pierce looked from one to the other of them. "I can only hope and pray that he is good to her," he said simply.

He went back to Malvern and tried to build over the emptiness which Sally had left. When he had told Lucinda all there was to tell, she looked at him in silence. She gave no sign of remembering the dreadful things she had said at White Sulphur, but he would never forget them as long as he lived. When Sally's letters began to come from Brazil, long letters in which there was not the slightest hint of repentance or of missing him or indeed of thinking of them at all, Lucinda read them once and then put them aside.

But alone in his library Pierce read them again and again. He was unable to tell whether she was happy or unhappy. Sally had poured her life into an unknown household and she was absorbed with it. Mother-in-law, father-in-law, aunts and uncles and cousins, the vigorous, voluble, brilliant family, he came slowly to know them in a strange, imaginative fashion through her letters. But the one he wanted to know most of all was the man who was her husband and of him Sally spoke the least, except at the end of each letter to stress again the underscored words, "Papa, I am happy. Dear Papa, I am *very* happy—"

He went on soberly building. The library wing was finished, a noble room, high-ceiled and paneled in walnut that he had grown on his own land and that had been five years in seasoning. When the room was done he hung in it the best of his paintings, one of them a gentle green Corot his grandfather had bought in France, and another a Romney portrait from England, of one of his own ancestors. Over the mantel he put his own portrait, painted when he was forty by Dabney Williams.

It did not occur to him that he would ever see Sally again. He did not want to leave Malvern for so long and he was sure that Lucinda would never receive Alvarez Lopez de Pre' here. Now that his dearest child was gone he tried conscientiously to know the children that were left. When Carey came home from law school at Christmas he made a chance to talk with him alone. He had always been uneasy with this son whose composure and cynicism, it seemed to him, had been born in his blood. Carey was like Lucinda's father, and old Rutherford Peyton had intimidated all young men who came near him.

"Want Lucinda, do you?" he had said when Pierce came to ask for her. "Take her and welcome! Daughters are a drug in a man's house after they're sixteen."

Lucinda had laughed but Pierce had been intensely indignant.

"Shall you practice in Richmond?" he now asked his second son one evening after dinner. According to Lucinda's rite, she and Lucie and Mary Lou left the table after dessert and Pierce sat on with his sons over wine and walnuts. He cracked a nut with the silver nutcrackers.

"No, Father," Carey replied. He had a clear tenor voice, pleasant but cold. "I'm going to set out for the new coal mines."

Pierce crushed the nut and let it fall on the plate. "The coal mines!" he repeated, stupefied. It was betrayal. He hated the mines that were scarring the face of the State.

"I'm going to be a big corporation lawyer," Carey said confidently. "My roommate's father owns the Woodley holdings, and it's a future for me. The way I see it"—Carey cracked a filbert with sharpness—"there is going to be increasing friction between capital and labor as unions develop—"

"Unions aren't going to develop," Pierce declared.

"It's my guess they are," Carey replied. "That means corporations are going to want their own private lawyers to hold down the unions. There's a fortune in it."

Pierce looked at his son with distaste. Carey was fair, like Lucinda, and he had her cool quiet manners. "You're going to get rich off the dissensions of men, are you?" he inquired.

Carey laughed. "There's no surer way of getting rich," he said lightly.

Martin poured his glass full of the port wine that Pierce was now making each year with increasing success. "Here's to the future!" he cried. "May dissensions flourish and wars multiply on the earth!"

"I'll drink no such toast," Pierce declared. But he lifted his glass and passed it back and forth under his nose. "There's real bouquet," he murmured. He forgot the foolishness of his sons and drank the wine down with relish.

Nevertheless, he was not pleased with Carey, and two months later he still remembered his displeasure and took sides against him and Lucinda in a quarrel between Carey and his third son John.

Of all his children Pierce had paid the least heed to John. Named for John MacBain, the boy had grown up as little as possible like him. Once or twice John MacBain, in undying longing for his own children, dead and unborn, had tried to befriend the son that Pierce had named for him. But no friendship had developed. John had frankly disliked Molly. "She paws me all the time," he said bluntly to Pierce, and he was impatient with old John. "He thinks about nothing but steel and locomotives and how to beat the unions," he told Pierce.

But if no friendship had grown there had been a result. Pierce's third son grew up with an intense disdain for business and business men, and a stern determination to hew his own life as he wanted it to be. Pierce knew that he went often to see Tom, and that he had long since ceased to ask permission or even to tell anyone when he went, and Tom's letters now made no mention of the boy. That, Pierce knew, was because John did not want his mother to know what he did. This being true, Pierce asked himself if he should not inquire into it.

Uneasily one day he faced the young man, and John admitted it at once. Of all his sons John was still the most like Tom in looks, and Pierce had the strange feeling when he saw him, that he was gazing at Tom's young self. But he

could not or would not acknowledge that the likeness went
deeper.

"Of course I don't want Mama to know I go there," John
said. "I learned when I was small that I couldn't tell her anything about myself—she has no sense of honor."

Pierce said sternly, "You are speaking of your mother."

John smiled, his eyes scornful and held his peace.

Pierce waited, and then took the lead again. "Your mother
has been brought up in the old tradition," he said formally.
"I confess that I have, too. We cannot change—"

"Don't put yourself in the same category," John said.
"You're a very different person. She's a woman."

"Then you should honor womanhood," Pierce said. His
words made him uncomfortable as he spoke them. There was
an echo in them of old dead grandeur.

"I feel sorry for women like Mama—that's all." John crossed
his long legs.

Pierce thought, "This boy has the most honest eyes I have
ever seen—far more honest than mine ever were."

"Sorry?" he repeated aloud.

"They're living in a world that's gone," John said. "They
don't know it—but they're afraid. They might know."

"That sounds like nonsense," Pierce replied.

"It isn't," John said pleasantly. "It's sad truth. Poor Mama,
she's hanging on by her fingernails to the old romance—pretty
white ladies living in lovely houses, protected by white men!
But we've betrayed them—we've sneaked out of the back
doors, after making sure they were quite comfortable, their
little slippered feet on satin footstools." He got up and walked
to the window. "God, how I honor my uncle Tom!" he cried
to the mountains beyond.

The room was very silent. Pierce could not speak. John sat
down again and looked at his father. "I propose to go North,"
he said. "I want to get away from the South. It's rotten. I
don't want to rot with it."

Here in his beautiful library, the great windows facing the
mountains, Pierce heard his son destroy his home. He made

feeble defense. "But this isn't the South," he objected, "we separated ourselves in the war."

"We've never dared to cut the placenta," John said harshly. "I want to go where my children never hear that a man's color dooms him and that because a woman is black, she is not a woman but a female."

Pierce winced and then smiled. "Where will you go?" he asked.

"I don't know," John answered, "but I'll go until I find the place."

"What will you do?" Pierce asked.

"I'm going to be a brain surgeon," John said. "I'm going to find out for myself that men's brains vary from the imbecile to the brilliant, but not from white to black."

Carey's voice interrupted them from the door. It was the first week of the summer vacation and the two young men were home together. "Is the dreamer dreaming again?"

"It's no dream," John retorted.

"Then it's madness and the same thing," Carey said gaily.

The two brothers did not love one another, and John lost his temper vehemently. "Leave my life alone, damn you!" he roared. "I don't say anything to your little pettifogging lawyer's plans! I'd rather cut my throat than make my living the way you're going to do!"

Lucinda, hearing the loud voice came in from the terrace where she had been sitting in the shade of a sycamore tree.

"Pray tell!" she said sharply. "What's the fuss now?"

John shut his lips together until they were white, but Carey smiled his bitter smile. "John is having heroics, as usual," he said. "He wants to go North where he won't see the horrid ways we have."

Lucinda turned to her third son. "Tell me instantly what you mean," she demanded.

Pierce interposed, "My dear, young men always quarrel. I advise you to go back to your seat."

But Lucinda did not heed him. "John, you are not going North!"

"Yes, I am, Mama," he replied. He stood, towering above her fragile whiteness. "I hate it here—"

"Indeed? You hate your home?" Lucinda's voice was tinkling ice.

"Not Malvern—exactly," John muttered.

"Oh—not Malvern, exactly," Lucinda repeated.

The mockery in her voice lit the wrath in her son again. "I take it back," he cried. "I do hate Malvern—and everything in it—"

"Oh!" Lucinda's hands flew to their place under her breasts. "Pierce—you hear him?"

Pierce bent his head sadly. "My dear—he must be free," he murmured. "We cannot make Malvern a cage—"

Lucinda turned from him and suddenly her hand flashed like the blade of a sword. She slapped John's cheek as once she had slapped Georgia's, Pierce thought in horror. "There!" she cried. "That's what you deserve—you silly boy!"

John gazed at her, shocked to the soul, and then turned and strode away. They heard him rush up the stairs to his own room.

"Lucinda, you have done something that can never be undone," Pierce said.

She burst into tears. "I don't care!" she cried.

"Don't cry, Mama," Carey said.

But Pierce answered, "Go away, my son. You ought not to be here."

Carey, hesitating, saw the look in his eyes, and went away and Lucinda wept on and Pierce sat silent and let her weep for he could not comfort her. At last her anger dried her tears and she went away without a word to him, and shut herself in her rooms.

All day she did not come downstairs and John did not appear until he had found that his mother had shut herself in with a headache. Then he came downstairs and to his father.

"I want to go away," he said.

"Of course," Pierce said. "How much money do you need?"

"A hundred dollars or so," John replied. His eyes were too bright, as though he had shed tears, and his cheeks were flushed. But Pierce asked no questions. He went to the safe behind the panels of his office and took out cash and gave it to his son.

"Tell me where you are and write to me every week," he said.

"I will," John promised him. And then in sudden gratitude, he cried out, "Papa, thank you—for—everything! And I'm going first to Uncle Tom's house."

"I thought so," Pierce said, and let him go.

# *Eleven*

THE YEARS SLIPPED PAST and he marked them by the growth
of trees he had planted in new orchards. The apple trees he
had put in on the south hillside began to bear and the chest-
nuts he had put on the west knoll were burred. He had to
order the sycamore over the east terrace cut back because it
shaded the house and the rhododendrons were rich on the
banks below the gardens.

There were more than trees to mark the years. Mathews'
children grew up and started livery stables and grocery
stores in the nearby towns, and inside his own house he had
two grandchildren and Carey, two years after he left home,
married the daughter of a millionaire mine owner.

Pierce did not like his new daughter-in-law. She was
effusive over the charm of Malvern but he heard her praise
with grim calm.

"It's delightful, isn't it, Carey? Such a wonderful background—" she exclaimed. Listening to her, watching her,
Pierce decided not to give Carey the MacBain house. It
would allow this young woman to stay too near. He'd keep
it. Maybe by some strange chance, Tom would come back
to Malvern. He dreamed of such strange things these days,
gazing at the mountains.

Pierce looked to the mountains increasingly now when
he was bored or lonely. He was often both. His Sally was
planted deep in South America, with children of her own.
Those people apparently did not believe in birth control—it
was their religion, he supposed. But he could not reach out
to Sally any more. And Lucie was Lucinda's own shadow.

He had never found a way to communicate with the child, though she was child no more, and engaged now to a young fellow from Baltimore—but he had no interest in it.

He met John MacBain sometimes, but John was tired and he was worried now by the talk of automobiles. If people bought cars of their own what would railroads do? There was even talk of freight being hauled by motor vehicles.

"It seems like railroads will never rightly come into their full glory," John MacBain mourned. "People are always inventing something new before they get the good out of the old. We've only just begun to think about street cars and automatic stokers and here they're plotting automobiles—"

Somewhere in the years John MacBain and Molly had reached the river which must part them or which they must cross together. Pierce knew of it, for John had sent for him abruptly one day from New York. Pierce had gone at once, with great distaste for that northern city, but with invincible loyalty to his friend. He found John and Molly together at the Waldorf in a state of mind that was iron on John's part and fire on Molly's.

Pierce was surprised to find them together in the same suite, for he had imagined that only Molly's broken promise and final desertion could have moved John to go to New York after her. He sat in the room with them both.

"Pierce, you decide," John announced.

"Decide?" Pierce murmured.

"Whether I'm being fair or not," John went on. "I've let her have her rein now for years. Pierce, you know the whole story. But the time has come to stop. If I'd been—a whole man—it would have been time to stop—even with me. She can just as well stop with another man—and I mean Henry Mallows, by Gawd!"

Molly burst into loud tears, but John refused to be moved. He turned to Pierce pathetically. "Pierce, either she can stay with me and grow old with me decently or she can leave me. My patience has given out." He pounded the table and overturned his glass of whiskey and water and the liquid spread over the floor.

Molly flew to mend the damage. "Oh, look what you've done, you big lout!" she cried in a trembling voice. She ran for a towel and wiped up the wet. "The table's spotting, too!"

"Never mind," Pierce said. He waited until she came back and then he went on, musingly. "Tables and chairs and things last so much longer than we do—I often think of that at Malvern. All the things I've gathered there—they'll be there, but I won't. There isn't much time left for nonsense—after fifty—"

His quiet words brought a still cold air into the heated room. John sighed and Molly wiped her eyes.

"You two," Pierce said affectionately, "I can't spare either of you and so you must stay together somehow. I don't want any more changes in my lifetime—whatever comes after."

He went home again after they had dined together and there had been no more talk. John and Molly went to Europe unexpectedly, and when they came back Molly had given herself up to fat and comfort and from then on John and she jogged along. Pierce looking at them wondered why it was that he and Lucinda could not do the same. But he could not, as John had, demand nothing but simplicities of marriage.

"I've given everything to my marriage," Pierce said to himself. John and Molly had come for a brief visit before going home to Wheeling. Then they were gone and the house was somnolent. Martin's family lived in the west wing, and when Pierce wanted quiet he drew a bar across the door between and it was understood that it remained so until he drew it back again. Mary Lou was compliant, never emerging, indeed, from the sweetness which she kept wrapped about her like a veil and through it Pierce saw her only dimly. But Martin seemed happy—as happy as he needed to be. Pierce knew his eldest son well enough now to know that he demanded little from life beyond comfort and security and these he took for granted from Malvern.

Then why, Pierce asked himself on one somnolent autumn afternoon, was he himself not content? He found himself increasingly and unbearably lonely as he viewed old age just over the horizon of the mountains. There it was, like the setting sun, and he must watch night come on. He dreaded it and he longed for closeness and nearness to someone, and to whom could it be, if not to Lucinda? They must be wed again to one another for age as they had been for youth.

So he set himself to win her once more, to court her with new love. He would study her, he told himself, and learn afresh her little likes and dislikes, her taste in colors and flowers and perfumes, things he had forgotten for years. And jewels—he had given her jewels for the children. Now he would give her jewels for herself.

It was not easy. Hardest of all to bear was Lucinda's surprise, cynical, half amused.

"What's the matter with you, Pierce?" she inquired. "What do you want?"

"Only to tell you that I love you, my dear," he said gently. But she seemed unable to believe him. She imagined with disgust that he wanted her body with some sort of recrudescent, elderly lust. He was too embarrassed to speak when he discovered her suspicions and for some time he refrained from so much as kissing her lips.

Then his loneliness overcame him and one November afternoon, when they had walked together through the woods, he sat down on a fallen log. When she sat down beside him he took her hand.

"I feel myself growing old, Luce," he said.

"It's about time," she said with the faint smile she used so often now.

"No, don't, my dear—" he begged her. "Don't be cynical, Luce. It's a desperate thing to grow old, and feel one's wife doesn't forgive him for something—he doesn't know what. Darling, come close to me—I don't mean—what you think—I mean—your heart, Luce—that's so far away from me. I must have your heart—because I can't grow old alone—"

She sat as still in the soft autumn sunshine as though she were made of marble. He felt something struggle in her. Her fingers still fluttered but he held them fast.

"Tell me what it is you have against me," he begged her. "Whatever it is, I will change it—do away with it—give it up —I promise you! But first you must tell me what it is or how will I know?"

She could not speak, or would not. But he held her fluttering, unwilling fingers and he told himself that if he were patient, loving but not passionate, if he could persuade her and make her believe him—

"I have no one but you now, to be near to me," he said tenderly. "See, dear, I want to be near to you, too, in the way we should be, each trusting the other. I want to devote myself to you—I thought I had all my life—but if there is something you think keeps me from you—"

And then bit by bit she began to speak, and he let her speak.

"But you do know what it is," she said.

"Indeed, I do not, Luce," he said gently. "That is why I beg you—"

"You know—you know—every time you go there—"

"You mean—Tom? My brother?"

"He's only part of it—you make an excuse of him—"

"Excuse for what, Luce? Tell me!"

"You go to see *her*—"

"Her?"

"That woman."

"A woman, Luce?"

"Georgia."

Now it was out. Now he knew. She sighed and drew her hand away. He sat staring at the tip of her shoe, peeping out from her long ruffled skirt. "Do you believe I have been unfaithful to you?" he asked abruptly.

"I don't—think of such things," she said faintly.

"Think of it for a moment, now. Do you?"

"You aren't—different from other men."

He felt his throat thicken with rage and swallowed it. He would be patient with her for his own sake, because he could not meet what lay over the horizon—alone.

"Will you believe me when I tell you that I have always been faithful to you—always?"

She did not stir or speak.

He went on. "Once and once only have I spoken alone to Georgia since she left Malvern, and there was not one word of love between us—I promise you."

"Then why did you speak to her?" Lucinda's words were like dry dead leaves fluttering to the ground.

He considered, remembering. "I want to be honest—I am honest when I say I don't know. Somehow it had nothing to do with me—what she was. It had to do with the far future. I—how can I explain to you? I think we've been taught wrongly, you and I—we can't change now. We belong to the past. But the future—"

He shook his head. He must not try to change her, for she could not change. He must not enter into that future, for he would not be alive when it came, and neither would she.

He said, "Georgia told me that day she was going to Europe with Tom's daughter."

Lucinda made a pettish movement. "But that's so silly," she exclaimed. "A niggra!"

He was patient with her. "It doesn't matter to us," he said reasonably. "We have nothing to do with it. We live here at Malvern. You and I—we'll grow old here."

She looked at him suddenly. "Do you mean you aren't going to see Tom any more?" she asked.

He looked down into her eyes. Ah, he knew her so well, all her little thoughts, all her narrow fears which she herself did not understand! He pitied her profoundly but to love her had become the habit of his life and he could not change.

He spoke slowly, with pain. "If I promise never to go to Tom's house again—will you forgive me?"

She fluttered her eyelashes, lifted them up and then let them down. "Yes," she said, "I'll forgive you—"

They rose, and she hesitated. Then she dropped her little handbag and her gloves and he felt her arms about his neck. She buried her face in his bosom and began to sob.

"Why—why—my darling—" he stammered.

"Oh, Pierce," she cried, "you're *good!*"

He held her while she wept, and could not speak.

Tom understood, of course. Tom did not blame him for anything. They met in a hotel in Baltimore and Pierce told him the simple truth in a few words.

"I want peace," he finished.

Tom listened and forbore. "You are a free man," he said at last, "as free as I am to make your choice." They had talked little after that, for there was no more to say. Tom had brought pictures of his children, and Pierce looked at them. Leslie was the father of a child now, and a successful writer. He had written a bitter clever book. Tom had a copy but Pierce did not open it. Small Tom was going to be a doctor and Lettice was married.

"Not one of them has crossed the line," Tom said calmly. "But they've my blood to help them when I am dead."

He took a big photograph from his bag. "This is Georgy," he said. "She's the vanguard."

Pierce looked down at a beautiful young face, confident and brave.

"You can see Georgy's not afraid," Tom said. "She'll sing, maybe even in Washington. That's her dream—to sing in Washington, where Lincoln was. Maybe she'll sing in the White House—some day."

Pierce could not speak. He had no heart to dim his brother's hope. Besides, perhaps Tom was right! Who could say what the future was to be except that it never could be like the past?

"I have a picture of Georgia, too," Tom said quietly. "Do you want to see that? She's—quite changed—from living in France so long."

Pierce did not speak for a moment. He kept looking down into Georgy's young and dauntless face. Ah, this was how Georgia would have looked—had she ever had a chance!

"Does she—look older?" he asked after a long moment.

"Younger—strangely younger," Tom said. "Very beautiful—

they've made a fuss over her there. Mademoiselle La Blanche they call her. She always wears white—"

Pierce's heart beat hard once or twice. Then he quieted it. He had chosen Lucinda for old age and for death.

"No," he said. "No—thanks, Tom—I'll just remember Georgy—"